The story of Jo C[...]g in her novels. Bo[...]-burn, Lancashire, [...]. Her parents, she says, brought out the worst in each other, and life was full of tragedy and hardship – but not without love and laughter. At the age of sixteen, Jo met and married 'a caring and wonderful man' and had two sons. When the boys started school, she decided to go to college and eventually gained a place at Cambridge University, though was unable to take this up as it would have meant living away from home. However, she did go into teaching, while at the same time running the administrative side of her husband's business, renovating the derelict council house that was their home, coping with the problems caused by her mother's unhappy home life – and writing her first full-length novel. Not surprisingly, she then won the 'Superwoman of Great Britain' Award, for which her family had secretly entered her, and this coincided with the acceptance of her novel for publication. She has now written nine novels which have all been widely praised.

'A classic tale . . . a born storyteller' *Bedfordshire Times*

'Tension and drama . . . a book to read at one sitting!' *Prima*

'A classic is born' *Lancashire Evening Telegraph*

Let Loose the Tigers

Josephine Cox

HEADLINE

First published in Great Britain in 1988
by Futura Publications

Reprinted in this edition in 1992
by HEADLINE BOOK PUBLISHING

10 9 8 7 6 5

ISBN 0 7472 4078 7

Photypeset by Intype, London
Printed and bound in Great Britain by
Cox & Wyman Ltd, Reading, Berkshire

HEADLINE BOOK PUBLISHING
A division of Hodder Headline PLC
338 Euston Road
London NW1 3BH

Dedications

My understanding husband, Ken.
Our two sons, Spencer and Wayne.
Special thanks to two new friends, Alice and
Toby.
And remembering my vast and wonderful
family too numerous to name. (Also Carole
and Bri.)
Always in my heart, Barny and Mary Jane.
May God keep them safe till we meet again.

Acknowledgements

Craig Brindle for dogged and detailed
investigations.
Staff of Blackburn Library.
Lancashire Evening Telegraph (Archives).
Not forgetting in particular the old codgers
who drink in the Robins Nest and Navigation
– and at different times have sent me home
legless!

Foreword

Some small part of the location has been
altered for purpose of story.

Part One

1965

Homeward Bound

But if the while I think on thee, dear friend,
All losses are restored, and sorrows end.
William Shakespeare

Chapter One

Rick Marsden had an ache in his heart. And that ache was Queenie. She had been gone some two years now, but in all those long empty days and nights Rick had never once stopped praying that at any moment he would look up and there she would be. She never was, though, and now he had grown fearful that he would not see her adorable face or gaze into those gentle grey eyes ever again.

It was a thought to haunt him, to fill his every hour with a dread too painful to contemplate. And he had tried – oh, how he had tried – to find her; until when all his efforts came to nothing, he began to think that Queenie had been snatched from the face of the earth. Yet he could not, would not give up his searching; for even if in the eyes of the law he was forbidden to marry her, there was no law in this life nor in the next that could command his heart to stop loving her.

At that moment, Mr Marsden senior turned his attention from the sombre procession which had this day travelled the streets of London, drawing a vast number of people from all walks of life, from every corner of the land, and indeed from across the world. This awesome State funeral, the first accorded to a commoner since the death of Gladstone some sixty-eight years previously, was a sight to behold. One hundred and forty-two men of the Royal Navy ranked fore and aft of the magnificent gun-carriage bearing a coffin ceremoniously draped with the Union Jack, upon which a cushion of velvet bore the insignia of the garter.

The many thousands of onlookers had gathered here to pay their humble respects and mark the state funeral of a man who had been hailed as 'the greatest Englishman of all time'.

On this 30th day of January, in the year of 1965, Winston Churchill, once leader of men, once Prime Minister, was ceremoniously laid to his rest. The nation mourned, and men of Mr Marsden's generation found much regret in the passing of one who had so valiantly refused to accept anything less than victory in the Second World War, and whose memory would ever be strong for that claim alone, if for no other reason.

The pomp and glory of such a send-off, and the unique character of the man being carried to his last resting-place, had rendered the whole affair deeply moving and emotionally exhausting for the onlookers. Now, his eyes moist, Mr Marsden had seen enough.

'Come on son. Let's make tracks towards home,' he told Rick, wending his way through the thronging crowd. He did not come to rest until he had successfully isolated himself from the jostling bodies. A moment later Rick too emerged from the crowd, to hear his father declare in a voice subdued by the occasion,

'*There* was a man, son! A man among men . . . and we'll not see the likes of him again I fear.' There followed a deep sigh, which had the curious effect of adding height to his appearance. 'Come on now,' he said abruptly, 'let's stop for a bite to eat before we get the train back to Wigan.'

Rick nodded his agreement, all the while searching the crowd for Queenie's face. But he was surrounded only by strangers, and amidst them all, he had never felt lonelier. His deeper thoughts ran on, unheeding his father's patter.

'I'm glad we were able to wrap that warehouse business up so swiftly. It would have been a great pity not to have caught a glimpse of Churchill's last journey.' Mr Marsden pursed his lips into a circle of deep crevices as he fell into dark reflective thought.

Sensing his father's brooding mood Rick exclaimed, 'Come on, Dad!' quickly propelling him down Fleet Street, through the thinning crowd, and along the streets of London towards the nearest underground station. Right now he had one thought uppermost in his mind – to get back to the familiarity of Lancashire and to resume his search for Queenie. It was true that he had accompanied his father to London under the guise of inspecting a warehouse which was up for sale. He had known it was too small, too insecure and too far from the docks to be of any real value to them but as always he had it in the back of his mind that he might, just might, catch sight of Queenie; even though his deeper instincts had always told him she loved Lancashire too much ever to leave it.

As he and Mr Marsden located seats on the train just preparing to depart from Euston Station Rick watched the older man surrender to the exhaustion of a long busy day. While his father slept, Rick gave full rein to his thoughts. In doing so, he found himself subject to many moods. Shock, at Katy Forest's revelation to him that the child which had been born to Queenie, and to Katy's thinking 'mercifully taken', was not, as Rick had strongly suspected, fathered by Mike Bedford . . . but by Queenie's (and sadly *his*) own father: George Kenney. As Katy was quick to point out, such a thing could only have been brought about by the worst act of desecration man could commit against woman, let alone father against daughter. It was a monstrous thing, which had caused Rick many a nightmare since. If George Kenney was not already facing his maker, Rick would have swiftly despatched him with his own hands.

That Queenie had not felt able to confide in either himself or Katy also angered Rick. Such anger though, had been tempered by recollections of Queenie's nature, and of how painful it would have been for her to shift her own troubles onto another's shoulders. Oh, but God in Heaven! she *should* have told him! Were not his shoulders broad enough to lighten *any* burden that would cause her distress?

Thinking on her now, the upsurge of love for her within him grew to such urgency that he could have got to his feet here in this train packed with people and, in loud defiance, proclaimed that same love; even in the knowledge that the woman he yearned to take for his wife was in fact his own half-sister. Would he *never* come to terms with it, as Queenie appeared to have done? In answer, all his senses screamed no in unison. He never could . . . not when it condemned him and Queenie to lives apart.

For a while, his thoughts melted into the rhythmic rumbling of the speeding train, his furtive mind growing quieter in the wake of his confident self-assurance that he *would* find Queenie even if it meant searching the four corners of the earth.

When he grew weary from gazing out of the window and marking the fast-changing countryside Rick turned to survey his father's sleeping face. Some two years had brought small change in Mr Marsden's forthright countenance. Still given to plumpness, there was much in him to try even Rick's patience, for he was a man of little compromise, occasionally riding roughshod over others when it came to a business deal or demands of his mill-workers.

Rick had come to know just how to handle situations often made fraught by his father's bull-headed, inflexible tactics. But what he found more difficult to cope with was the manner in which his father blatantly sought to marry him off to Tad Winters' daughter, Rachel. Lovely though she was there would never be anyone for him but Queenie. Rick resented, too, the way his father bristled at the very mention of Queenie's name. It struck him yet again, to wonder at the full consequence of his mother's affair with George Kenney all those years ago. Had she confided in Mr Marsden that Rick was not *his* son? Or was it a secret kept only to Rita Marsden herself, and did her husband to this day believe Rick to be his? There had often been times since Queenie's disappearance when Rick had been on the verge of probing the subject deeper with his mother, but on each occasion he had refrained from doing so, because a haunting sadness in his mother's eyes always cautioned him from raking over the coals of the past. There had been enough pain.

He looked at the sleeping man before him, the man

he had always known as his father, and of a sudden he hoped that his mother *had* kept safe her secret; because for all Mr Marsden was a hard-nosed taskmaster, often ruthless and unforgiving, Rick knew without a doubt that this man loved him deeply. And it was surely an unnecessary thing to hurt the innocent if it could be avoided.

Feeling himself somewhat worn by the rush of an unusually busy day, Rick relaxed into the seat and closed his eyes. At once the smiling image of Queenie came into his mind, causing him to wonder where she was at that very moment. If she thought to elude him for much longer, she had greatly underestimated his determination. After the short letter Katy had received from Queenie some weeks back, he was convinced it was only a matter of time before Queenie was found.

Chapter Two

It was Friday night: the last hour of the working week and, for Queenie, the last day at Naylor's Plastics Factory.

One by one as the women left their work benches and clocked out before making for the outer door and freedom, they came into the small partitioned office, to say their farewells to Queenie again.

'You've been a good supervisor, Queenie,' said Big Bett, 'and we'll miss you.'

'Look after yourself dear,' said another.

When they had all gone and the place ached with quietness, Queenie emerged from the office to make her final check about the machines.

A great feeling of loneliness came upon her, as it always did at this particular time of day. Strange, she mused, how these past two years or more she had kept close her own company in spite of working in daily contact with nigh on a hundred women, all of whose names, strengths and weaknesses she knew. She had laughed with them and lent a sympathetic ear to their problems; she had worked alongside them until her fingers and back ached as theirs had done. But outside work-hours Queenie had extended friendship to no one, man or woman.

Some time back, because of her exceptional devotion to work, together with a good personal working relationship with the women, Queenie was made up to supervisor. The promotion brought support and congratulations from one and all.

For a while now Queenie stood outside the office, her quiet eyes sweeping the length and breadth of the vast shop-floor, of which she knew every nook and cranny. This was the upper floor of a building that was once a long row of cottages. Now, with the inside partitioning walls removed, the ground floor had been converted into a huge warehouse. This floor, which was Queenie's domain, was little more than a sweatshop, where plastic macs of all colours, shapes and sizes were turned out in their thousands.

Welding machines, with flat metal platforms and numerous foot pedals, flanked either side of the long, crowded work area. Close to these iron contraptions stood wooden horses piled high with brightly-coloured shapes of plastic mackintoshes in various stages of development. One woman on her machine would weld together the sleeves, another the collars, and yet another would shape and turn the long tie-belts. All these pieces would be conveyed down to the end of the line, where a group of women seated at monstrous machines would weld them all together into a recognizable mackintosh. That done, the female baggers would shape each one into a flat, attractively-packaged garment, complete with label and guarantee. Finally the trolleys, stacked ceiling high, would be pushed down the ramps to the warehouses below, for loading onto the trucks waiting to carry them countrywide.

Every day was a busy one, and not a moment was

wasted by any worker. They were paid good wages, tied directly to production, but they earned every penny.

Queenie's job was to oversee the entire procedure, keep the floor clear and maintain a steady flow of garments from the cutting area through the welding process and down to the loading-bays. She worked harder, and longer, than any other employee, and there wasn't one person at Naylor's Plastics who envied her that burden of responsibility in spite of the extra £4 weekly it brought her.

Eager now to be on her way, Queenie checked that every machine was shut off and that the main outer doors were all secured, before returning to the office. Then she took a moment to relax after what had been an unusually hectic day. Her thoughts quickly came to the letter in her overall pocket which she now withdrew, her eyes drawn to the bright red stamp at the top of the envelope indicating that it had been posted from one of Her Majesty's prisons in Manchester.

'You were never really a part of it here, were you, Queenie?' The man had come up on Queenie so stealthily, that she had not perceived his approach. Startled by the unexpected intrusion, she swiftly thrust the letter back into her pocket, at the same time closing the ledger and rising smartly to her feet. 'Oh . . . Mr Roderick, I didn't hear you.'

'Got your mind on other things, eh?' The floor manager was a burly fellow with a large plain face and an insincere smile, which he now displayed as he lowered himself onto a packing case. 'Never could make you out,' he remarked quietly, at the same time regarding her closely. With her slim figure, striking grey eyes and soft hair braided across her head, Queenie was a pleasant sight, 'Young woman like you . . . good-looker as well! It's a while since you first came to Naylor's and *still* there's nobody knows anything at all about you outside these walls.'

'I've told you before – there's nothing *to* know.' Queenie smiled brightly and handed him the bunch of keys from the desk. Then taking her coat from the back of the door, she took her leave of him, saying, 'I've checked round and everything is as it should be, so I'll be away. Look after yourself, eh?'

'I'll do that, and mark *you* do the same, Queenie girl, wherever you might be going!' His flat round eyes followed Queenie's attractive figure with a regretful look. There wasn't a woman in this place that ever said no to him – a favour for a favour was his motto, and his position of advantage ensured him a steady stream of bedmates. Oh, but the one he yearned for most was the only one beyond him. Yet he wouldn't blame himself for that, because Queenie was different. She kept herself to herself, and in a way there was something about her that brought out the best in a man, even in a fornicating bugger like himself! he mused. Everything about her was deep and untouchable; she gave nothing away, with the exception of her warm nature and appetite for hard work. He'd admired the way she never asked the women to do anything she wasn't prepared to do herself. It wouldn't be an easy task to replace her, but in all truth he wished her well. As he went about his business Mr Roderick sighed, put Queenie out of his mind and cheered himself up with the thought that her replacement might be a little more receptive to his offer of 'friendship'.

Once outside the red-walled factory, Queenie did not look back. Instead, she quickly made her way along the Woburn Road past the rows of Victorian houses with their smart brown doors and pretty net curtains, then on towards the station, where she would board the bus which countless times had carried her to Bedford and to the place she called home since leaving Blackburn.

The cold light of a February day had given way to a groping blackness, cut with a sharp spiteful breeze. Queenie quickly pulled the black beret down over her brow then flicked up the deep collar of her brown tweed coat and drew the lapels across her throat as she stepped smartly towards the bus which had just drawn in. Another moment and she was seated halfway down the aisle on the bottom deck, her face stiff cold from the biting wind yet ready with a smile when the conductress made her way along to collect the fares. There being only one other passenger besides herself, Queenie found little to attract her interest, so after buying her ticket she began to dwell again on the matter of the letter in her pocket. In doing so she was drawn to search her conscience and to suffer a degree of guilt for not having kept better faith with old and cherished friends such as dear Katy, Father Riley and Mrs Farraday. But she had needed to distance herself from such luxuries as friends, and after the many hours of soul-searching, she was still of the mind that there had been little alternative.

Now, however, it was as though Queenie had never left Blackburn, so disturbed was she at the discovery from a national newspaper article that Sheila Thorogood, as was, had been locked in prison. Ever since learning of this, Queenie had been saddened, because she herself knew the awful loneliness of such a thing. Hadn't she too been in a prison of her own making? She had permitted herself only two contacts with the past, one some twelve months back when she asked one of Naylor's delivery drivers to post Katy a letter from Lancashire with the intention of directing Katy from the real truth that Queenie was nigh on two hundred miles away.

In her letter to Katy, Queenie had assured the darling woman that she was very well, in good work and prospering . . . hence the enclosed handsome sum of money, which would pay one of Father Riley's poorer parishioners to keep tidy Auntie Biddy's resting-place as well as those of George Kenney and the child. It was a warm letter, full of love and gratitude, but Queenie was exceedingly careful not to reveal how desperately lonely she was and how much she longed to walk again the streets and ginnels of her beloved Blackburn. Nor did she admit that the money had been painstakingly scrimped together by making sacrifices over a period of many months. It was important to Queenie that Katy should have peace of mind about her. She also suspected that Katy would mention the letter to Rick. It was for this reason that she had included the postscript. 'Give my love and regards to everyone, Katy – tell them I'm carving a new life for myself, and I'm very happy.'

It took more courage to write those few words than anything else she had ever done. But she didn't want anybody fretting on her behalf although she couldn't stop *herself* from fretting. She had been convinced that the passage of time would soften the pain of an ill-fated love. The heartache did not cease, however, and the only way Queenie had learned to cope with it was to deliberately close her mind and her heart to the persistent bitter-sweet memories.

Queenie had lost count of the number of times she had suppressed the strongest of desires to telephone Katy. It was more often than not in late evening, when she would come from the awful solitude of her room and stand before the pay-phone on the landing. Some few minutes later, she would return to her bed, having yet again resisted the temptation; one part of her certain that Katy could be trusted to be discreet and the other filled with dread that in her misguided best intentions, Katy might feel prompted to impart Queenie's whereabouts to Rick. Queenie would then argue with herself that Rick was a strong and sensible man who might even by now have settled in a church career. And anyway, how could Katy guess where she was from a telephone call? But for all the arguments Queenie presented to herself, the deep-seated knowledge persisted within her that Rick had abandoned the church and was even now searching far and wide to find her. As for Katy, she was wily enough to somehow discover *anything*, even in a telephone call. Queenie could not risk it.

All of this had changed however, on the day Queenie read of Sheila's downfall. She had telephoned Katy, and determined as she was not to impart more information than was necessary, Queenie had not reckoned on her own deep need to confide in an old trusted friend. And she could never have anticipated just how great an emotional shock it would be to hear Katy's kindly voice again.

It took only Katy's gentle persuasion and promise of total confidence to bring Queenie's resolve to its knees. She told Katy of her lonely existence in the South; of how never a day went by but she didn't long to be home in Blackburn, and of her intention now to go to Sheila in her trouble.

'Oh, Queenie . . . Queenie, lass!' Katy had cried, the tears spilling into her voice which rose now and then in great excitement. 'I knew it! Soon as ever I clapped eyes on that article, I said to Father Riley that'll fetch our Queenie back, sure as eggs is eggs!'

'Katy, I don't want *anyone* to know where I'm to be found! You must believe me, please.'

'I've given you my word, lass, and I'll tell no one. But I can't for the life of me understand it! Father Riley can do you no harm, and since Rick's taken on the lion's share of running his father's business we see less of him than we'd like. And I know for a fact, he'd be overjoyed at seeing you!' Katy said nothing about Rita Marsden's failing health, for she saw it as serving no purpose. Instead she continued, 'Oh, what is it, lass? Are you in trouble? Is somebody after you?'

'No Katy, I'm not in trouble.' Queenie's assurance was firm. 'But I'm not ready to show myself and I don't want to be found. And especially, you must promise not to tell Rick that I've been in touch.' Queenie had been right in her perception that Rick had abandoned his career in the church, and she was equally certain that he would never accept the utter futility of the love they felt for each other.

So, in the face of Queenie's desperate pleading, Katy had given her word not to tell a single soul of their conversation, or of Queenie's intention to come to

Sheila's home at Lytham St Anne's on the outskirts of Blackpool, less than twenty miles away from Blackburn. But Katy did not take kindly to such secrecy, and when she eventually put down the phone, on an assurance that she herself would go to Rirkham Prison and see the way of things with Sheila, Katy was puzzled and anxious. She had waited for Queenie to mention that poor child in the churchyard and the business of how it was begot, but there had been nothing.

It was all a strange how-do-you-do, she'd told herself. Queenie living all this time in some alien place down South, pining and fretting to come home, yet afraid to do so. Katy was more convinced than ever that the lass was in love with Rick Marsden. Yet undoubtedly it *was* Rick she was hiding from. There had been *something* amiss between those two before, and it had not changed. Katy had half a mind to go back on her God-given word and go straight to Rick this very minute. But she'd bide her time, until Queenie arrived. And mebbe when the two o' them were face to face, Queenie would bring herself to expand on the information left with Mrs Farraday . . . that George Kenney had fathered the boy-child born to her.

Queenie's thoughts had run along the same lines in the days following her call to Katy. In spite of Katy's promise she couldn't help but feel afraid that if Rick was to find her, there would be no barrier wide enough to keep them apart, because she knew that confronted with the powerful magnetism of his love she would forget the teachings of a lifetime, throw caution to the winds and fall locked into his arms forever. It was a terrible thing, this relentless force that forbade her the love of a man she would gladly spend the rest of her life with, and by the self-same stroke, denied her the love of a brother.

Time and time again, it was as though she kept her sanity only by persuading herself of two things: firstly, that in time Rick would build a new life without her, and secondly that if he had not yet accepted the way of things between them, the only course *was* the one she had taken! At least until he saw the degree of her determination.

Yet Queenie knew also the strength of Rick's own determination, which, together with the memory of his angry departure from 2 Parkinson Street on that fateful day, filled her with all manner of apprehension. He had in him a fearful rebellious streak against the blood ties between them. Queenie's heart told her that his love for her was no less torturing than her own for him. Sometimes, after awakening in the night from an uneasy sleep, she would imagine the sound of Rick's voice calling her, would feel an overpowering sense of his closeness . . . and then Queenie most feared this man she loved. For in the depths of their forbidden love lurked the awful power of destruction, and in her most vulnerable moments Queenie was tempted to go to him whatever the consequences. But always, in the hard light of day, Queenie shrank from the temptation.

'Bedford Bridge!' The conductress rang the bell, then as the bus shuddered to a halt, she gave Queenie a cheery smile, adding, 'This is you, dear!'

'Thank you,' acknowledged Queenie, gathering her bag and her wits as she hurried off the bus. Steeped in thought, she hadn't realized it was her stop so soon. Normally, when she alighted from the bus here, there would be a heaviness in her heart at the prospect of returning to the loneliness of her bed-sitting room. But not this evening!

As she made her way across the market square, devoid of stalls but alive with people all hurrying their different ways, then down the embankment which bordered Bedford River and was already bedecked with little raised gardens of wallflowers, Queenie found herself humming a song.

In no time at all, she had turned into Ridgeway, a short avenue of vast Victorian houses each with wide double doors atop a broad expanse of stone steps, every house still resplendent in its decaying grandeur. These dwellings had long ceased to be the private residences of doctors, councillors and the like. Now they were a maze of bedsits, housing the Italians who had settled in Bedfordshire to work in the nearby brickyards, together with souls like herself, reaping some shrewd landlord a handsome income.

Queenie's room was up the first flight of stairs, sandwiched between the ground floor and the upper reaches, where from both directions the private lives of other occupants filtered unashamedly into her own little domain. But she learned to live with the intrusion and had worked at making her room into a home.

Queenie entered through the arched door, switched on the light and for a long moment, she stood by the doorjamb, her wise grey eyes taking in the scene before her.

The long rectangular room was arrayed with tweed-covered chairs and sparse, dark brown furniture. At the far end, behind a curtained rail, there stood a single bed and a small cabinet. Beside the cabinet stood a narrow dark-wood wardrobe. Situated in the corner by the bed was a small triangular hand-basin.

During the morning, when the sun came up beyond the river and shone straight in through the two deep windows, the room would be filled with light. In the afternoon when the sun moved away, the room would suddenly be plunged into an unpleasant grimness, cold and unwelcoming.

By nine pm, Queenie had eaten eggs on toast, enjoyed a refreshing bath, spoken in passing to the old man who resided in the room next to hers, and now, after a last cup of tea, she was ready to go to bed. She could hardly wait for morning, because then she would leave this place to make her way home – home to her own Lancashire· to see her old familiar friends. Now that the decision had been made, she could hardly wait.

Queenie sat on the edge of her bed, slowly undoing the thick golden plaits which had been attractively crossed over her head and were now hanging one over each shoulder down to her lap. As she performed this nightly ritual, with her long legs tucked up beneath her slim form, Queenie's lovely face was quiet in thought. Her mind was on Sheila, as it had been since she first read the newspaper article some two weeks ago.

With slow, deliberate movements Queenie brushed her hair, and gathering it into her two hands, she lifted it over her shoulder to drape loosely down her back. Then she leaned towards the bedside cabinet and took from one of the drawers a folded-up piece of newspaper, which she opened out. It was the article which had informed Queenie that Sheila, together with her mother, Maisie Thorogood, had been charged with keeping an improper house in Lytham St Anne's near

Blackpool. There was irrefutable evidence that the premises had been frequented by clients said to have been entertained by the two women concerned, and by others already known to the police as street-prostitutes.

Queenie replaced the article in the drawer, turned out the bedside lamp and settled down into the bed, murmuring 'Oh, Sheila! Sheila! What's to be done with you?' Well, she thought, the outcome was clear enough. Although the judge had merely fined Maisie and released her on probation because of her deteriorating health, Sheila had been the 'instigator' and as such had been sent down for a period of five years. In spite of the fact that Sheila had responded to Katy's visit with a curt note to Queenie saying, 'Thank you for your kind thoughts, but I won't see you if you come. Stay away! 'Taint no place for angels!' Queenie had not been deterred. She was convinced that the brief, forbidding letter contained an underlying cry for help. It was *too* brief, *too* forbidding, and too lacking in Sheila's typical humour.

Just before Queenie closed her eyes to sleep, she spoke into the darkness, her voice firm and cheerful. 'You *will* see me, Sheila Thorogood! And often, until the day they turn you loose and I'm waiting at the gates to take you home!'

At ten-fifteen the next morning Queenie went by way of Bedford River, then along the broad pavements of the High Street towards the sprawling bus station, where she boarded a coach which would take her to the North.

The few precious minutes she had spent watching the swans on the river almost cost her dearly; there had been no time to purchase a ticket at the coach office on the far side of the bus station, and it was fortuitous for her that it was still possible actually to pay for passage en route. As the driver informed her, 'Given a few more weeks, all that will change!'

Breathless and concerned that the coach would pull out without her, Queenie had surrendered her suitcase, climbed aboard and negotiated her way down the aisle to a vacant seat at the back. She drew many admiring glances; not just for the flattering manner in which her blue woollen dress with matching swagger coat emphasized her tall, elegant figure, nor for the way her dark wide-brimmed hat sat forward across her brow at just the right angle. It was Queenie's vitality and friendliness which shone out to entrance all who saw her. With the tension of the last two years gone from her face, her smile was radiant.

Some three hours after Queenie's coach had departed, a well-built, handsome young man dressed in an expensive suit and overcoat made his way from Bedford railway station to tread the very same path which Queenie had taken, along the embankment and on towards Ridgeway.

He strode swiftly and with purpose until he reached the door of the house where Queenie was reported to be staying.

Rick Marsden could hardly contain the powerful emotions which surged through him as he dwelt on the wonderful prospect of seeing Queenie at long last, after all this endless time of searching.

In answer to his determined knocking came a gruff call of 'All right! All right!' and straight away a man of advanced years cautiously opened the door, his face wrinkled up tight in concentration as he peered hard into Rick's warm brown eyes. He listened with some impatience to the enquiries regarding his former tenant, then, his face falling loose in surprise, he exclaimed, 'She's gone! Left early this morning.'

'Gone, you say?' Already the fear in Rick's heart had coloured his voice.

'That's right . . . left for good.'

Rick's heart sank. 'Do you know *where* she's gone? Is there a forwarding address or anything?'

The landlord set his bushy grey brows down over his piggy eyes and surveyed Rick with some curiosity. 'Nope! That one kept herself to herself. Can't tell you no more, I'm afraid.' And no more he could, because Queenie had not confided her destination to anyone.

'Do you know which direction she took, or of any means by which I could find her?' Rick was clutching at straws. Then, as the landlord shook his head and made to close the door, their eyes met for a moment. In that moment, the old man felt a pang of compassion for Rick, and Rick in turn derived a degree of comfort from the knowledge that, not long before, Queenie had looked at this man's face and had in all probability smiled at him. It was a link, a delicate and poor substitute for having lost Queenie yet again . . . but somehow he suddenly felt closer to her.

'Sorry.' The old man gave out the semblance of a smile, then before quickly closing the door, he offered, 'Had a suitcase with her. Try the bus station, or the railway.'

Some two hours later, Rick had tried both; together with all the local taxi-firms and even the car-hire companies, for he had no way of knowing whether

Queenie had learnt to drive. But at each place, the answer was the same. No one could recall a girl with warm grey eyes and honey-coloured hair, braided in thick soft folds. And from the way he described Queenie to the ticket-clerk at the bus station he declared, 'There's no likelihood of me forgetting a beauty like that!'

So, with dejected heart, Rick started his long journey home, thinking all the while of Queenie. His instincts now told him to leave Queenie free to choose her own way, to accept as she had obviously done, that it would never be in their power to become man and wife.

He felt like a man torn asunder, filled with fury and yet brimming with tenderness and love.

These last two years had been little short of a nightmare, what with Queenie gone and every obstacle seemingly put in his way to delay his finding her. Then there was his father, grown even more cantankerous and hell-bent on seeing the daughter of a wealthy business colleague brought into the family as his own daughter-in-law; his ambition fired by the handsome shares she owned in her father's business, one of the largest cotton-exporting concerns in Lancashire.

On more than one occasion, Rick vehemently condemned his father's brazen intention to couple him with Rachel Winters. He attached no blame to Rachel herself, for it struck him that she was probably just as embarrassed and angry at their respective fathers' misguided matchmaking as he was. Rachel was charming company, and undeniably a strikingly beautiful woman. But she was not his darling Queenie . . . and she was not for him.

These past eighteen months, his mother had been a

source of great anxiety to Rick. Struck down by an unusually vicious bout of shingles, she had recovered at length, only to be left in a constant state of nervousness which of late had seemed to Rick to have lapsed into a certain weakening of her mental faculties.

Rick had quickly become aware of her condition and had immediately sought the best of specialist advice. His father, on the other hand, had refused to come to terms with this pitiful development in his wife's illness, and for a long time adamantly refused to discuss the matter with anyone. In a row which had erupted between Rick and his father, Rick accused him of acting as though he was ashamed of his own wife, and declared that if his father was not up to his responsibilities, then he himself would take the whole matter in hand, and if such a thing was to become gossip, he might have even *more* cause to be ashamed.

The passion of Rick's indignation at his father's lack of moral fibre – or perhaps it was the threat of the news spreading amongst his business colleagues – stirred Mr Marsden into appointing a nursing assistant and a permanent housekeeper. He straight away showed more tolerance towards his wife. These were measures which on the surface might be made to satisfy Rick, and he welcomed them. But in all truth he was saddened by the ever-yawning distance between his father and mother, for while one was growing less able to convey the love she must surely still feel, the other was unwilling, unyielding and unapproachable. It was an unhappy situation; often when in the presence of his mother, who at odd times seemed perfectly well, Rick pondered on how much the knowledge of his love for Queenie had contributed to his mother's ill-health. In rare coherent discussions, Rita Marsden would ask after Queenie with interest, and though it was a matter ever close to his heart, Rick would make light of the subject, then when his mother retreated into herself, he was convinced that the burden of knowing half-brother and half-sister had fallen in love was too heavy for her. And his despair was twofold.

The decision to relinquish his search for Queenie was prompted not only by the apparent fact that Queenie wished it so, but the inherent hopelessness reflected so cruelly in his mother's illness.

For all his resolution, there stayed with Rick an overwhelming certainty that without Queenie he would never be complete. How could he not go on searching? If he could only convince Queenie that nothing mattered except their love for each other, wild horses would not tear them apart.

Chapter Three

Queenie had telephoned Katy during the rest period when the coach stopped en route, to let her know that she would arrive in Blackpool between four and four-thirty that afternoon. As the time passed and the coach travelled deeper into Lancashire, Queenie's heart began to beat faster, and for the life of her she could not sit still. The prospect of seeing old Katy again was all she could think of; Queenie wondered whether these past years had been kind to her old friend. She wondered also whether there might even be an awkwardness between them, on account of their prolonged estrangement. For which Katy would surely chastise her, thought Queenie with some amusement.

After some six hours of travelling, the coach pulled off the main road, rounded the corner into Blackpool Boulevard – and there was Katy dressed in a dark coat down to her ankles and sporting a navy-blue boater, firmly secured to her head with two enormous hat-pins. The sight of the dear soul, straining her neck to search the coach as it drew to a halt, sent a great painful lump into Queenie's throat. Even before she alighted from the coach and rushed into Katy's outstretched arms, Queenie was crying helplessly.

Katy too was crying, hugging Queenie to her bosom
and patting her on the back and every now and again
blurting out 'Oh, lass! My lovely lass!' Queenie had
not fully realized until that moment just how very much
she had missed this warm wonderful lady.

'Now then, my girl!' Katy sniffled, taking a hanky
from her handbag, '. . . let's have a look at you, eh?'
She stepped back a pace, dabbed the hanky about her
wet eyes and afterwards blew her nose long and hard.
For quite a moment she took stock of Queenie, notic-
ing how gaunt she had become, and how devoid of
colour were her lovely features. She noticed too, even
beneath the present smile, how subdued were those
exquisite grey eyes, grown much darker now, and she
observed with some compassion the way Queenie's
long, fine fingers nervously twisted themselves about
each other. Katy's heart was never more brimming
with love for this dear creature than it was right now.
Of a sudden she had clasped Queenie to her again,
and was holding her in such a grip that might never let
go. 'I ought to spank you!' she declared, a mood of
anger straightening her face, 'taking yourself off the
way you did!'

'I know, Katy . . . but I had to.' Queenie disengaged
herself from Katy's embrace, a soft apologetic smile
lighting up her face as she kissed the old lady's forehead. 'Oh, Katy. It's so lovely to see you!' Queenie
noted that in spite of Katy's hair now being snow-white
and the bright eyes enveloped in fleshy rises, there
was comfortingly little change in her dear friend. At
seventy-three years of age, Katy Forest was remarkably
full o' fettle.

'Ah! Changing the subject is it?' Katy demanded,
her face set one minute in mock reprimand and the

28

next in a great beaming smile. 'Go on! Pick up your case 'afore somebody makes off with it and we'll find a quiet place for a bite to eat and a chin-wag, eh?' The seriousness came back into her face. 'There's a lot I want to know, my girl! And I'm not letting you out of my sight again, I can tell you. Not this fine day, and not ever!'

In the quaint and cramped tea-rooms opposite the pier, Katy regretted the fact that even though it was out of the holiday season, there were too many folk about to afford her and Queenie the private conversation she would have liked. But that did not prevent her from talking as though she might never stop. She told Queenie of Rita Marsden's illness, of how old Parkinson Street was scheduled to be demolished and how already folks had started moving out. The Farradays had gone some fortnight back . . . no! they didn't say where. And that Mrs Bedford! Mike's mother. Well, *there* was a story! Rumour was that she'd been in and out of prison for all manner o' things like petty theft and vagrancy; and the latest rumours told how she'd set herself up as a fence, buying and selling stolen articles from criminals hereabouts. It were said that she'd tekken a posh place on Preston New Road and had certain dubious characters on her payroll. That Mrs Bedford had turned out to be a right bad 'un and no mistake!

After imparting this information, all of which had marred Queenie's homecoming, Katy began to question Queenie, lightly at first, then with some bombardment. Queenie gave her answers as thoroughly as possible. Then came the one question she had been dreading.

'What a blasphemous fellow was George Kenney!'

Queenie had stated with contemptuous disgust after learning the truth of how Queenie's dead child had been conceived. 'But what of the man who would have stood by you, child? What of Rick? Oh, Queenie. Have you any idea at all of how much he loves you eh?' At the mention of Rick's name, Queenie's face filled with apprehension. 'Don't worry, Queenie lass, I've spoken to no one about your movements.' Katy reached out to cover Queenie's hand with her own, as she continued, 'You love him too, don't you? I've known it from the first. What is it, lass? What is it that keeps you apart? Can you tell me?'

For a long moment Queenie gazed at the old lady, the whole of her being longing to divulge the knowledge that had lain so heavy in her heart. Yet it seemed to have driven itself so deep within her, to have been shut away in some dark untouchable corner, that to bring it out into the daylight now would resurrect too much pain. Rick had obviously kept the knowledge of their relationship quiet, no doubt thinking the matter best left alone; much as she might want to, Katy could do nothing to change the truth which would be an unhappy weight for her also to bear. With these considerations in mind, Queenie gave the only answer she could.

'Katy, I'm going to ask something of you. I hope you won't think hard of me?'

'Of course I won't, child – go on!' Katy urged.

Queenie smiled at Katy's fondness for calling her child. 'Thank you Katy,' she said. After a pause she continued, 'First of all, you're right in thinking that there *was* a degree of feeling between me and Rick – but it's over! And we have no future in the way you imply. It's *over*, Katy, and best left that way . . .' Here, Katy would have interrupted, but Queenie raised her hand in protest. 'No, Katy! Rick and I will not see each other again. It would serve no purpose for either of us. So please, Katy . . . I'm asking you to continue keeping my whereabouts secret. Will you do that for me?'

Katy gave her agreement, but it was not given graciously, because even in the face of Queenie's insistence her instincts persisted in telling her that something was amiss. Yet she had no option but to go along with Queenie's wishes, for here was not the helpless, tragic girl who had been driven away from Parkinson Street, but a woman, emerged from tragedy and unhappiness with a strong, capable character and a will of iron determination. And Katy had no mind to risk losing her again.

'Don't worry yourself, Queenie lass,' she replied softly, her eyes smiling into Queenie's, 'just so long as I can see you regular, and know you're well, I'll keep the information to myself.'

It was seven pm when Queenie saw Katy back to Blackpool Boulevard. The two of them parted company, Katy to board the bus which would carry her the short distance to Blackburn, and Queenie to collect her case from the property desk. She intended to board a tram for Lytham St Annes, some two miles up the coast.

'Now, you watch that Maisie Thorogood!' Katy was saying as she clambered onto the bus. 'If you ask me, my girl, you're throwing yourself right into the lion's den!'

'Oh, Katy! I shan't *stay* at Maisie's house. I'm

31

booked in nearby, just till I see how the land lies.'

'Well, you watch your step, else you'll end up getting dragged into all manner of trouble! I still say you should let me come with you!' Katy impatiently declined the bus conductor's help as she negotiated the step from the boarding platform. 'Oh! Dear me,' she tutted, of a sudden stopping to dip into her coat pocket. 'Queenie! I forgot to give you this.' She turned around to hand Queenie a small flat package. As she did so, the conductor ushered Katy to a seat, rang the bell and the bus moved off, with Katy's voice calling, 'I got that from Mrs Farraday. Look after it – and you telephone me like you said!'

When Queenie opened the package, she was amazed to see that it contained Mr Craig's lovely golden locket. 'Oh, Katy!' she murmured, her heart heavy with memories, and filled with gratitude at Katy's thoughtfulness. 'Thank you. I'll not let it go ever again.' So Katy had got the locket from Mrs Farraday, who no doubt had straight away taken all the information concerning Queenie to Katy Forest. The sale of the locket had been intended to pay for the child's Christian burial; Katy herself must therefore have footed the bill. What a darling she is, thought Queenie, somewhat guilty that she had not been able to confide her innermost secret in such a friend. But that was a door which must stay closed.

It took but a moment for Queenie to collect her suitcase, after which she boarded the coastal tram, her mind already looking ahead. There were things to be done now, arrangements to be made and people in authority to see. If there was any chance at all of getting Sheila out of prison, she would take it. Yet in the back of Queenie's mind Katy's warning lingered. 'She's a bad one! Bucking the authorities and forever causing trouble. Sheila Thorogood will find herself in deeper water unless she mends her ways!' Of Maisie she had said, 'If you ask me, that house is just as much a whorehouse now as it ever was . . . never mind that Maisie Thorogood is an ill woman. I tell you it's still going on!'

Katy's grim warnings had disturbed Queenie. But she was here to help, and nothing she had heard from dear Katy would make her change her mind.

Her thoughts firmly settled as to her purpose here, Queenie shifted about on the wooden-slatted seat and stretched her neck to peer out of the open-topped tram. It was bitingly cold up there on the top deck, with the wind sailing in from the sea and skimming the tram like a knife-edge. Her nose burning from the cold, the wispy fringes of hair driven back from her forehead and ears, she felt the wind like the sharp crack of a whip. But in all of her life Queenie could never remember experiencing such exhilaration. The tangy salt air flooded her nostrils and the rhythmic clatter of the tram's iron wheels against the metal sleepers reverberated through her like a second heartbeat.

Queenie's eyes were alive with excitement as the tram shunted along. She greedily stored every sight: before her the tower of Blackpool rose up from the skyline like a giant twinkling ornament, providing a beacon for everything below.

Many of the shops would stay closed until Easter, when their windows and forecourts would display multitudes of colourful nonsense and little souvenirs for the merry holidaymakers to take home, for keeping alive the memory of a week or a day at Blackpool's seaside.

The gaily-painted gypsy wagons festooning the broad promenade, where the weathered-skinned women held a client's trembling hand, to foretell a fortune of coming riches and maybe a tall, dark-skinned lover, were tightly shuttered against the unloving winter. Hanging overhead down the mile-long road hugging the promenade, Queenie's eager gaze feasted on glowing lamps and lighting paraphernalia of every shape, size, colour and description – of elves and gnomes, glass coaches and diamond stars. As Queenie gazed up at them, entranced as the small child who had once dreamed of coming to Blackpool, it was like a wonderland she knew she would never ever forget.

Queenie tried to keep her emotions under control. But when of a sudden a beautiful black open carriage, pulled by the most graceful bay filly she had ever seen, sauntered past, decorated by long white feathered plumes which danced in the breeze, the smile on Queenie's face grew and spread and sparkled until it might light up the sky. 'Oh,' she breathed. 'It's all wonderful! Like I always knew it would be!'

In that exquisite moment the years rolled away, carrying Queenie back to the Ragged School, to Father Riley and inevitably, to her darling Auntie Biddy. A deep contentment spread through her, renewing her energy for the unpleasant task in hand.

Chapter Four

The wail of the ambulance preceded its arrival into the yard of Marsden Mill and in a matter of minutes the injured man was put on a stretcher and placed in the back of the ambulance which lost no time in ferrying him to Wigan Infirmary.

'All right, men! Let's have you back at your work – sharpish!' Ted Lampton, the works foreman, thrust himself in amongst the workhands, who had gathered in small groups to murmur of the latest and worst in a string of accidents at the Marsden mill. In the face of the issued instructions they stood firm, their expressions defiant and sullen. One man in khaki dungarees took a step forward, and at once the other workhands moved in behind him, their mood silent and morose, heads nodding in agreement as he spoke.

'You can threaten us all you like, Lampton, but Ryan's likely to lose a leg over this last business. These bloody machines are bound to take a life if something's not done – and done quick!'

'You'll get back to your work. Now! If you know what's good for you!'

'All right Ted, leave it to me.' Rick Marsden had seen the ambulance safely from the premises and now he came face to face with the anger of his father's millhands. 'I know how you feel, men . . . and something *will* be done,' he told them in a serious voice.

'Aye, but *what*? And when? That's what we want to know! No disrespect, but you're not aware of how strong the men feel on this one, what with you away most of the time looking after other concerns!'

There were murmurings of support from the men backing him, and Rick couldn't blame them. He had only this day learned of the dangerous state of some of these old weaving and spinning machines. They had every right to look out for themselves, to expect the same safety standards which he himself had introduced into the other Marsden mills. What in God's name was his father thinking of? This particular factory was the Marsden first, the 'baby' which for Mr Marsden held great sentimental value; on his father's express wishes, Rick had not interfered with its running. He reproached himself now; a fury roaring inside him as he realized that at this very moment his father was looking down on the scene with complacency, from the window of his office high above the factory floor.

Rick faced the irate men before him. 'Take an early break, men,' he told them, his voice commanding yet not domineering. 'I'll be back here in fifteen minutes with something constructive. Trust me!'

For a moment there was no response. But in that moment the workhands weighed up this man, whom in the past they'd had occasion to respect. They took stock of his broad upright figure, of his rolled-up sleeves which bore the stains of Ryan's bleeding limbs; they admired the way he had of looking a man straight in the eye with that dark honest gaze; and to a man they trusted him.

'Fifteen minutes!' Lampton said in a hard voice, and the men nodded their agreement; but the one in khaki dungarees kept his eyes on Rick, saying, 'We'll not break! We'll stay right here and wait!'

Rick gave the slightest nod before turning away towards the run of wooden steps which would take him up to the office. Once inside he confronted his father, who by now was seated behind his desk, drawing on a cigar and preparing to head off the heated discussion which he sensed was unavoidable, and from which he had every intention of emerging victorious. At the same time Mr Marsden was under no illusions concerning Rick's forceful powers of persuasion when he knew himself, and the men, to be in the right.

'Well?' Rick spat out just one word, but it spoke volumes. As he towered above the older man's desk his face, dark with anger, darkened further at his father's first words.

'There'll be no *new* machines! A good overhaul of the existing ones will suffice . . .'

'No, father! It will *not* suffice, and well you know it. I want the best of that lot to undergo complete renovation and updating. The rest can be scrapped. I'll get you a good price, which will help with the installation of new machines to take their place. And all of that done over a matter of *months* – not years!'

At this, Mr Marsden was on his feet, his expression stern, his teeth digging hard into the cigar held between them as he hissed, 'You've got a free run with the rest of the business, lad, and I've never had cause to regret that . . . but this one's *my* baby, always has been! And I'll thank you to leave me to deal with it! *I'll* talk to the men. They'll get their machines overhauled.'

'I say no! That won't do.' Rick stood his ground and

the two men faced each other, one counting the possible cost in money, the other counting the daunting cost in men's lives and limbs. 'They deserve better, and I'll not leave here till I have your promise of it.' Rick knew that once he had that word, his father was not the man to go back on it. 'Or I'll leave the business altogether, and go my own way. You know I will – and if the men have a mind to follow me, then so be it!'

As Mr Marsden took in the meaning of Rick's words, he wondered whether it was an idle threat made in the heat of the moment. One look at Rick's face told him otherwise, and though he cursed beneath his breath, there was no denying the pride he felt at this man whom he had brought up as his own son. He loved him dearly, and needed no-one to tell him that without Rick, the Marsden textile business would not be the flourishing concern that it was. Competition from foreign parts was fierce nowadays, even though local mills were closing down at an alarming rate.

But for all that, Mr Marsden had no intention of giving in graciously. So the row continued and the men waited below.

Twenty minutes later, Rick emerged from the office to inform the men that his requirements on their behalf had been agreed in full.

This time Mr Marsden did not come to the window. Instead he stayed at his desk, deep in thought and frustrated in defeat. At one time he might have been able to handle Rick more easily but since Rita's illness, and more so since the disappearance of that Bedford woman, Rick had grown into a formidable adversary: more of a man than he himself would ever be. Rick, who had once looked to the church for strength and who had always been of a quiet placid nature, yet had it within him now to fight the world and to drive himself to impossible lengths. Not only was he a man of integrity, greatly respected and accomplished in matters of business, but above all he was his own man.

Mr Marsden had followed Rick's determined search for Queenie Bedford with discreet attention. He considered it a good move on his part to have ferreted out the identity of Rick's private investigator. It was amazing how much 'loyalty' a few hundred pounds could buy.

Up until now, such cunning had ensured that Rick's relentless efforts to find Queenie Bedford were constantly thwarted, so effectively that Rick had put the investigator under one month's notice to come up with something, or find his services dispensed with in favour of an investigator who *would* earn his money.

A slow smile spread over Mr Marsden's face as he drew deeply on his cigar. He was not too concerned, just as long as he could stay one step ahead of the situation – something he intended to do. He also intended to see Rick wed to Rachel Winters, and he would not rest until that happened. Not Queenie Bedford nor anyone else would be allowed to upset his plans on that score.

At this point in his thinking Mr Marsden's scowl deepened, and in an almost inaudible voice he murmured, 'You drove your husband to distraction, Queenie Bedford . . . but you'll not ruin my son! Your damned father took my wife and left her carrying his child. I can't forget that . . . and I can't forgive! Kenney's badness is in *you*, and I'll see you beggared before you wed into my family if it's the last thing I do.'

A fortnight later a threat to Mr Marsden's plans for Rick and Rachel Winters emerged in the form of Mr Snowdon. Mr Edward Snowdon was a solicitor by profession, and a long-standing colleague and confidant of Mr and Mrs Marsden.

Rick knew very little of Mr Snowdon's personal background. He had known him over the years as a business associate of his father's and as an occasional guest at their dinner-table. He thought him to be a forceful authority on matters relating to law, and he always found him polite yet reserved in manner.

Mr Snowdon, on the other hand, knew a lot about Rick's background, for it had fallen upon him some twenty-five years ago to defend Rita Marsden's sister, Hannah, Rick's real mother, against the charge of first-degree murder of her husband. The charge had been commuted to manslaugther, the punishment to a life sentence, and only Mr Snowdon and certain authorities held the secret of Rick's subsequent adoption into the Marsden family. Rita and Mr Marsden had been the only remaining relatives of the unfortunate boy, so the transaction had been swift and discreet.

Since Rita Marsden's illness, and Mr Marsden's persistence in disowning Rick's real mother, it had fallen upon Mr Snowdon to keep track of Hannah and to provide for her, as best might be in the circumstances of her long imprisonment.

The dinner tonight had been a success and Rita Marsden's face, though thin and devoid of its former vibrancy, lit up with the pleasure of accomplishment. Her delicate blue eyes smiled around the table, fleeting from her husband to Mr Snowdon, then to Rachel Winters, whose exquisite beauty never failed to take

40

her breath away. In spite of that fiery red hair and
vivid green eyes, there even so was a certain coldness
about Rachel Winters that Rita Marsden had sensed
from the first, a feeling which had persisted ever since.
Resting her gaze now on Rick, she suggested in a voice
bereft of energy yet not conceding to weariness, 'Please
excuse me . . . I think I'll call it a day.'

At once Rick was on his feet to help his mother from
her chair. 'That was a wonderful dinner, mother,' he
told her, leaning to kiss her forehead, 'and you look
very lovely.' His compliment was heartfelt; he was glad
to see her of better presence than she had been for
some time. It had been longer than Rick could easily
remember since his mother had taken such trouble with
her appearance, and the royal-blue silk dress she had
chosen to wear this evening had always suited her to
perfection. Her growing awareness of people in general
and of herself in particular signalled to Rick that at
last she might be on the mend. He had mentioned as
much to the doctor earlier in the week and even the
doctor's advice on caution had not diminished his optimism for his mother's recovery. Indeed, it had been a
week for optimism – what with the old machinery at
Wigan Mill being dismantled in record time, and
because of it the men being in a healthier state of mind
than for many a long day, in spite of his father keeping
well away from the factory floor, burying his head in
paperwork and on every occasion grudgingly referring
to the enormous cost of 'all that bloody fancy iron-
work'. Yes, it had been a good week, thought Rick.
All that was needed to make it perfect was news of
Queenie.

'Away with you!' Rita Marsden pulled herself up on

the strength of Rick's arm, and smiling into his rich dark eyes, which always gave her a feeling of well-being, she added, 'you should save such compliments for Rachel, and not waste them on me!'

'I'll do no such thing!' Rick retorted good-naturedly, his gaze swinging to where Rachel Winters sat, with her easy smile fixed on Rita Marsden. 'I'm sure Rachel gets more than her fair share of compliments. Come, I'll see you to your room.'

At this, everyone bade Rita goodnight. Mr Marsden came to her side and placed a fleeting kiss on her temple, after which Rick gently led his mother across the room, past the long mirror-polished sideboard with its display of crystal glasses, matching decanters and enormous range of spirits and liqueurs. Then along by the deep casement windows, hung with curtains of rose-pink velvet, and on into the vast hall from which rose the ornate stairway to snake away into a galleried landing above.

The first door at the top of the stairs led into Rita Marsden's room, a bright feminine room fitted with delicate cream Regency furniture and warmed by the cherry red of cushions, curtains and bedspread. At his wife's request a year ago Mr Marsden had moved his own belongings into a bedroom some way down the landing.

'There you are, mother. Will you be all right?' Rick eased his mother into a chair and straightened himself up. She looked tired, he thought. In his opinion, the dismissal of her nurse two weeks back had been an irresponsible action, but it had been on his mother's express instructions and in spite of his arguments and his father's attempts to dissuade her, she would have it no other way. But it did his heart good to see a glimpse of her old fighting spirit. Strange though, how it never reached her eyes, those pretty blue eyes which seemed too tired even to smile. They were looking at him now, and the question his mother put forth was so unexpected that for a moment he was caught unawares. 'You're unhappy, aren't you, son?'

'Now what put such a thing into your head? Of course I'm not unhappy.' How perceptive she is, he thought; and he hoped she had not guessed the reason for his unhappiness. Yet although it was never mentioned between them, his instincts told Rick that his mother had long known of his love for Queenie. And such knowledge could only add to her illness. 'The only thing that has concerned me is your getting better . . . and now you're improving by the day, so we'll have no more talk about my being "unhappy", he reassured her. 'Nothing could be farther from the truth.'

'You know your father has it in mind for you to marry Rachel?'

'Father has *many* things in mind . . . but they don't always happen. Rick squeezed her hand and went on 'I'll marry when *I* decide – you should know that, mother.'

For a long moment, their eyes held each other's gaze and even before she spoke, Rick had the uncanny feeling that she knew what was running through his mind. 'Strange how Queenie just disappeared like that,' she murmured, her gaze still holding fast his own. 'Too much tragedy in that girl's life . . . lovely girl don't you think, son?' Her voice had tailed off and the blue eyes had softened into vacancy as she shifted her eyes to the floor.

43

Rick got to his knees, his fists wrapped tightly about his mother's small hands. 'Mother, mother,' he coaxed, crooking his finger beneath her chin, lifting her gaze back to him, 'you must not concern yourself about Queenie or about anything else that might bring you pain. Just concentrate on getting well again. Queenie Bedford made her own choice . . . she's gone, and I don't expect we'll ever see her again.' The blatancy of his deceit at such a statement filled Rick with uncomfortable guilt. But his reward was a smile the like of which he had not seen on his mother's face this past year.

Relief welled in her voice as she told him, 'You're right, son, I must *not* worry myself over matters that don't concern me. You know, I don't think you should altogether rule out marriage to Rachel Winters. You *are* fond of her, aren't you?' He had to be fonder of the woman than she herself was Rita thought. But then again, Rachel Winters was a good catch by any standards, and she did appear to be in love with Rick. A marriage between them whatever small misgivings there might be, *must* be more successful than one between her son and Queenie. That union would bring down the wrath of Mr Marsden, and her husband could be a formidable enemy if he put his mind to it. No, such a marriage would be ill-fated and would divide her husband and son forever. So, in a way, Rita Marsden was glad that Queenie was gone. She wished her well wherever her journey had taken her, but it might be better if she never came back.

'Oh, so *you're* trying to marry me off to Rachel as well, eh?' Rick got to his feet and smiled down on his mother. 'I'm beginning to think it's a conspiracy. And talking about Rachel, she'll think I've deserted her. Goodnight, mother.' His tone left Rita Marsden in no doubt that the conversation was brought to an end.

Downstairs, Rick learned from the maid that his father and Mr Snowdon had retired to the library, and 'Miss Winters' was in the drawing-room. It was here that he found her, seated on the chesterfield sipping sherry.

'Is your mother all right?' she asked, and on Rick's affirmative reply, she patted the cushion beside her. 'Come and sit down.'

Rick did not accept the invitation. Instead, he crossed to a walnut cabinet by the fireplace and helped himself to a small measure of brandy. Instead of drinking it, he kept the tumbler between the flat of his hands and rolled it back and forth. There was much still on his mind, not the least of which was the discovery that Queenie appeared to occupy a good deal of his mother's thoughts.

'Hey! A penny for them.' Rachel Winters had got up from the settee and was standing before him, her hands up against his chest caressing his coat lapels. 'I'm not used to being treated like part of the furniture!'

Rick gave no answer, but when he looked down at her upturned face he was moved by her beauty. She was everything a man could want, he knew that. Her body was sensuous, perfect and desirable, and she was offering it to him right now. Beneath his gaze, her sea-green eyes had narrowed with desire and the well-groomed mass of titian-coloured hair brushed teasingly at his neck. All he had to do was to reach down, take her in his arms and taste that exquisitely-shaped mouth which breathed pleasure. He felt only a heartbeat away from doing just that because, much as he might regret such an action later, he was a man after all, with a man's urgent desires.

Rachel Winters at once sensed the dilemma within Rick, and in a moment she was on her toes sliding one arm up around his neck, with the other taking the tumbler from his hand and placing it on the mantelpiece; all the while holding that dark intense gaze which was not easy for Rick to draw away. In the closeness of their bodies she felt his need of her, and like so many times before, her own desire was heightened. Oh, she had been in Rick's arms in as intimate a way that a man could take a woman. They had loved and found something together but she knew that Rick remained out of her reach. There was a part of him that always held back from her, in spite of her employing every trick she knew.

When Rick's mouth came down on hers, wanting, demanding, Rachel Winters felt within herself a thrilling sensation, a feeling of power and a surging need to possess this man wholly. His arms were about her now, pulling her into him, enveloping her, his urgent kisses hard and bruising. As she moulded herself to him, the woman in his arms felt that at last, he was hers for the taking.

But she had reckoned without the enormous reserves of strength which in spite of all the odds against him, had driven him to pursue the one woman he could ever love. Yet there was agony in his groan as he drew from her, and the heaviness of passion was still in his rich brown eyes as he told her hoarsely, 'I'd best take you home – now!' But even as Rick went to collect her coat, Rachel Winters would not admit defeat. She had never wanted him more than at that moment. She meant to have him, and *nothing* would stand in her way. Before the year was out, she intended to be Mrs Rick Marsden! Oh, she knew of the woman, Queenie Bedford. Mr Marsden had made no secret of his dislike for that woman, and of his son's obsession with her. Well, it would take more than a girl from the back-streets to defeat Rachel Winters.

At that very moment however, had she but known it, there was a discussion going on in the library that could very well deter Rachel Winters from her desire to be Rick Marsden's wife. For the talk was of Rick's real mother.

'I trust you will continue to be discreet in your handling of this affair, Snowdon!' Mr Marsden was clearly agitated as he paced back and forth across the room, now and then spinning an anxious glance to where Mr Snowdon stood, his back against the desk. 'The fact that Rick's mother . . . my sister-in-law, is imprisoned . . . a murderess! It must be kept the secret it has been all these years.'

'Count on me. I haven't let you down yet. I can't stop the authorities moving her to Rirkham Open Prison, but I can and will monitor the situation with extreme caution.' Here, Mr Snowdon paused before continuing, 'Will you keep the news of the latest development from your wife!'

At this, the other man stopped his pacing and swung round. 'Of course! I'm convinced it's all this damned business that brought my wife's illness on in the first place. Of course I'll keep it from her! From everyone! And you can rest assured that my wife *won't* be setting foot in Rirkham prison or any other place they might choose. For the moment, she is content in the belief that *I* make regular visits.' He commenced his pacing again, then of a sudden, as though stopped in his tracks by some unseen hand, Mr Marsden came to a halt; and with the germ of a smile moving his face, he said, 'In fact, it might be the most charitable thing for Rita if she were to receive news of her sister's demise.' He came to within an inch of the other man's face, his smile deepening to deviousness. 'Can such a deception work, do you think?' he asked. 'More's the pity it *needs* to be a deception! It would have been a blessing to us all if Hannah Jason had departed this earth years ago!'

'I don't see why we couldn't engineer such a deception . . . if you really feel it's for Mrs Marsden's peace of mind,' the solicitor replied.

At this Mr Marsden laughed aloud. 'Good! Then we can bury the whole bloody business along with her! Get on to it – you'll know what to do. I'll see to it that Rita gets no ideas of attending funerals and the like. It shouldn't be too difficult, eh?'

Mr Snowdon headed for the door. 'Will you require me to visit her on the odd occasion as before, remain as go-between?' he said before he went out.

'Yes, yes! I need to be kept informed of the situation. But you must ensure that all information comes to me through *you*. I don't want prison authorities getting in touch with this house direct. That will be even *more* important now, if we are to succeed in divorcing Rita from the situation altogether.' He knew though that the matter could not be discarded as easily as all that, for all his cunning.

One day in the future, Rick must know of his true background: but not yet, not for as long as it could be kept from him. And certainly not while there was every chance of the Winters girl, and her father's business, marrying into the Marsden family.

Part Two

1967

Old Friends, New Beginnings

When miles between bring loneliness,
Oh, for a smile, a word or caress.
Nothing in the world will ever replace
A fond familiar loving face.

J. C.

Chapter Five

Queenie wasn't sure she liked the changes that had developed with such swiftness these past two years, since her return to the North.

Nineteen sixty-seven showed girls with long straight hair and tiny mini-skirts that would have made Queenie blush to wear them. And round almost every corner where there had been bombed sites and old-fashioned two-ups two-downs with their tiny dark rooms and outside loos, the flurry of demolition and re-building programmes had greatly intensified.

Folks seemed to have more brass in their pockets too, in spite of the fact that many of the old familiar cotton mills had been closed down. Queenie remembered how Auntie Biddy had related to her that Gandhi himself had visited the Blackburn cotton mills in the thirties. She wondered what Auntie Biddy would have to say about the fact that Lancashire was now *importing* cotton from India. And what on earth would she say about this latest idea from Harold Wilson's Government, to introduce decimal currency. Things seemed to be moving so fast, it made Queenie feel sad.

'There you are, dear,' the prison officer said as he handed back Queenie's pass, 'there's a table over there. Sit yourself down and I'll have Bannion brought across.' His eyes smiled down on her as she thanked him and turned from the desk. Taking quiet stock of her large and wonderful eyes set in a face of refined features, he found himself wondering how such a creature had associated herself with one of the inmates here. It was even more surprising when that inmate was Sheila Bannion, a bad lot if ever there was one! But this young woman, Queenie Bedford, she'd been attending some two years now, regular as clockwork and always as lovely a breath of air as the likes of him were ever to be blessed with in a place like this. Funny thing though! She couldn't be above what . . . twenty-four? Twenty-five? But she never flaunted her youth the way some young women did . . . with skirts up to their arses, hair all shapes and enough make-up plastered on their faces to frighten the dead! No . . . this one always wore her hair in thick shining plaits, layered across her head . . . oh, but he wouldn't mind seeing those plaits broken and the hair cascading naturally . . . bet it was a gladdening sight! And the clothes she wore, none of your cheap plastic stuff, but quality without being too expensive . . . like that green corduroy two-piece she had on today . . . a smart fetching outfit, with its straight-cut skirt and loose three-quarter coat. Queenie Bedford, eh? Well she was certainly a sight to brighten up a day and no mistake!

Queenie went in the direction he had indicated, smiling to herself at his reference to Sheila Thorogood as 'Bannion'. It was the name of her ex-husband, and since he'd seen fit to take himself off to Australia with their two children, Sheila had disowned all three of them and had made no secret of her intention to revert to her maiden name once she was released.

Queenie sat stiff and uncomfortable in the chair. She had never learned to relax during these regular fortnightly visits. At least this time, she thought, they had put her near a window, where she could look out over the beautifully-manicured lawns and shrubberies.

For a brief moment, Queenie looked around her, and as always, she was intrigued by the great number of visitors. Some already chatted to the particular prisoner they had come to see, while others, like her, still waited for them to be 'brought across'. It amazed her to see the high proportion of very young people here, both inmates and visitors. It seemed a very sad thing, she thought, mentally wishing them well.

The room where visitors came to see and encourage their unfortunate loved ones Queenie presumed to be a canteen of sorts. Fitted with plastic stackable chairs, all uniformly set round endless rows of white circular tables, the whole area was cold and unloving. No curtains or blinds adorned the windows, and both the entrance and exit doors were guarded by serious-faced prison officers.

At the furthest end of the room, opposite the door through which Sheila ought to appear at any moment, stood a long counter arrayed with trays of sandwiches, cups, saucers and two large shiny urns. On visiting days, it cost Queenie only half-a-crown for two good strong cups of tea and a healthy pile of sandwiches. Sheila's appetite never failed to amaze Queenie. It wasn't surprising that she had grown to the mirror image and ample proportions of poor old Maisie, who was now bedridden, and who, according to the doctors Queenie had consulted, would not see out the end of the year.

Queenie had refused their suggestion that Maisie

should go into a convalescent home, and had taken the responsibility of Maisie onto herself. The income from the small hotel was now such that it well afforded a private nurse for keeping Maisie comfortable. It had not always been so. Queenie's thoughts reached back to the day when she'd first set foot inside Sheila and Maisie's house. It had been something of a shock, although she should have been prepared for it by the outside appearance of that place. Nestled in a row of large Edwardian houses, the Thorogood residence stood out, conspicuous by its dirty steps, broken railings and grimy grey net curtains. Inside the house had been a shambles, with the great entrance-hall made dark and dingy by the failure of daylight to make a way through the dirt-encrusted casement-windows flanking the great front door.

Throughout its fifteen rooms, five on each of its three floors, there had lingered a smell alien to Queenie's experience, but more unpleasant than any she could remember. It weighed heavy in the air, sweet and heady, thick like a tangible cloud which seemed to fog a body's reasoning. It was not a bitter smell, nor was it sickly; Queenie had thought of it as being like a smell of bodies, as though many people had come and gone from the house, each leaving their own unique aroma. No fresh air had been allowed in through door or window to sweep them all away, so the aroma had built up undisturbed.

The closed curtains in each room hung tatty and colourless with ingrained dirt. Ceilings and walls were patchy-brown from pipe, cigar and cigarette smoke. It was a depressing scene, the only saving grace to cheer Queenie being the beautiful furniture, now sadly neglected.

In every room without exception, there were items of furniture of the same Edwardian period as the house: heavy and square-set, fashioned in warmest walnut wood. Queenie's first thoughts were that the house must have been purchased complete with all its furniture, something Sheila had later confirmed.

Following Sheila and Maisie's convictions for keeping a brothel, the house had been closed down by the police. Yet on Queenie's arrival there were enough unsavoury characters who had since crept back and were now making an establishment there, that gave her cause for concern. And poor old Maisie was in no fit state to show them the door.

Queenie had made this observation to Sheila straight away, on her very first visit. At once, afraid for herself and wary of an extended term of imprisonment, Sheila had implored Queenie, 'For Gawd's sake! Get the buggers out! Tell 'em to piss off outta there, and that *I* said so . . . else they'll face the bloody consequences when I get me 'ands on 'em! An' if that mother o' mine kicks up a fuss . . . kick 'er out an' all!' Then, with her temper spent, she had softly pleaded, 'Queenie, gel! Turn that place around for me, eh? Them other places along there makes a bloody good living . . . y'know, taking in guests an' the like . . .'olidaymakers! You manage it, tek a wage. Look 'ere, if anybody can do it, *you* can. Will you do it for me an' me Mam, Queenie?'

In the face of her friend's asking, how could Queenie say no? Truth be told, it would be a wonderful challenge, just the thing for Sheila to look forward to. And with Sheila childishly excited and insisting that her friend be now regarded as her 'manageress' Queenie took on the role with a sense of serious responsibility.

So, in the wake of old Maisie's jeering, the threats of violent retribution from the house's unwelcome tenants, Queenie had flung open every door and window through which she then threw the protesting rebels. Like a whirlwind, she swept through that place, pulling down every curtain and remnant, sweeping, scrubbing, dusting and polishing everything in sight. Maisie, too, was treated to her first proper soap and water bath for years although the way she screamed and hollered, Queenie feared the old woman would surely have a heart-attack.

Afterwards, with the place spick and span, the windows brightly shining and bedecked with a brand new sign proclaiming 'Bed, Breakfast and Evening Meal – Vacancies,' Queenie baked old-fashioned recipes taught her by Auntie Biddy – hot-pot, bacon-dumpling, spotted-dick pudding and the like. It was only a matter of time before the word got around that the guest-house newly named 'Kingsway', and under fresh management, was a force to be reckoned with. Even Maisie crept out of her room more often, to see what was going on.

Since then, the little guest-house had gone from strength to strength.

Some instinct now caused Queenie to gather her thoughts and look across the room to where Sheila stood, flanked by two officers and scanning the sea of heads in search of her visitor. At once, Queenie got to her feet and gave a small wave in order to catch Sheila's eye.

The prisoner had stepped away from the officers, and in a moment Sheila was facing Queenie across the table, her eyes wide and bright as she grabbed Queenie's arm. 'Like me escort did you? Waiting for

me they are, Queenie gal! So give us me fags quick,
else they'll 'ave me away 'fore I gets a bloody drag!'

'Oh no!' Queenie groaned, glancing nervously at the
two officers by the door, who did appear to be biding
their time. 'You haven't been up to no good again,
Sheila?' Reaching into her bag she withdrew a packet
of cigarettes, and before she could hand them across
the table, Sheila had seized them. 'A light, gal!' she
urged, impatient for the matches which Queenie
quickly produced.

'Naw! I *ain't* been up to no good! It's just, well . . .
I get blamed for everything that goes on round 'ere.'
She paused to draw long and hard on the cigarette.
'Must 'ave believed me, gal, eh? Else they wouldn't
even 'ave let me see you at all! The other two had *all*
their privileges tekken away. I've got ten minutes with
you . . . and I've to miss next visiting time.'

Queenie had already been told by the governor that
Sheila had done nothing to rid herself of the tag of
'known trouble-maker'. 'Unless she comes to her
senses,' he'd said, '. . . she'll get no remission!'
Queenie had related this to Sheila, who had dismissed
it out of hand. 'Got it in for me, gal!' was all she would
say. Queenie despaired.

Their conversation had to be brief. While Sheila
smoked incessantly, Queenie told her that Maisie was
no worse, that she sent her love, and that the little
hotel was doing well – the accounts were there for
Sheila to see when she came home.

'Aw! I don't need to see no accounts, Queenie! I
wouldn't understand them anyway. You've done me
and me mam proud and I can never repay you,' Sheila
told her.

Queenie felt embarrassed. 'Don't be silly!' she

retorted, before changing the subject to ask after Hannah, an elderly woman who according to Sheila had not received a single visitor for well over a year now. The subject of old Hannah, put away some twenty years or more ago for the murder of her husband, was a regular topic between Sheila and Queenie. Of late, Queenie had begun to leave a small hamper at the gate for Hannah. Messages of thanks would come back via Sheila, and in answer to Queenie's questions about Hannah's background and family, Sheila could only tell her that Hannah's mind wandered so much, you could never tell whether she was talking sense or not. But by all accounts there had been a lad who was adopted.

'She's harmless enough, Queenie. I can't believe she really *murdered* somebody. The authorities can't think she's dangerous though, eh?' asked Sheila one wary eye on the officers who were now moving in her direction, 'else they wouldn't 'ave brought her from Manchester to an *open* prison, now would they?' She was puffing the cigarette furiously now.

'On your feet, Bannion – time's up.' The officer placed a hand on the back of Sheila's chair, and as Sheila returned what was left of the cigarettes and matches to Queenie, their hands touched and held for a moment, during which time Queenie said quietly, 'Sheila, please try . . . for Maisie's sake, if not your own.'

Sheila squeezed Queenie's hand. As she got to her feet she laughed, 'I'm not as bad as I'm med out to be!' And winking at one of the officers, she added, 'There's worse than *me*, wouldn't you say, eh?'

The officer removed his hand from the back of

Sheila's chair and gestured for her to move, at the same time half-smiling as he retorted, 'I doubt it, Bannion . . . I doubt it!'

But there was no smile on the second officer's face as he stood to one side, jerking his head to intimate that it was time for Sheila to go. This she did, calling out to Queenie, 'Keep up the good work, Queenie. Hey! Why don't you come anyway next visiting and see old Hannah! Be a treat for 'er, that would!'

Queenie watched until she could no longer see Sheila's brown head, devoid now of the bleach which even Maisie had long denied herself. Then, with Sheila's suggestion running through her mind, she sat patiently waiting until the duty officer told her she could go, after which she left to make her way back to Lytham St Anne's; where she knew Maisie would be waiting for news of her wayward daughter.

Some forty-five minutes later Queenie alighted from the bus on the sea-front at Lytham St Anne's, and as was her way, she did not make straight for the hotel. Instead, she crossed to where the iron railings cordoned off the pavement from the beach below. Here she leaned on the railings, fetching her thoughtful gaze far out to where the sea heaved in fits and starts, every now and then spitting out jagged lines of white foam which quickly folded into themselves and disappeared.

Queenie loved to look out across the sea, especially in March when there was an angry turbulent freedom about it which held her in envy and fascination. Yet that same turbulence which caused the sea to gyrate and writhe as though in a strange fit of anguish never failed to bring a sense of contentment to her. Like magic, the deep ache which ever held her heart from being free would ease for a while. In these moments, she could look back over the years, draw out the memories and savour them without pain. Memories of Parkinson Street, of Auntie Biddy . . . and most of all memories of her and Rick together and in love.

The image of Rick loomed up in her mind's eye, and just for the briefest moment, a tear threatened. It didn't matter how hard she tried to dismiss what the two of them had shared, or how wide grew the span of time since their last meeting, she loved him until at times she thought she *must* seek him out. But these desperate urges were allowed only the smallest element of consideration, for Queenie had learned well how to keep them under control.

Other, nastier thoughts crowded her mind, uppermost in them that of Mrs Bedford, Mike's mother. According to Katy, she had become somewhat of a dubious character, dealing with rogues and living on the wrong side of the law. It seemed also that she was a person whose wrath you must not provoke.

Queenie couldn't help but smile cynically at that particular thought, for if anybody had provoked that woman's wrath it was Queenie herself. All the same, it was not a matter for smiles of *any* description. Mike had tried to make her a good husband, and in spite of his crippling jealousy and smothering possessiveness, he had done the best that was in him to do.

At this point in her thoughts, Queenie sighed, her heart heavy for wasted years and for the unfulfilment of those dreams which had belonged to others than herself. Not for the first time since that night years ago when she had lost both a husband and a child, she wondered whether there might have been anything, any word or action, that could have halted such an avalanche of tragedy. And back came the same answer as always. No! There was nothing, not a single thing she could have made herself do, that could have truly altered the course of things. She knew that, yet still she searched for the fault in herself.

After a while, when the sharp incoming breeze had pinched her face and numbed her ears, Queenie turned her back on the sea, to gaze across the road to where a row of grand Edwardian houses stood typically big and square with coloured glass fanlights, strong broad windows and a proud rising of steps to each stained-glass front door. Towards the centre of the row was a house made conspicuous by its sparkling windows and absence of net curtains as well as by the polished brass number and nameplate fixed to the door post. As always when looking at Kingsway Queenie was filled with a sense of satisfaction, never dulled by the fact that she was only temporarily managing the house until Sheila could take over. It had demanded every minute of every day since her arrival here first to rid the house of its bad reputation, then to lift it out of the guest-house league and into that of a small hotel. Under the new name she had given it, and with a great deal of hard work and determination, Queenie had succeeded in creating a reputable establishment with an enviable name for quality and service.

Waiting by the kerb for a taxi to pass before the road became clear, Queenie thanked God that Sheila would have something worthwhile to come home to. When her time was served and her debt to society paid,

Sheila deserved a new start. Queenie was glad that she had been able to help. The matter of her own future was not a priority.

As she started across the road, Queenie was interested to see a regular guest, by the name of Miss Taylor, emerge from the hotel with her arm wound round a man. There was nothing unusual about that in itself, but something about the manner in which the man shook himself free as she giggled alerted Queenie to the suspicions she had developed about 'Miss Taylor' since the woman checked into Kingsway three nights ago.

Her suspicions were now instantly confirmed by the man reaching into his waistcoat and handing the woman what looked to Queenie like a clutch of bank notes.

At once, Queenie vowed to despatch that woman from the premises without delay and to make sure she never returned. But then Queenie glanced at the man's face and all but froze in her tracks.

It had been so long ago that she could not be sure, yet she was certain enough to turn her face away for fear he might recognize her. As she walked away, the knowledge of his identity had set Queenie trembling; for it *was* Mr Marsden! Rick's adoptive father. Somewhat looser in build than he had been and more bent at the shoulders, but it was him right enough, paying that woman, presumably for certain pleasurable entertainment. And on Sheila's premises! Queenie was in doubt as to what the authorities would have to say if this became known. No matter how Queenie tried to persuade herself that she might be mistaken, there was no denying the transaction which had so obviously taken place.

Keeping watch from the end of the street, Queenie waited until Mr Marsden took his leave and the woman disappeared inside. Then she hurriedly made her way down the street and into the hotel, to seek out 'Miss Taylor' to satisfy herself that she had not misinterpreted the entire incident. What followed would be determined by the outcome of that. But Queenie did not intend to stand for any nonsense.

So intent on her errand was Queenie that she did not see Mr Marsden pause in his departure and glance back to witness her entry into Kingsway. Queenie Bedford . . . the woman whose very name, and that of her dead father, caused him to cringe. The woman who took delight in tormenting his son, and who was playing a game he had not yet fathomed. Though he'd been given an inkling by the investigator that she had returned north some time back, he had not pushed for her exact whereabouts since it had been enough for him to block Rick's own efforts to trace her. Recently though, the whole matter had become more urgent because having grown increasingly frustrated in his fruitless search for Queenie, Rick had dispensed with the idea of using a third person and had taken it upon himself to track her down. These last few weeks he had been relentless in his determination and judging by Rick's excited nature recently, he was close to finding Queenie Bedford. There'd be no shaking Rick off now. He would trace the woman, there was no doubt on it. And by God! here she was, going into that place . . . a place of pleasure for those that could pay and which he had discovered only recently, through a business colleague. Well! Well! Well! So Queenie Bedford was no more than a trollop, eh? Hadn't he always said as much!

What intrigued him, and had done these past years, was why the woman hadn't taken Rick for all he was worth. She must know he doted on her. And that a Marsden was a good catch. There was something very odd about it, unless she was no fool and knew that being a Marsden would demand more of her than she'd got to give. Or happen there was a deal more dirt about her than she wanted to reveal, eh? Whatever the reason she didn't take advantage of his son's feelings, here was *one* who was glad of it and who intended to keep it that way.

Mr Marsden's initial expression at recognizing Queenie had been one of shock and surprise. But now, with such a delightful train of thought running through his mind, his face held a look of dark conniving.

As he hurried away from there, he actually laughed aloud. There was meat on this here bone he'd found, and like a dog, he did not intend to let it go.

Inside the house, Queenie stood for a moment in the centre of the hallway, and as her searching gaze moved from door to door and then upwards beyond the wide curling stairway, she could not even in her state of anxiety wholly suppress that pleasant surge of pride she felt on seeing how beautifully shone the relief carvings on the walnut dresser which displayed pamphlets offering all manner of holidaying information. And the little wooden panelled reception-counter fitted so neatly into the spacious alcove beneath the stairs, sparkling and bedecked with signing-in ledger, dining-room menus and a little brass hand-bell.

The floor of the hall was dressed in its original Edwardian tiles of blue and brown ceramic. Now, as Queenie strode across it, her heels rang out a resounding rhythm which had the effect of echoing her frustration. There was no sign of anyone! Where *has* the woman gone? she thought. Queenie headed upstairs to continue her search.

Once up the broad carpeted stairs and onto the galleried landing, it took only a moment for Queenie to locate 'Miss Taylor'; for both her and Maisie Thorogood's voices could be heard emanating from Maisie's room some three doors down. First there was laughter, quickly followed by anger.

'Right!' muttered Queenie as she marched off in the direction of Maisie's room. The stern look in her eyes and the grim set of her lovely mouth proclaimed her ready for anything. When she reached the door, however, what she witnessed fair took her breath away.

Maisie's sick-room door was open, and there she was, her ailing body hitched up in bed, wrestling a bundle of notes from one of the other woman's hands. 'Miss Taylor' for *her* part was bent forward over the bed, her left fist locked onto a hank of Maisie's thinning white hair which she was viciously yanking backwards and forwards as she screamed, 'You old cow! I should pull every last bloody piece of 'air out by the roots and I'm buggered if I won't! Unless you let loose o' that money! Share and share alike, I said, not me earn and you bloody take!'

For just a split second Queenie stood by the door, rigid with shock. Then her fury took over and springing across the room she grabbed the woman's arm which in turn caused her to pull on Maisie's hair, and Maisie to scream at the top of her voice like all hell was let loose.

Undeterred, Queenie swung the woman round, her

own voice fearsome as it yelled, 'Out! Get yourself out of here! Now! Before I've time to change my mind and call the police!' Sheila's release being uppermost in her mind, Queenie hoped the woman wouldn't recognize the bluff for what it was. The very last thing on her mind was to expose Maisie's part in all of this.

'All right! I'm going!' The woman's painted eyes were wide open and defiant. 'It ain't *me* you oughta throw out! It's *that* one!' she accused. And thrusting a fist in Maisie's direction, she added vehemently, 'Greedy old sod! Worst bloody pimp I've 'ad yet, so she is!'

'Go on then! Sod off, you baggage!' came Maisie's reply. She had clung hard to the bank notes and now with a swiftness which belied her weak state of health, she thrust them· under the mattress before returning her full attention to the matter in question. 'Seen better whores down the market earning more in a day than *you* could fetch in a bloody week! Go on! Be off with yer!' she jeered.

At this point, Queenie was beginning to see the funny side of it in spite of everything. To Maisie's warning she swiftly added her own. Turning to the woman, she instructed, 'Exactly! Be off with you!' In a matter of minutes, she and Maisie were left alone.

Seated on the edge of Maisie's bed, Queenie asked in a gentle voice, 'Maisie – whatever possessed you? Have you so little thought for Sheila?'

For a long moment, Maisie gave no answer but lay rasping and wheezing, her puffed face devoid of colour and her fist protecting the place into which she had squeezed her money. Then very slowly and with seeming great pain, her features crept into the shape

Queenie had known as Maisie those many years ago down Parkinson Street. With her lips curled into a smile, she chortled, 'Useless baggage! Eh! I could 'a shown that one a thing or two in me time, Queenie gel! Allus set the pace did Maisie, eh?' The artfulness of Maisie Thorogood rose to kindle her old eyes, growing bright like a candle flame in its last throes. And Queenie knew the futility of chiding her. Instead, she gave the old rascal a disapproving shake of the head, tucked her up, and left her quietly chortling to herself.

The twinkle never came back to Maisie's eyes. The next morning she was found lifeless and the money, amounting to more than a thousand pounds, stuffed into a slit in the mattress.

The doctor said Maisie had died of a 'riotous heart'. But in view of what she'd found out, Queenie believed the cause to be more like riotous living.

On hearing the news from Queenie, Sheila launched into a fit of giggling. 'The artful bugger!' she said over and over again, chuckling until the tears spilled down her cheeks and her laughter turned to sobbing. 'Oh, but I'll miss the old cow,' she cried in a hoarse whisper.

'I know, Sheila love,' Queenie consoled her, but there was a tightness in her own throat, which might just hold until she was out of Sheila's presence. 'The days won't be the same without Maisie,' she conceded.

It was in low moments like these that Queenie's thoughts turned to Rick. But for now, even that gave her small comfort.

The prison authorities allowed Sheila to go to her mother's funeral. It was just as well that she was under escort, because several times throughout the service she whispered to Queenie, 'First chance I get, Queenie, gal, I'm off! The buggers won't be expecting me to abscond at a time like this. But they'll be wrong won't they, eh?'

It took all of Queenie's powers of persuasion to convince Sheila that she'd do well to forget that particular idea. After all, if she watched her Ps and Qs especially now she had lost poor Maisie, there was every chance that Sheila might get a deal of remission. She could be out within the year. And hadn't she got a grand hotel and a fair bank-balance to come home to? This had been swelled considerably by the addition of the thousand pounds found in Maisie's mattress – a sum rightfully described by Sheila as 'a bloody fortune'. It was all there waiting for Sheila to do with as she saw fit; the money Maisie had left, together with every penny profit made from the guest-house, all dutifully deposited in Sheila's name.

Found with the money in Maisie's mattress had been a grubby piece of paper folded into a brown envelope and addressed to 'My gal, Sheila'. The message it contained was only just decipherable, scrawled as it was in spidery infantile lettering. But the legal representative Queenie sought out had no hesitation in declaring the piece of paper to be a valid will; being duly dated and witnessed, and requesting that on Maisie's demise, legal rights to the deeds of the house and everything in it should, in Maisie's words, 'Go to my las, Sheila. And as I've not set eyes on that bloody wandering lad of mine since he buggered off years back, I intend he'll get sod al!'

So, in view of Sheila's now considerable nest-egg, Queenie demanded whether all of that was worth the silly-minded notion to 'abscond'. And if that wasn't enough to convince Sheila, Queenie instructed her quite forcibly that unless these foolhardy ideas were given short shrift, she would find the hotel under new management. 'You needn't expect *me* to stay around and see you locked away forever!' she whispered harshly.

'You wouldn't desert me would you, Queenie?' Sheila had asked. But one look at Queenie's stormy grey eyes told her differently. After that, there was no more talk of Sheila 'absconding'.

After the funeral, Queenie and Sheila hugged each other and Sheila thanked Maisie's nurse for having looked after her mam. Then the handful of mourners went their separate ways – the nurse to her next patient, Sheila back to Rirkham prison, and Queenie home to ring her darling Katy and to draw comfort from her voice.

Chapter Six

On the Friday following Maisie's funeral Queenie made her usual fortnightly visit to Rirkham prison. On this particular occasion however, it was not to visit Sheila, whose privileges were still withheld; but to take up the opportunity to see Hannah, who by all accounts would welcome such a visit.

Certainly, if the bright smile with which she greeted Queenie was anything to go by, Hannah was clearly delighted. 'You'll be Sheila's friend then?' she asked, 'the one who leaves me hampers?' The moment she had seated herself, Hannah reached across the table to grasp Queenie's hand, and for a long time she made no sign of releasing her hold.

'Yes . . . I'm glad we've met at last, Hannah.' Queenie's returning smile concealed the shock she had experienced on seeing this dainty little woman, who looked pathetically out of place in such an institution as this. According to Sheila, Hannah was in her mid-fifties; but she looked older. Now, as she leaned forward towards Queenie, her small reddened eyes narrowing to slits, it was painfully evident that her sight was deteriorating. She was a tiny creature, whose delicate chalk-white features caressed by a soft halo of snow-white hair put Queenie in mind of a doll.

During the time allowed Queenie discovered many things about this endearing little woman, who was prone to rambling with such zeal that she hardly paused to take a breath. Queenie had let her talk on without interruption, reminding herself of what Sheila had pointed out: that Hannah had not received a visitor for over a year.

'I've got a son you know! Oh yes, 'e'll be going on thirty now,' she said proudly. With a look of sadness she went on, 'Don't know where 'e is . . . or even what 'e's called . . . taken from me when . . . when . . .' Her voice faltered and caught within itself. Then, artificially brighter, it continued, 'Adopted you see . . . the only way . . . give 'im a fair chance.'

'Have you heard nothing of him since?' Queenie had taken the little woman to heart, and it grieved her to think of the tragic circumstances which had deprived such a sad lonely creature of her only child. 'Heard nothing! The lad won't want me . . . an' who could blame 'im? Likely as not 'e don't even know I'm alive. Some woman used to come visiting me . . . told me lies she did!'

'Lies? In what way?'

'Said she was me sister. Well, I've never 'ad no sister . . . nor brother. I think it were that one as 'ad my boy . . . I don't know. It's all best left alone! The lad's gone now . . . they've *all* gone, and thank the Lord for it.' Her voice cracked and, looking away, she continued to mumble in so incoherent a voice that Queenie could not make sense of it. 'Do you want me to go, Hannah?' Queenie asked, fearful that in some way she was upsetting the little woman.

At once, and with such swiftness that it caught Queenie unawares, Hannah got to her feet. 'No dear,' she said in a hushed tone, as though planning with a conspirator, 'they watch everything 'ere. *I'll* leave first . . . draw them away from you.' And with a parting smile she headed towards where the wardens flanked the doorway, pausing but once to look back at Queenie and ask, 'You will come and see me again, won't you dear? I like you . . . I can trust you.'

Queenie's answer was to smile and nod her head. Was it any wonder, she thought, that Hannah appeared to be losing her mind? Twenty-five years locked away, her family destroyed by her own hand, and nothing to look forward to but the rest of her life imprisoned. Well, there was one thing at least that Hannah could look forward to now, resolved Queenie, and that was regular visits from herself. She would let the poor unfortunate creature talk to her heart's content in the hope that it might ease her burden.

All the way home, Queenie reflected on Hannah's ramblings. She wondered about the woman who had claimed to be Hannah's sister . . . was she *really* her sister? And if so, why had she stopped visiting? Then there was the son, who must have been little more than a baby when taken for adoption. Where was he? Had he been told of his mother, and perhaps because of the nature of her imprisonment chosen to turn his back on her? Or was Hannah right? Happen he didn't know of her at all.

Whatever the answers, one thing was certain to Queenie's mind. That poor woman back there in Rirkham prison was being punished twice over for her dreadful deed. She bore the guilt of murdering her husband and was rightly deprived of her own freedom because of it. But to lose her child also . . . and this last year to have no visitor from the outside world! Surely that was more punishment than a body could endure. The matter of Hannah had played on Queenie's mind, waking her several times during the night, and getting her from her bed at the unusually early hour of five on Saturday morning, with a stirring headache which resisted all manner of medication.

Saturday was always a busy time at Kingsway. It was the beginning and end of a week, and the day on which most guests came and went. Queenie was never later rising from her bed than six o'clock, for there was so much to be done – and tonight there was a special guest arriving, because Katy was coming to spend a few days.

It seemed old Katy thought Maisie's absence might be somewhat made up for by her own presence and she was right, bless her old heart, thought Queenie, as with renewed vigour she had bustled about making sure everything was in order. Three times before breakfast, she'd gone into the dining-room to satisfy herself that the ten pretty circular tables were dressed with fresh ivory linen tablecloths and set smartly for breakfast. She must have checked the buffet-table at least a dozen times. Was there enough butter? Were the wicker trays filled with warm fresh-baked rolls? Had the cereal containers been topped up? And had Nelly, the little live-in help, put out the condiment-sets and made sure of enough cups and saucers?

As usual everything had been in perfect order thanks to Nelly, a bright young thing of seventeen whom Queenie had taken on some twelve months back together with a middle-aged woman called Maud who was taken on a casual basis only, when Queenie was in need of her.

Between Queenie and the two helpers everything was done like clockwork. Breakfast was served, cleared away after and the washing-up done. Beds were changed, bathrooms were scrubbed, every nook and cranny was scoured, lunch was taken and evening dinner prepared. Days were hectic and demanding, especially in the height of season, but Queenie loved every minute of it. Never on a single day did she regret taking on such responsibility.

But now, it was eight o'clock in the evening, the dinner things were all put away and the tables set ready for tomorrow's breakfast. Nelly was in her own little bedsit on the first floor, some of the guests had packed and gone (leaving only five, and they were out) and Queenie was relaxing in her own sitting-room on the ground floor. Queenie's living area consisted of the sitting-room and a single bedroom off which was a bathroom of diminutive proportions, but with which Queenie was perfectly satisfied.

Queenie wasn't expecting Katy for at least another fifteen minutes so when the outer door-bell rang, she looked up with some surprise. In a moment she was hurrying across the hall into the vestibule, where she flung open the door in eager anticipation.

The growing smile which had anticipated Katy's presence hardened into a look of shocked surprise when she saw who it was standing out there in the night.

His name fell from Queenie's lips as she involuntarily took a step back. 'Mr Marsden!'

Taking swift advantage of Queenie's small retreat, Rick's father set his foot inside the hall and before she might protest he had closed the outer door, shuffled past her, then with himself on the inside and Queenie on the outside he faced her, saying, 'I understand you've had a recent bereavement, Mrs Bedford. Please accept my condolences.' His voice was charming and gave away nothing of his devious thoughts.

These last weeks he'd made it his business to find out more about this place. And he was glad that he'd done so for he could easily have made both a costly mistake and a fool of himself. Yet he would much have preferred his first impression, that Queenie Bedford was living and working in a house of prostitution, to have been the right one. Instead of this his enquiries had told him just the opposite, that she had dragged it from a place of dark reputation to a thriving establishment catering for holidaymakers and boarders. There had been those, the bed-ridden owner especially and some long-time acquaintance of Queenie Bedford, who had been loath to let go the flow of money got from 'other' pursuits, the same which he himself had followed here with great relish.

'What is it you want, Mr Marsden?' Queenie had not moved, and in spite of the shock his arrival had given her, there was no betrayal of it in her voice.

For what seemed an age to Queenie, but was in fact only a matter of seconds, Mr Marsden let his gaze move over the young woman before him. He admired the way she faced him, tall and forthright, hard in her expression, yet beautiful and commanding. He could see instantly that the frightened girl over whom his son had made such a fool of himself that night at the house was not so very evident in this woman who looked at him now so indignantly, and yet in such a way that she stirred a deep desire even in him. Such a revelation was so repugnant to him that he became all the more determined to be rid of her once and for all and to pay whatever price might be demanded for the release of his son from her magnetic thrall.

Something in her manner, in her calmness and control, cautioned Mr Marsden to take the whole thing slowly. He did not want to leave this place without having achieved what he'd set out to do. With a mingling of cunning and admiration that caused his smile to broaden and his voice to take on an uncommon mildness, he said, 'Please forgive me if I've intruded, but I would like to talk to you about my son, Rick. Could we perhaps go inside?'

'I think not, Mr Marsden. There is nothing at all I need to discuss with you!'

'Ah, but there is! With regard to . . . certain matters, I think you *will* want to talk.'

Queenie did some quick thinking. This man, Rick's adoptive father, did not like her, had never liked her. From the first moment she'd met him that evening at the Marsden house, she had been aware of his hostility towards her. Bearing in mind that he had brought up the son of his wife's former lover as his own and then had seen that same man's daughter in his own house and playing on the affections of a young man who was her own brother, Queenie was forced to ask herself how in all truth could she blame Mr Marsden. Was he not acting in the way *any* man would act, how she herself might act in such circumstances?

All of these considerations might have persuaded

Queenie to be more sympathetic to Mr Marsden's attitude had it not been for two things. One was the unpleasant deviousness about this man which always put her on her guard. The other was the fact that he had frequented this house to procure the services of a prostitute. And, according to Katy, his own wife ill at home!

Her first instinct had been to see him off as quickly as she knew how. But she felt compelled to hear him out, because he had stated that his business was to do with Rick.

Coming into the hall she met his gaze unflinchingly, and in a clipped voice she told him, 'Go through into the dining-room – we won't be disturbed there.' Queenie had no intention of showing him into her *own* quarters. As he stepped sideways to let her pass and lead them on, she remarked, 'I was sure you'd know the way, Mr Marsden, as you are no stranger to this house!'

He made no reply, and Queenie chose not to pursue the matter. In a moment, the two of them were in the dining-room, she standing before the big open fireplace and he with his back to the window. Then in a gruff voice which conveyed to Queenie a measure of embarrassment and which at the time surprised her, he started talking. When he spoke, he took to pacing the floor, as though irritated by his own words. 'I don't really know how to start, Mrs Bedford . . . I don't know what *you* yourself have in mind as regards my son.' He lifted his gaze from the polished tops of his shoes to look questioningly into Queenie's face, and when no help came from that direction, he gave a small grunt, cleared his throat and continued, 'Very well! I'll come straight to the point. If you've a mind to get in touch with Rick, you'd do best to forget it. I'm very well aware of what was going on between you two and that he might have given you the impression there'd be summat of a future for the both of you.' At this point he stopped in his pacing, flung his fists together behind his back, stretched himself up and looking straight at Queenie, he said with some deliberation, 'Rick is to be married shortly, and I'll not have anything put in the way of that! I know you've designs on him . . . playing tricks to whet his appetite, and biding your time to mek a move. I'm here to ask you to keep away. Name your price!'

Queenie had stood in silence all the while, listening to his words as all manner of emotions raged through her. What kind of man was he! And what measure of woman did he take *her* for! What was that he'd said: 'designs on Rick' . . . 'biding your time to make a move'. And all of that leading to a demand for her to 'name a price'! Did he really think she wanted anything other than for Rick to find happiness, to find in another woman's arms what she so much wanted to give him, yet could not. So it seemed that Rick had indeed found someone to love and to return that love. Queenie was glad of that, because it meant that at last he could build a secure future for himself. He would have someone to bear his children, to give him a family, which Queenie knew in her heart she herself would *never* have.

There had been one marriage in her life, a disastrous arrangement she would never forget. It had been a means of escape, a flight from reality, and the price paid had been a cruel one with the newborn child dead, Mike killed, and herself a fugitive in a foreign land.

Yet, though Queenie found a degree of comfort in the knowledge that Rick was planning to marry, she also experienced a great hollowness within her, a digging pain of bitterness and regret. Even though she told herself that these hurtful feelings would pass, the evidence of her pain was there in the cut of her voice as she addressed Mr Marsden. 'Don't judge others by your own standards, Mr Marsden. How could you think I want *anything* other than Rick's happiness?' She had stepped towards him now, the rise of her indignation bright in the look she gave him. 'I am *not* "biding my time to make a move" as you put it. I want *nothing* from you . . . I have *no* mind to "get in touch with Rick", and the news that he is to be married is wonderful!' Queenie was close to tears, afraid that if he did not leave then and there she would surely betray herself to him.

Mr Marsden made no move. His mind was churning over what Queenie had just said, and the conclusion he came to was that either she was a bloody good actress and intended to give nothing away, perhaps playing him for a bigger reward; or there was something going on here that for the life of him he could not get to grips with. He'd have it out and be damned to it all!

'What's your game?' he demanded. 'Don't tell me you haven't been playing hard to get and leading my son a dance these past years? What! The man's spent a bloody fortune chasing you about . . . thought about nowt else but Queenie Bedford! Queenie Bedford! Like a man possessed he's been, and within the week he'll be knocking on that bloody door, I'm telling you!' He jerked his head to the street outside and became so agitated that he brushed past Queenie and took up pacing to and fro from one end of the room to the other, his voice thick with anger. 'Oh aye, he's found a woman, the best catch in Lancashire by *my* reckonings! But it's *her* as is doing all the running . . . *her* as is ready for mekking the vows. As for Rick, he still hasn't got *you* out of his system! I'm here to change that, don't you see? So don't be trying any of your cunning on *me* because I'm wise to your bloody sort. Let's have the truth, eh? What'll it tek to shake you off him . . . come on! Let's have it straight out!'

And now Queenie's anger was a match for his own as she sharply brought herself into his path, and facing him square on, she uttered in a calm, though trembling, voice, 'What kind of monster are you, Mr Marsden? No! I won't deny that I love Rick, and that if it was possible, I'd go to him this very minute, any way he wanted me! I won't deny either that Rick and I believed in all innocence that our love was untainted. When we learned the awful truth that George Kenney was father to us *both* it was like a nightmare! That was part of the reason I left Blackburn, and well you know it! So what right have you to bring yourself here, making such damned accusations?' In spite of her efforts to remain in control, Queenie found herself shaking from head to foot. 'I'm playing *no* games! I've kept away in order to give Rick every chance to get me out of his system and I'm sorry that he's been looking for me, but I know how he must feel. I *know* because I feel the same way. Oh, but don't you worry, Mr Marsden, if he does come knocking on that door it won't change anything.' She gave a small painful laugh. 'Fate does seem to be callous don't you think, letting brother and sister fall in love. Well, you needn't worry, Mr Marsden; nothing can come of it. Nothing *will* come of it. And now, I'll thank you to leave!' Queenie crossed to the door, which she held open, her whole being feeling spent. 'Please just leave,' she said.

Silenced beneath Queenie's astounding verbal attack, there had burst open in Mr Marsden's quick mind a whole boxful of explanations. Explanations as to why little had come of the passion Rick and this one so obviously had for each other. It also explained a certain mellowing towards him by his son, no doubt because he believed himself to have been adopted by a man big enough to take on the child of his wife's lover. It was not in Rick's make-up to openly broach a subject which might cause his family any pain. So *that* was the real reason for Queenie Bedford's disappearance and for her intention that Rick would not find her. He could see a lot of things now, which had not made sense before. But even now, so help him, he couldn't find it in him to trust her.

Mr Marsden could also see how it might have come about that George Kenney, who presumably had been the one to spill such malicious information, might have deduced that Rick was the boy born to Rita as a result of their affair! Nobody except a handful of folk knew that Kenney's child had died young and that Rick was the son of Rita's sister Hannah who was justifiably rotting in jail for murdering her husband. Oh yes! Such a mistake was understandable, and such a 'fortuitous' error could now be turned to his advantage, because if he could see *anything* at that moment, it was that Queenie Bedford really did love Rick, and was willing to make quite a sacrifice on his behalf.

Of a sudden, Mr Marsden's face displayed a warmth which took Queenie by surprise. 'I *will* leave, Mrs Bedford . . . but I think there are things that still have to be said. I take it you would rather see Rick married and settled than eating his heart out for something that can only spell trouble – am I right?' he said in a kindly voice. Queenie kept her gaze to the ground and only nodded in response to Mr Marsden's question, all the while her heart sore to the point of breaking.

'There is one *sure* way of deciding all this. When Rick does track you to this address, if he finds you married – *happily* married, perhaps with a child – I'm sure he'll content himself that there's no place at all for him in your future. I can arrange such a situation. There are those who would willingly play the part for a small payment . . .'

If Mr Marsden had thought his devious plan would be welcomed, he could not have been more wrong. For while he'd been talking, Queenie had lifted her head in disbelief at the length of trickery to which this man was prepared to go. She looked at him now with blazing eyes, and with all the control she could muster she flung wide the door, instructing him, 'Take yourself out of my sight! What you suggest is shameful and I'll have no part in it!' When he took a small step forward then hesitated, she yelled, 'Out! And don't bother making your way here again. If Rick knew what you'd suggested I'm sure he'd despise you!'

For just a fleeting moment, Queenie thought she detected a look of shame in Mr Marsden's countenance. But it was not there when he pursed his lips into a thoughtful expression before saying, 'You could be right Mrs Bedford . . . but I'm sure you'll spare us all a deal of aggravation by keeping such matters to yourself.' Then straightening his shoulders, he nodded slightly and made for the front door. Here he turned, to warn Queenie in a quiet voice, 'If you really do have any feelings for my son . . . *your* brother, remember! then you'll keep to your word and send him back to the woman who's been by his side these past years. She'll make a grand wife, the best! You've got my word on that.' He stayed still for a while, his look one of pleading.

Queenie kept her eyes on him, as though searching his face for some measure of honesty. And she saw it there, in his deep love for the man he'd brought up as his own son. When she spoke, there was reassurance in her voice. '*I* love Rick too, you know,' she murmured, 'and I'll never knowingly stand in the way of his happiness.' In a strange way, she could sense the man's desperation as being something akin to her own. Knowing that, she gave him a small smile. 'I hope this woman knows how very lucky she is . . . Rick is a wonderful man,' she said.

At this, Mr Marsden stroked his chin, his eyes still held fast to Queenie's and his face a thoughtful study. Then, without saying a word, he nodded his head several times, gave a grudging smile, and left.

For some time Queenie stood leaning on the doorjamb, her thoughts in a turmoil. With a small shock she found herself believing Mr Marsden's suggestion to be a good one, one which might just send Rick away. To see her as a happily married woman with a child would certainly satisfy him that she really had cut him out of her life and out of her heart.

But Queenie could never take part in such deception. She had deceived Rick once, when she'd done her best to convince him that she loved Mike in a certain way. That in itself had been a painful thing to *both* of them. No! She had decided there would be no more hiding.

There in that hallway, which was still alive from the anger between her and Mr Marsden, Queenie's voice uttered out loud the thoughts in her mind. 'Queenie my girl! If and when Rick Marsden finds you, there'll be no weakness on your part. You must send him away from you and into that woman's arms. Or there'll be no peace for *either* of you in this world!'

Chapter Seven

Rick's mind was in a turmoil. It had been so all night
and now the restlessness of that night and many nights
before showed on his face. Half-circles of deep
shadows had drawn themselves beneath the serious
brown eyes and in the grimness of his mouth and in
the expression shaping his features an air of despondency hung heavy.

He had left the house at ten minutes past six that
morning, driven by the germ of an idea which had
presented itself to him in the first light of morning, and
which would not now go away.

Rick had been convinced for a long time that the
key to Queenie's whereabouts lay with Katy Forest.
He was sure that if Queenie had felt the need to confide
in anyone, Katy would be the friend to whom she
would turn. Yet this had always been, if not denied by
Katy, evaded. She had changed the subject and used
delaying tactics that would have done a politician
proud. Not once, in all the different ways he'd
approached her concerning Queenie, had she ever
actually given him any hope or lead by which his search
might be made easier.

These last few months he had experienced something

within himself which he could not readily explain, a sense of nearness to Queenie, an expectation of sorts stirring great excitement which would not be stilled. Lately, when he'd spoken to Katy, he could have sworn that she was on the verge of imparting something to him. There was a hesitance, a certain suggestion in her voice which had set him off on a particular train of thought. Yet when he'd pressed her, Katy had clammed up in that infuriating way she had. Now he intended to pin her down . . . to draw from her whatever it was she knew, and he had no intention of backing off until she had given him at least a discreet hint as to Queenie's whereabouts.

Rick had sat in the car these last few minutes, realizing that tackling Katy successfully would not be easy. In her advancing years, she could be extremely cantankerous and obstinate. After deliberating his tactics, Rick could see only one way to deal with her.

With the fire of determination in his eyes, he started up the Vauxhall Victor, engaged the engine and set off in the direction of the vicarage. 'Head on, Katy! he said aloud. 'You'll find that I can be just as cantankerous and obstinate when needs must!'

It was ten minutes to seven when Rick arrived at the front door of the vicarage and pulled on the bell-chain. It was early, he knew, but Katy and Father Riley would have been about since before six that morning. And being Wednesday, there was an early morning service to be held.

As he waited in the porch, Rick looked about him, and as always he derived pleasure out of letting his gaze wander over the expanse of grounds fronting the old vicarage. The attractive lay of lawns and the abundance of mature shrubs and conifers always gave a feeling of serenity. But on such a day as today, in the early hours of a warm April morning, it was enhanced by the singing of birds and the perfume of buds just beginning to blossom. Rick was reminded of how much Queenie loved this place, and his determination to find out what Katy knew was strengthened.

It seemed a longer span of time than was usual before Rick could hear someone hurrying to answer the door. He quickly recognized that the steps he heard were not those of Katy but of Father Riley.

On seeing Rick at the door, the black-frocked priest gave a beaming smile, saying, 'Rick! Come in, come in. I don't know what fetches you here *this* time of a morning, but you're in time to share some breakfast, if you've a mind.' Then, without waiting for an acknowledgement, he swung about and in a moment had crossed the hall and disappeared into the kitchen.

Rick closed the front door and followed him into the kitchen, where he found Father Riley already seated at the table.

'There, sit yourself down. The tea's just made. Now then, d'you want a bite to eat?' The older man indicated a chair opposite himself, then when Rick was seated he filled two mugs from the big brown teapot.

He replaced the teapot onto its wrought-iron stand, pushed one of the mugs in front of Rick and took a careful gulp of the scalding liquid from the other. 'Grand!' he smiled. 'Like Katy always says, there's nowt to beat a good cup of tea, eh?'

'It's Katy I've come to see,' offered Rick, looking round in a search. 'Is she not about?'

While Rick was speaking, Father Riley had spread

a thick layer of marmalade over his slice of toast, which he was now consuming with gusto. 'Katy's gone gadding about,' he said after swallowing. 'Been gone these last four days . . . took off on Saturday, she did.' He picked up his toast and tore off another chunk, which he appeared to be thoroughly enjoying.

Rick's disappointment at Katy's absence was not easily disguised. In fact, if he hadn't been in the presence of a man of the cloth, he might have blurted out something a bit stronger. As it was, he rapped out a series of questions. 'Gone? Where? Did she say?'

At this Father Riley gave a chuckle. 'That's Katy! She tells me precious little these days. If I didn't know better, I'd say she was hiding a man-friend!'

'She's being secretive, is she?' This information was welcomed by Rick. Now he was *convinced* she was keeping trust with Queenie.

'Well perhaps not "secretive" . . . just guarding her privacy . . . as is the privilege of someone her age. I think she's made off to her sister's. Those two haven't been close these many years, you know.' Father Riley unashamedly ravaged the last of his toast. 'I'll not be sorry when she's back though,' he added. 'When it comes down to it. I'm not much cop at looking after myself, in spite of the lass who comes in daily.' He pointed at Rick's tea. 'Here, get that drunk while it's still hot. As Katy's not here, is there anything I can do?'

Rick shook his head. 'I don't think so,' he answered, mentally looking for the next move as he supped at the tea – aware now that Father Riley had got to his feet and was standing with his back to the cold fireplace, filling his pipe with tobacco and regarding Rick with questioning eyes.

Father Riley had guessed that Rick's business with Katy might somehow concern Queenie Bedford. Much as he would have liked to help, he was not able to do so. In certain instances old Katy played her cards very close to her chest, and woe betide anyone probing for information.

With the two men quiet in their respective thoughts, the music from the radio was a welcome intrusion. But when it stopped to make way for the seven am news the brisk male tones imparting the progress of Britain's latest application to become a member of the EEC, Father Riley lost no time in switching it off, saying, 'I'm not so sure being a member of this "Common Market" is such a good thing.' He paused to allow for a comment from Rick. When there was none, he continued, 'Perhaps it's time this Labour government was given a rest? . . . but then it's to be wondered if the Conservatives are likely to fare any better! Times are certainly restless, what with wage freezes and such like! Here we are in 1967, and looking back these last twenty-odd years since the war, I can't help wondering what progress has been made. Look at that business last year, that seamen's strike! Goods piling up in warehouses . . . choking the docks to a standstill . . .'

'Yes, that *was* a bad business . . . caused us a few headaches trying to shift stuff,' Rick said as he got to his feet. 'So you don't know how I can reach Katy?' he asked, his foremost thoughts running on.

Father Riley shook his head, 'She'll be back the morrow, I'm certain,' he said, clenching his pipe firmly with his teeth and talking out the side of his mouth. 'Old Katy never strays for very long.'

But such a reply gave Rick small comfort. He couldn't wait for Katy's whims to fetch her home, because he knew if he could find Katy *now* then without a doubt he would find Queenie.

Without further ado, and heading off the long conversation his old friend evidently wanted to embark on, Rick explained that he would make it his business to call again within a few days, when the two of them could talk at more leisure. For now, he'd best be making tracks as all manner of business was calling. The latter observation reminded Father Riley sharply of the imminence of his early morning service, due in less than an hour.

At the front door the two men shook hands and parted company; Father Riley to help himself to another mug of tea before going into the vestry to prepare for the service and Rick to pursue the matter dearest to his heart.

Since Queenie's disappearance Rick had grown adept at following up a body's movements, and in less than an hour he had located not only the name of the company whose vehicle had collected Katy from the vicarage on the previous Saturday, but also the name of the man who had actually driven the taxi. From this man, he discovered that Katy had gone to the railway station; where, according to the ticket clerk, the old lady with a forceful character had purchased a weekly return ticket to Blackpool.

Without delay and with a heightened sense of achievement which spurred him on, Rick drove the twenty-odd miles to Blackpool. Once there, he parked the car as close to the railway station as was possible, and made straight for the taxi rank that served the passengers using the station. Here he gleaned little information and it seemed as though Katy's journey had come to a full stop right there. Nobody remembered an old lady of Katy's description and temperament.

'An' I was 'ere Saturday! We were *all* 'ere!' The man took off his cap and proceeded to scratch his head with the greatest deliberation, as though doing so might aid his memory. 'Nope! I can't recall no such woman!' he said, shaking his head and lovingly replacing his cap.

Desperate now, because this driver was the last in a long line and each one telling the same empty tale, Rick urged, 'Think man! Is there anything, *anything* at all you can remember . . . an elderly lady . . . snow white hair and large in build. She's got a sharp tongue if put out . . . and knows how to speak her mind. She got off the train from Blackburn, on Saturday . . . early evening!'

'No, it don't bring nothing to mind! Nothing at all.' Here, the man paused, then stroking his chin, he said, ''Ere! Just you bide yer time a minute and I'll 'ave a word wi' yon.' At once, he had taken off from Rick's side, to amble in the direction of an enormous fat man who was leaning on the side of his taxi and digging his way through a great doorstep sandwich. 'Hey! Sat'day, late afternoon . . . did you 'appen to notice if Fred parked at the station?' asked the first man. 'Fred? Aye, 'e did! Not for long though.'

Rick had been sharp on the heels of the first driver and now further questioning of the big man produced information that Fred was a self-employed driver – a 'one-man band' who ran his own car and answered to no one. He *had* been running fares to and from the station on Saturday morning; but whether he'd picked up this old lady, nobody could be sure.

Having secured a telephone number and at least a semblance of hope, Rick followed this up by locating the nearest telephone kiosk, where he rang the given number and asked to speak to Fred. On learning that the man in question was out on a long fare and that he wouldn't be home for some three hours and that only he himself could supply information regarding his fares, Rick took the address and arranged to call around eleven-thirty; taking great care to stress the importance of his call and assuring the woman that Fred would be compensated for any possible loss of fares which might arise from this arrangement. That done, he went back to his car, drove to the sea-front and decided to kill time by strolling along the promenade.

In his light brown trousers, black polo-necked sweater and dark jacket flapping open to the breeze, Rick looked a handsome sight, drawing more than one admiring glance as he came to lean on the rails overlooking the beach. When from below came the teasing shout, 'Hello there, gorgeous!' followed by a flurry of girlish laughter, Rick laughed too, before moving on.

On this lovely day, with the promise of a glorious summer in the air and the sound of fun-loving folk all around him, he felt certain he would find his Queenie. Such a wonderful prospect brought a lightness to his step and wings to his heart.

For the first time in a long while, Rick felt at peace in himself and able to cope with anything.

Leading from the main promenade and almost exactly opposite where Rick's tall figure was throwing a shadow on the flagstones, was a broad lamp-lined street festooned with gift shops and quaint little tea-rooms. It was from one of these tea-rooms that Katy and Queenie now emerged; Katy looking decidedly uncomfortable in her navy calf-length coat and chequered headscarf, and Queenie bright and summery in a straight lemon skirt with high-heeled shoes and short loose-fitting white jacket. 'Oh Katy, it's been wonderful having you with me these last few days. *Must* you go back tonight?' she said, smiling radiantly.

'Aye, lass . . . I must. Heaven only knows what chaos Father Riley's preparing for me. The poor man's helpless! Helpless as a babby! I'm telling you!'

'But you'll come again, soon, won't you Katy?' Somehow, with Katy close, Queenie felt happier in herself.

Before answering, Katy halted, undid the large chrome buttons of her coat and eased it slightly open, then flapped the coat back and forth by its lapels, blowing out exaggerated breaths. 'Phew . . . it's looking like another warm day, Queenie lass!' Now she grasped the knot of her headscarf to undo it, and thrusting the scarf into her handbag, she laughed aloud, 'Best take that off, eh? Afore me brains cook!'

Queenie laughed with her, then put her arm through Katy's as she repeated her earlier question. 'You will come and stay with me again, won't you, Katy?'

The two of them were standing in the middle of the pavement, and irate holidaymakers, anxious not to waste a minute of their precious time, began to push past, letting it be known by loud tutting and quiet comments about 'folks blocking the way' that Katy and Queenie were causing some irritation.

But there they stood, Queenie awaiting her answer

and Katy looking at her with a little smile on her face and a host of loving memories in her heart. In her mind's eye she could see Queenie as the lass who'd been brought to the vicarage all those years back. A tormented slip of a thing who even then would not sell her pride for a sure place in Katy's kitchen. Queenie had come a long way and survived things too dark for thoughts to dwell on. Oh, aye! she was med o'good strong stuff an' not easily brought down. But the past hadn't altogether left her, observed Katy, for there was still a scarred reflection of it in Queenie's eyes, in spite of their beauty and brightness. Katy wondered if she'd ever see the day when those grey eyes were free of pain altogether. Oh, how she did hope so! For the moment however, there were a few hours of exploring ahead of them, and the idea was to enjoy every blessed minute.

'Now, what sort o' daft question is *that* to ask?' she chided Queenie, taking her hand and shaking it. 'O' course I intend to come and stay again! You try an' keep me away, that's all!' Setting off now, and taking Queenie with her, she urged, 'Come on, lass! Let's tek us-selves onto yon promenade an' find a couple o' deck-chairs. We'll let the sun wash us faces for a while, eh?'

That was exactly what they did. Queenie had stopped at the ice-cream cart to collect two cornets of strawberry-flavoured delight, topped with a chocolate flake and sprinkled with chopped nuts, for the two of them to enjoy whilst lazing in the deck-chairs which fronted the promenade.

Some few minutes later, while Katy dozed in the gentle warmth of the sun, Queenie leaned forward onto the rails to gaze out at the sea. It was calm today, peaceful, she thought, just like these last few days. What sights she and Katy had seen, and what fun it had all been! There had been a fascinating afternoon spent in the amusement arcade, where Katy had sat in a booth and piloted an aircraft and she herself had lost the price of a pair of sandals by feeding coin after coin into a waterfall of money. She wouldn't be tempted into doing *that* again.

The day before yesterday, when the rain had poured from the sky in bucketsful, trapping her and Katy in the doorway of Woolworths, Katy had caught sight of a big blue policeman in a glass case on the forecourt.

In spite of the rain, Katy had gone to the case, put a coin in and waited to see what would happen. What happened was that the policeman commenced first moving and then laughing with a gusto that had Katy and Queenie shedding tears of delight. The numerous folk squashed into Woolworths' doorway felt obliged to come out and take part in the fun; one little boy was so fascinated that he went round and round the glass case, gazing up at the gyrating policeman, his fingers in his ears and his eyes so wide and great they looked set to pop from his head.

It had been a wonderful few days in Katy's company and though Queenie was sorry it was coming to an end, she knew also that her own time was in great demand, what with guest bookings flooding in and all manner of accounts to be done, not to mention the making of time in between for Sheila and Hannah.

Getting to her feet Queenie stood with her back to the sea, the breeze teasing out long wisps of hair from beneath the soft braids and blowing them about her face, so that when she gazed down on Katy, it was necessary to draw her hands across her temples in order to see without hindrance.

With Katy in a deep snooze, Queenie brought her attention to the people thronging by. It fascinated her to see the many forms of fashion. Some girls looking to be sixteen or more dressed like baby dolls in loose, short ruffled cotton frocks and flat slippers . . . their hair bobbed into severe lines about their ears. Others were dressed like little old grannies, with frilly dresses reaching to the calf and often half-covered by a fringed shawl about their shoulders. Some of them wore small rimless spectacles and pale pearlescent lipstick. The boys had taken to sporting narrow trousers, collarless shirts and bright peacock colours. Though Queenie herself liked soft bright colours and feminine clothes, she could never have seen herself in some of these wayward fashions – especially those 'baby-doll' smocks which came almost up to the thighs . . . and on which Katy had commented with some unusual exasperation, 'They've only to bend down an' nothing's left to imagination!'

'Queenie, lass. You wouldn't fetch me a cuppa tea, would you? I'm that parched.' Katy had opened her eyes and was screwing them up against the sun which silhouetted Queenie from behind. 'That's what comes o' lying in the sun, eh?' she went on ruefully.

In no time at all, Queenie was on her way down the steps which led to the beach and on to the little red kiosk that sold sandwiches, beach-balls and pots of tea.

At the same moment as Queenie began making her way down the beach, Rick waited patiently while the man in the red kiosk passed over a triangular-shaped package of cheese sandwiches and the few coppers' change. Then, thanking him, he followed the track back up to the promenade by way of the slope at the far end. Glancing at his watch he saw that the time was almost ten o'clock, giving him something of an hour before he should make his way to that particular address. Having strolled up and down the front until he'd begun to feel that people might notice and think him strange, Rick thought the next hour might be pleasantly employed by going up to the far end of the pier, where he could eat his sandwich. From here, he could watch the people who saw a good day's enjoyment in throwing a fishing line off the side of the pier and into the waters below.

Blackpool pier was considered to be one of the most popular in the country, and Rick could see why. It was an attractive old pier, built with great thick planks of wood, slatted together for walkways and leaving gaps between, showing the sea below. Right up the farthest reaches where the pier ended and the waters stretched out into an endless horizon, some of the boards had rotted and one or two of the handrails had warped and split because of the relentless salt winds.

This particular area was duly cordoned off against the public and detailed for a considerable sum of money to be spent in restoration; a conspicuously-placed board warned people away.

Rick found a bench close by and there he sat to eat his sandwich, gazing towards where the sea lurched and slapped against the thick sturdy pier-legs; his mind conscious of little except that soon, quite soon he would find Queenie.

So steeped in thoughts of Queenie was he, that what happened next took him by complete surprise, triggering a reflex action which gave him no time for caution.

The child came out of nowhere, a flurry of red-chequered dress glimpsed out of the corner of his eye. Even as Rick stood up, she was dipping beneath the balustrades and already running towards the rail at the end of the pier. Without delay, he was after her and running across the cordoned-off area, with shouts of alarm from somewhere down the pier ringing in his ears. He could also hear his own voice, terrified for that child and urging her to stand still, to stop and stay exactly where she was . . . and though his heart trembled at the danger she was in, his voice came out to her in a calm controlled manner.

Now he could hear a woman screaming behind him, and when in a nerve-destroying sound of renting, splintering timber the child fell out of sight and into the swallowing waters, the woman's screams filled Rick's brain until he could see and hear little else.

It was only a matter of seconds before Rick had thrown off his coat and shoes and had launched himself into the air above the spot where he'd seen the child go down beneath the waters.

The pier had come alive with activity. The police ushered the people back and the coastguard launched immediate rescue. When they reached Rick, he held the live bundle up for them to take safely into the craft. And in that instant, the jagged timber made precarious by the child's fall wrenched itself loose to come crashing down about his head and shoulders. In his exhaustion Rick was unable to fend off the avalanche and, unconscious, he slithered from the sight of those who had watched in helpless horror. In his darkening mind he could see only Queenie and with her image came the sensation of it all being too late, for she was lost to him forever!

Katy and Queenie had been making their way towards the coastal tram when their attention was drawn by the wail of sirens together with the sight of hurrying ambulances and fire-engines. Two police constables were running towards the pier and a large crowd had gathered at its mouth.

'Good Lord, Queenie lass!' cried Katy, her face drained of colour, 'whatever's happened?' Queenie had no idea, but it was obvious that someone somewhere was in trouble. She said a quiet little prayer beneath her breath, then seeing the pitiful state of Katy, she suggested they make their way home. Katy seemed glad of that idea.

On the tram, there was talk among the passengers of someone having been drowned. It was a man, they said, 'a young man who had given up his life to save a child'.

On the short journey back to Lytham St Anne's, Katy and Queenie were silent, lost in thought . . . their enjoyment in each other's company subdued by such tragic news.

Queenie's heart went out to the young man and his family. It was good that a child's life had been saved, but heartbreaking that it had been at the taking of another. And she wondered with bitterness at the cruel hand of Fate.

Chapter Eight

'One more rack of toast, Mrs Bedford, and that's it!' Nancy chirped, waiting for Queenie to butter the toast fresh from the grill. Then, when the toast was quartered and slotted into the little chrome rack, she swooped it up and made off towards the dining-room.

Queenie gave a sigh of relief, stretched her aching back and poured two cups of tea out for herself and Nancy. Then she removed the apron from round her waist, took her tea and went to the back door, where, leaning against the door-jamb, she looked out over the pocket-sized yard. There was no garden here, no grass or trees . . . just a flagstoned yard strung with a washing-line and surrounded by a thick stone wall covered in unhappy-looking clematis. There was no garden at the front either, much to Queenie's disappointment, for people who came to the guest-house more often than not arrived in cars. Cars needed parking space and so the area at the front was covered in loose gravel and decorated here and there with wooden flowerboxes which Queenie filled to bursting with blue alyssum, crimson salvia and yellow marigolds in the summer, and multi-coloured wallflowers in the winter. These little beds with their bright splashes of colour were a

105

great source of pleasure to Queenie and guests often commented on their delightful appearance.

As Queenie's thoughts turned inward her gaze fell away from the yard and looked on nothing in particular. She felt unusually restless this morning, almost uneasy; and she could not put her finger on any particular cause.

True, Katy had gone home last evening and she had already begun to miss the dear old lady, and on top of that there had been a letter in the early post which had given Queenie cause for concern. It was from Sheila, telling that Hannah was poorly and had asked especially to talk to Queenie. As a result she had already rearranged her visit, in order to take advantage of this afternoon's visiting period. The duty officer to whom she'd spoken this morning had agreed that after seeing Sheila, Queenie would be allowed to have a few words with Hannah – but she could stay no more than ten minutes in the prison sick-ward.

All of this had meant a hurried rescheduling of the day's work arrangements, but when Queenie phoned, Maud had readily agreed to come in this afternoon instead of Saturday. Providing Queenie left instructions regarding the dinner arrangements that evening, everything would be taken care of.

It had all been a bit of an upset, but Queenie had taken it in her stride, and although she was both concerned for Hannah and curious as to why she had asked specially for her, she was not unduly alarmed. After all, Hannah had no other visitors, so it was natural that being poorly she might turn to one who had shown an interest.

No! It wasn't the fact of Katy's leaving and the letter

from Sheila that had brought about this strange feeling in Queenie. There was something else gnawing at her, making her almost want to cry. And the only other recent distressing event was that tragic happening yesterday, on the sea-front in Blackpool. There had been talk of nothing else in the dining-room that morning, and in between cooking fourteen breakfasts and rushing in and out to help Nancy serve, Queenie had been subjected to reports of 'such a bad thing' . . . 'handsome young gentleman by all accounts . . . lifeless when they took him from the water' 'Oh yes, the little girl will recover . . . but it's such a dreadful thing about the young man who drowned'.

The tragedy had the effect of forcing Queenie to recognize just how short life can be, and how unpredictable. Another reason for snatching at any small happiness that might come your way. Inevitably she had thought of Rick and of how happy they had been together before discovering the awful truth which had driven them apart and which was now keeping them apart. She felt angry that things were the way they were. And angry with herself, for not being able to throw aside the moral aspect which dictated her course of action. As for the *legal* side of it – well, why not move right away where no one knew, where they could know happiness!

Yet even as Queenie threw these questions up in her mind, answers stared her in the face. It *was* morally wrong, it *was* legally wrong; and how could they find happiness in such circumstances? How could they feel content, knowing they were not man and wife but brother and sister? And what manner of love would it be that forbade the creation of children?

Queenie asked herself too whether she could be any more unhappy with him than she was without him, but in all truth she knew that happiness itself was not the only issue here. It was tied in with right and wrong, and such issues were indelibly ingrained in her, fostered by her upbringing and coloured by a woman whose life had been hard but whose values could never be brought into question.

Queenie dwelt for a while on the sweet memory of Auntie Biddy. Then, slowly draining her cup of the now-cool liquid, she gave a sigh of such intensity that it raked through every inch of her body and left her trembling. She recalled Mr Marden's words of how Rick was contemplating marriage, and she prayed with all her heart that he would be content with this woman who appeared to love him. That in itself did not surprise her, for Rick was an easy man to love.

Shaking off the troublesome mood which had settled on her, Queenie came back into the kitchen where she found Nancy seated on the stool by the worktop and finishing off her tea. Queenie smiled at the girl, noting how wearily she appeared to be slumped on the stool, her narrow plain face even paler than usual. She asked Nancy, 'Tired, are you?' to which the girl quickly replied, 'No, course not! It's just that I've got a splitting headache which won't go away.' Getting up off the stool she crossed to the sink, where she put down her cup before taking her two hands up behind her head to secure the brown ponytail. 'I'll be away upstairs and get started on the rooms.'

At this, Queenie put her hand on the girl's arm, saying in a firm voice, 'No Nancy, I'll start the rooms. You see to the breakfast things. It'll be easier for you.'

Queenie allowed no argument and eventually they settled that Queenie would go upstairs where rooms needed hoovering and polishing, bathrooms awaited cleaning and beds were ready for changing. Nancy was to take two aspirins before clearing away and washing the breakfast things. Then, if she felt able, she could follow Queenie upstairs for a bit of dusting and polishing or if the headache persisted, she could phone and get Maud in a little earlier than arranged, and take herself off to bed for a while.

As it happened, the girl took the latter course and after making small talk with guests departing for another day of pleasure, Queenie fled through the mountain of work like a thing possessed. By the time she put away the cleaning box and cumbersome upright hoover, her arms felt as though they'd been wrenched from the sockets and the small of her back seemed to be carrying the weight of a lorry.

'Oh, Mrs Bedford! You should have called me sooner. That work's more than enough for *two* let alone one!' Maud Sharples was a sizeable woman, with short greying hair, big round eyes and a deadpan face. As far as Queenie was concerned, no one else would come in at short notice and justify every penny she was paid as readily as could this woman. Here she was, the downstairs all spick and span and a freshly-brewed pot of tea on the wait. Unfortunately, Queenie did not have time to waste so she thanked Maud for her help, quickly gave out the list of things required from the shop and set out the ingredients for lunch. Fortunately only four guests had opted to return for the midday meal today.

Half an hour later Queenie emerged from the pink

and cream bathroom and came into the tiny bedroom, a pleasant room with warm brown furniture and matching cherry-red curtains and carpets. There she collected from a wardrobe a long-sleeved blue printed dress with a swirling skirt and open-necked collar, the fitted waist secured by a dainty cornflower-blue belt. The dark-blue sandals with two-inch heels and open toes complemented it perfectly. Before laying the dress on the bed and the shoes below, Queenie took from the top drawer of the chest a white matching bra and panties and a full-length slip of the palest blue. After putting these on, she sat at the stool in front of the dressing-table where she rubbed the towel into the considerable length of her thick tangled hair. Following this, she brushed and brushed until the hair sprang to life, draping itself down the whole length of her back like a shining golden waterfall.

Next, she slipped the dress over her long slim form, drawing the belt about her small waist. Then she put on her sandals. Finally she parted her hair and deftly wove two braids which she draped and styled into a neat attractive frame over her head. Having done this, she quickly checked her hair in the mirror, at the same time applying the merest hint of cream powder to her nose and forehead. Then a touch of soft pink to her lips, a smile at Auntie Biddy's picture on the dresser, Mr Craig's locket about her neck, and she was ready!

On her way out Queenie snatched the time to peek in on Maud, who could be heard clattering about in the kitchen. Nancy was feeling better and was laying the tables for lunch. Already, the air was pregnant with delicious smells, the scent of the morning's polishing now entirely overcome by the aroma of gently baking

110

fish and spiced apple-pie, and percolating above all that, the unmistakable fragrance of bubbling coffee.

Queenie had just fifteen minutes to get down Rosamund Street and catch the bus which would take her to Rirkham open prison in time for the gates to open at two o'clock.

Making her way along Jacob Road, which ran into Rosamund Street, Queenie felt much lighter of heart than she had done early that morning. Most of the housework aches and pains had dissolved into the bathwater. In spite of everything, there was a little song in her heart as she found herself looking forward to spending some time with Hannah and Sheila. Sheila's special brand of humour in particular never failed to gladden Queenie's heart.

'You're a bloody breath o' fresh air, Queenie, an' no mistake!' Sheila and Queenie sat facing each other across the small circular table; every now and then Sheila emitted a rush of smoke from her busy mouth as she puffed away and chattered incessantly. 'You're a saviour to me, gel! This 'ere reg'lar pack o' fags is a godsend, I'm not bloody kidding!'

'That's a matter of opinion, Sheila,' Queenie answered. Queenie herself had never seen the attraction in smoking, but there was no reproach in her voice, for whatever gave Sheila an ounce of pleasure was her own business. 'I'm not sure it's a good idea for you to try and get through the *whole lot* before visiting time's over, though!' she told her, her eyes wide with horror as Sheila kept up the pace, lighting one cigarette from another until both she and Queenie were all but enveloped in a cloud of smoke.

'Away with you!' Sheila protested, her face opening up into a lopsided grin which immediately displayed the accelerating neglect of her yellowing teeth. 'Can't take the buggers back inside with me . . . them sort o' privileges 'ave to be *earned*! Sodding daft ideas they've got in this place!' At this, her face straightened itself, then sucking in a further helping of smoke, she screwed up her eyes to exhale a thick choking blanket which obscured her face.

'Going to see the old 'un are you, gel?' she asked, in between spurts of breathless coughing.

'Well, yes. I've got permission, but it does mean pinching ten minutes or so off the tail end of *our* time. You don't mind, do you Sheila?'

'Naw. Poor old cow! I've only seen 'er just the once since she's been poorly but if yer ask me, the old sod's getting more addled by the day! Oh, I don't mean ter say as 'ow she's altogether *barmy*, don't get me wrong, Queenie. I feel sorry for the creature . . . but there's summat preying on 'er mind, an' *that's* a fact!' Sheila gave a small laugh, and winking cheekily, she instructed Queenie in secretive tones, 'Look over there! D'you see that little woman, the prisoner talking to that other fat lump?' Keeping her eyes fast on Queenie, she jerked her head in the direction of the door, where at the table to the left there sat a great bumble of a woman wearing a red beret and smoking a cigar. Opposite her was positioned a tiny figure with cropped brown hair and soft squashy face. The two women were deep in conversation. 'I see her,' Queenie said, feeling somewhat like the man who peeps through keyholes.

'Right! Now d'you see that woman prison warden

112

by the door . . . the one standing with 'er legs that far
open you could drive a bloody bus through?'

To this, Queenie nodded.

'Would you believe it . . . them two . . . that warden
and the little 'un . . . they're having it off! *'Aving it
off*, I tell yer! It's common knowledge from one end
o' this place to the other!' Sheila nodded her head
vigorously; then lit a fresh cigarette from the butt of
the last one and drew her breath in hard. Her eyes
wide, muttering out the corner of her mouth, she told
Queenie with some bitterness, 'An' the buggers locked
me away for no more than bringing a bit o' pleasure
to a few lonely fellas! Hmph!'

Queenie couldn't help but burst out laughing, for
which she was immediately chastised. 'It's all right for
you to laugh, Queenie gel! I'm telling you it's a partic-
c'lar sort o' justice for one, and another sort for the
next poor sod!' Sheila told her reprovingly.

For the next hour the conversation followed a pre-
dictable pattern, with Sheila offering all manner of
advice on the goings-on in that place and her opinion
on how the values of folk in higher places were coming
a tumble. Now and then, she would broach the subject
of the guest-house, questioning Queenie as to the run
and character of those frequenting it. Once, very
quietly, she spoke of Maisie and of how it was sad we
couldn't all have a say in the time and manner of our
departure from this world. Finally, when the visiting
period was drawing to a close, she pointed out that
Queenie should be making tracks. 'Go an' give the
poor bugger a bit o' comfort, gel,' she told Queenie.
After Sheila had departed with a warden, Queenie
bided her time until that same warden had returned to

lead the way across the outer yard into a red-brick building, where she was taken into a small, sparsely furnished room and asked to wait for a moment. Queenie did so, feeling forced to wrinkle up her nose at the clinical smell of disinfectant which seemed to cling everywhere.

A few minutes later, there emerged a kindly-faced woman of middle years dressed in a white smock. She led the way down a narrow corridor of green-painted walls and shuttered windows, into an airy open room containing eight beds, beside which were placed sturdy armchairs. Three of the beds were occupied by sleeping bodies; one had in it a young woman sitting upright and engrossed in her knitting. The remainder of the beds appeared to be empty, but two of the chairs were occupied, one by a bent-up elderly woman, and the other by a dainty little creature with snow-white hair and china features. This was Hannah. Queenie was taken straight to her. 'Ten minutes dear . . . no more!' the woman in the smock told Queenie before disappearing.

Queenie nodded and fetched a stand-chair from the table in the centre of the room, which she placed directly in front of the watching Hannah. With a warm smile she took hold of the woman's hand; at the same time astonished at how feather-light and frail it was.

'How are you, Hannah?' she asked, her quiet voice reflecting her concern for this poor soul.

For a while, the little woman sat quite still, her frightened eyes looking first at Queenie, then down the room towards the open door, as though in anticipation of someone coming through it. Then, appearing satisfied, she leaned forward and in a voice not much above

114

a whisper, she confided, 'I've been poorly, dear, but today I'm feeling more well in meself.' Of a sudden, she drew her hand from Queenie's and appeared to shrivel into herself. 'This lot needs watching! You never know what they're up to.'

'It's all right, Hannah,' Queenie assured her, gently taking the woman's hand in her own again, 'there's nothing to be afraid of, I promise you. Nobody's going to harm you, please believe that.' Such a pitiful sight as this dear little soul suspicious and afraid had moved Queenie deeply.

'You're Queenie, aren't you?'

'That's right, Hannah, you wanted to talk to me.'

'I did! Yes I did!' In an instant, the little woman had leaned forward again to place her other hand on top of Queenie's pressing it down with such urgency that Queenie felt the nails penetrating her skin.

'Sheila's told me about you . . . said you were a clever 'un, running that "Kingsway" an' all! Telled me you were a *real* friend, someone to be trusted, eh?' She paused and waited until Queenie had given an encouraging nod, then away she went again, all the while furtive and close. 'Well, there's summat I want you to do for *me!*'

'If I can, Hannah,' promised Queenie.

'I want you to find my boy!' She nodded now and her whole body visibly relaxed as though shedding a great weight. 'My lad as they took from me. I *want* 'im. I've to tell 'im the way of things, don't you see? I deprived the lad of a father, an' it needs explaining. I've to see 'im . . . put things right afore the Lord sees fit to call me. Say you will, Queenie – say you'll find my lad!' Her voice was broken and Queenie could see that she wasn't far from collapsing into tears. She wanted to help if it was possible. But how? Where would she start?

As though in answer to Queenie's silent questions, Hannah's voice brightened with a suggestion. 'That legal gent! The one as used to come a' visiting . . . Snow . . . Snowford, or some such Christmassy name. Find that one, an' I'm convinced you'll find my lad! That legal fella knows more than 'e ever let on! I'm no good wi' such uppity folk . . . but 'appen you'll ferret the right information out of 'im. You'll do it, won't you? You've *got* to. I've a feeling I'm not long for this 'ere world, an' I *must* put things right. I *must*, don't you see?' She began to cry, softly at first, then bitterly and with pain, her head bowed down.

Queenie lifted her hands to place them about Hannah's face, and gently raising the little woman's head so that she must look into Queenie's gaze, she told her, 'I'll do all I can, Hannah. I promise you, if there *is* a way to find your boy, I will. But it's been a long time, hasn't it? And you've given me little to go on.'

'That legal gent, Queenie. Find that one an' you'll find my son – I *know* it!' Hannah cried. Then seeing the smocked orderly approaching, she snatched herself away from Queenie, fell back into her chair and feigned sleep.

Queenie made no further address to her. Instead she got to her feet, returned the stand-chair to its place at the table, and made for the exit, thanking the woman in the smock as she left. It was on her mind to question the woman as to how an appointment with the governor might be secured but she thought better of it, seeing how such a question would immediately indicate that she required to speak to the governor about Hannah. It might be wiser, she told herself, to make such inquiries at the main gate, where it could be arranged more discreetly. Even smocked orderlies were human, she reflected, but if her inquiries were to be misconstrued as complaining of Hannah's treatment here, then such a possibility, however remote, must be avoided. This was, after all, a place of correction, where relationships might be easily strained. No, better to go back to the main gate and broach the matter from there. If *anybody* was in a position to give her information concerning this 'legal gent with the Christmassy name', then who better than the governor?

As it was, Queenie was first fortunate, then unfortunate. In view of her assurance that the matter *was* of an urgent nature, the governor found time to see her straight away. But he could not agree to imparting what little information he had concerning the solicitor, a man by the name of Mr Snowdon, and his involvement with the prisoner in question. 'I'm sorry, Mrs Bedford, but I have no authority to convey such information to anyone,' he told her.

After ten minutes of explaining how she had in fact been asked to talk to this man, whose name she had cleverly drawn out by the use of stressing the first syllable, and to make every effort to trace Hannah's son, Queenie already felt defeated. She could also see how much trouble could be unleashed by Hannah's fearful request: trouble, and possibly pain.

There was no escaping the fact that Hannah had murdered her own husband, and that such a tragic act had consequently robbed the boy of both parents. So, Queenie had to remind herself that if the child had subsequently been adopted, it was highly unlikely that his adoptive parents would want to expose the boy to such an appalling background. It might even be the case that they themselves had not been told. Then there was the further possibility that the boy might have been made aware of the dreadful circumstances of his effectively orphaned status and, being in possession of such crippling knowledge, had found himself unable to forgive his mother, who he had then disowned.

Queenie knew without the slightest doubt that here was a Pandora's box which might best be kept closed. But she had given her word and she would not purposely go back on her promise to Hannah. Yet, at the same time, she knew only too well that every step of the way must be cautious, not only for Hannah's sake, but for her son's also; for was he not now a grown man, possibly with a family of his own?

'You do understand my position, Mrs Bedford? I'm sorry I can't help you.' Now, in replacing his rimless spectacles and by the impatient manner in which he settled his considerable bulk of a body back into the leather-bound chair behind the desk, the prison governor was in effect dismissing Queenie. Sensing the consultation to be at an end, she ventured one last but vital question.

'I do appreciate your situation . . . but there is one thing I'm sure you could do for me, without compromising your position of trust. Would you allow me to write out a short note and have it delivered to this Mr Snowdon?'

At this, the governor looked up, his face set into a serious mask as he appeared to ponder Queenie's request. For what seemed to Queenie to be an excruciatingly prolonged span of time, he tapped a pencil against his square white teeth, his piercing gaze fixed unnervingly on her.

All the while he had Queenie under scrutiny, a torrent of possibilities rushed through the governor's quick mind. He had a soft spot for Hannah Jason, thinking her to be a woman ill-fitted for the title of murderess. In his opinion a mild-mannered little thing like Hannah must have been driven to such an act of extreme violence. She was frail and had grown more so of late. What harm could come of forwarding a letter to this Mr Snowdon, a man of more devious character than *ever* Hannah could be and that was a fact.

And here was this delightful woman before him, a creature of such striking looks that a man might sell his soul for. Quality! That's what she possessed, quality and a rare sort of compassion to have befriended Hannah, whose mind was apt to wander in a most irritating fashion. Much as he might convey to this lady here that he was not aware of the contents of her 'short note', it was not the case. In her sleepless wanderings and dire need to confide in somebody, Hannah Jason had often betrayed a desperation to find her boy.

Of a sudden, in so unexpected a move that it startled Queenie, the governor leaned across the desk to grab a small writing pad, which he thrust, with a pencil, towards Queenie. 'All right! Make it brief. I'll see that he gets it.' Stepping forward, Queenie thanked him. She quickly wrote down a request to Mr Snowdon that she would be very grateful if he could contact her at the address below, with a view to meeting. It was of extreme urgency and concerned Hannah Jason, an inmate of the prison who was desperate to find her son, presumably adopted at the time of Hannah's imprisonment.

Queenie signed the note with her name and added the telephone number and address of Kingsway. Then, ignoring the governor's outstretched hand, she asked, 'Could I have an envelope, please?' thinking it best for the matter to stay as quiet as possible, for Hannah's sake.

'I'm sorry, Mrs Bedford . . . but *all* correspondence in and out of this establishment must be vetted!'

Queenie was not deterred. In her most charming voice, she reminded him, 'I realize that you do need to vet prisoners' mail, both going out and coming in. But that is *not* the case here, surely? I'm not writing to one of your inmates, nor is this note *received* from an inmate. I am an outsider writing to request a meeting with a solicitor and you in your generosity have agreed to forward the letter on. Isn't that so?'

A surprising smile lit up the governor's features. 'Well, it *is* something I've not come across before so I'll give you the benefit of the doubt,' he conceded. He took an envelope from the desk and handed it to her. 'There you are . . . I'll see it's properly addressed and posted.'

Queenie folded the note, placed it in the envelope which she sealed and returned to him; then without further conversation apart from farewells she was on her way out of the office, out of the prison and within fifteen minutes she had boarded the bus which would carry her to Lytham St Anne's and Kingsway.

All she had to do now was wait. She had no reason

to believe that this Mr Snowdon would not get in touch. According to Sheila's information, it had been Hannah herself who'd created such a fuss about Mr Snowdon's visits that he had eventually stopped making the effort.

Queenie wondered what she had taken on. Who was this 'legal gent' and why had he been visiting Hannah in the first place? Surely that wasn't usual, thought Queenie. But if for some reason he *did* have Hannah's interest at heart, then he would be only too pleased to respond to the letter.

Beneath her breath, Queenie murmured 'I hope so,' but somehow she got the feeling that it wasn't going to be as straightforward as all that. Some twenty-seven years had passed since Hannah Jason's sentence. It was half a lifetime and time enough for many threads to become entangled in a way that could never be straight again.

The bus wound its way along the lanes leading from the prison gates until it reached the main Blackpool Road where it got up speed and soon left behind the little white-painted houses with their concrete fore-courts and swinging boards declaring their ability to provide bed and breakfast.

Normally, Queenie took pleasure in gazing across the open fields which now stretched out on either side of the broad trafficway. But not today! Her mind was busy, filled with recollection of Hannah's misery and her plea for help.

Queenie consoled herself with the reminder that she had taken the first step, indeed the *only* step as far as she could see. Now all she could do was to wait, a frustrating prospect.

But for all that, when Queenie disembarked from

the bus, her spirits were not daunted by the task in hand.

Making her hurried way along Rosamund Street, Queenie smiled wryly to herself. She had been up against bigger obstacles before. Now to help one less fortunate than herself, she had started down a particular road. And she would see it through, however it might twist and turn.

Chapter Nine

'She's what!' Mr Marsden's voice exploded with such force that his eyes popped from his head and set his jaws trembling. 'The *devil* she is!' Snatching the paper from Mr Snowdon's hand, he lifted it to his face, and hunched over it as he directed his whole attention to the reading of Queenie's note.

It appeared to the onlooking solicitor, from the slow deliberate steps with which the other man now paced the room, that all had become calm again.

This misguided impression was abruptly shattered when Mr Marsden came to a halt and let his arms drop as though they had carried a great weight. He turned to regard the waiting solicitor with thin, vicious eyes. Just for a moment, Mr Snowdon imagined how messengers might have felt when in days of old they were rewarded for bringing bad news by the loss of their heads.

'When did you say this came to you?'

'It was there when I returned to my office from a business trip this morning. I brought it straight round, knowing how vital the contents to be.' He pointed to the envelope lying on the desk. 'If you examine the postmark, you'll see that it was stamped last Saturday, a week ago today.' He waited, watching the other man's face with a degree of apprehension.

'Hmm . . . let me think! I've got to weigh this one up carefully.' Mr Marsden stood up straight, levelling his back until the shoulderblades could be seen almost touching. Then, after a minute of aimless wandering about the study, during which he looked out of the window and across the lawns to where the hired gardener was pruning some overgrown shrubs, he came back to the swivel chair at his desk and absent-mindedly swung it to and fro in a half-circle.

Of a sudden, he stopped the chair's movement and then sat in it, looking up at the other man. All the time Mr Snowdon had stood quite motionless; he was greatly relieved to see the blazing fury gone from Mr Marsden's face and in its place the usual kind of cunning he could easily recognize. But if he had at first been lulled into a false sense of relief, Mr Snowdon's blood chilled when the following words fell on his ears. 'That woman's coming dangerously close to unearthing things long buried. She's been a thorn in my side for too long. It's time she was removed once and for all!'

'Removed? What do you mean, "removed"?' Mr Snowdon had taken several swift steps forward, until he stood now, his hands grasping the desk, his eyes wide and fearful and his face emptied of colour, 'I'll not be a party to murder! Cheat the taxman, keep a secret or two yes! But if it's anything stronger you count me out, do you understand?' At this Mr Marsden leaned back in the chair, gently rocking from side to side; all the while his eyes glued to Mr Snowdon's frightened face. Now, he gave a low throaty chuckle before assuring the poor man, 'Relax . . . relax, I tell you. There are more subtle ways than murder to get rid of something unpleasant. I'll not ask you to take part in any such plan but I *will* ask you to do something for me, and double quick! I want the information set before me no later than Tuesday. Not *one minute* later than noon on Tuesday, mind!' He was leaning forward now, the gaze in his deep eyes becoming a drilling stare which held the other man paralysed. 'That husband of Queenie Bedford's . . . got killed, didn't he . . . you remember?' He waited for the other man to nod, then he continued, 'Word is she led him a right dance, and if that night of Rick's party was anything to go by, it's clear enough. Often a time I've heard rumblings coming up through the workers, about how the mother of Mike Bedford would give an arm and a leg to get even with the woman as took her son!' He was on his feet now and coming round the desk he draped an arm about the other man's shoulder, at the same time propelling him towards the door. 'Find out if that's really the case! Get the woman's address and see if there's any truth in the rumour that this Mrs Bedford lives and works aside . . . what might be called the "darker" elements of our society. I want to know. Get to it, man!'

'I'll do what I can . . .'

'No! You'll ferret out what I want by *Tuesday noon*, together with any other snippet of useful information. Right!'

They were at the door now, Mr Marsden waiting for an acknowledgement before letting the other man out. When he got one in the form of a reluctant nod, he opened the door and smiled. 'There'll be no problem – you've never let me down yet,' he said. 'Oh – of course you'll not reply to that letter! Now, I'd best move myself. I'm taking Rita and Rachel down to the infirmary to see Rick.'

'Oh. How is he?'

'Out of the woods, thank God!' Mr Marsden's voice fell low, and to the watching solicitor, it was plain that here was a man who doted on his son, who loved as no father had a right to and would turn over heaven and earth if anything was to threaten that relationship. Mr Marsden was speaking again, and he appeared a different man from the one who had stalked this study not five minutes back. 'There was a time when we thought we'd lose him, you know. He was in a dire way when they brought him out of the sea; busted ribs, broken leg and a fractured skull. But thank the good Lord, he's pulled through. All we want now, his mother and me, is to see him back on his feet and him and Rachel wed!'

While he had been talking, Mr Marsden had surrendered to a brighter mood, but now his face darkened as he reminded the solicitor, 'So you can appreciate the urgency of my requirements!' Upon which, he ushered the man out of the room and out of the house. Then he called out, 'Rita! I'll be ready for off in ten minutes,' from the bottom of the stairway. Afterwards he immediately returned to his study.

Here he stood with his back to the door, leaning heavily against it, his jaw working in quick impatient movements, his eyes tightly shut and his furtive mind going over and over the conversation that had taken place in this room but a few moments ago. The subject still weighted the atmosphere, drawing it tight about his head and throat until he thought he must surely suffocate.

He felt weary, haunted and more than a little afraid. Queenie Bedford was like an itch that wouldn't stop; she was a threat to whatever slender security he had achieved. If this box of fireworks exploded, Rick would learn of the deceit all these years in as cruel a way as was imaginable, he would be exposed to the facts of his background, of his father's murder and of his mother's imprisonment. It would also be inevitable that another deception would come to light, that of his own carefully laid plans to delude Rita into believing that her sister Hannah had died behind the bars of her own making. And he had suffered no qualms about that lie, because as God was his judge, Rita had been more her own self since. It was like a weight had been raised from her shoulders. He had been most surprised at the mild manner with which Rita had greeted the 'sad' news. There had been a few quiet tears, but few questions and an acceptance which had convinced him that with her sister at peace after all these years, Rita could shed that misguided guilt which he was so sure had pulled her down for so long. There had, it was true, been days following Rita's knowledge of the 'demise' of her sister Hannah when she had seemed to withdraw tearfully into herself. Even so he felt no cause to regret his action, for he had been, and still was, convinced that it was the *right* one.

Finally, his thoughts came to dwell on what would undoubtedly be revealed should Queenie Bedford persist in following up what she had now started. Above all others this was the issue which caught fiercely at his heart and hardened his determination to be rid of her. With the revelation that Hannah Jason was his mother and the late Edward Jason his real father, it would be swiftly apparent to Rick that he and Queenie were after all unrelated and thus free to marry.

At such a prospect Mr Marsden took to pacing the floor, his hands in front of him; one clenched into a fist and hitting the other open palm with even hammer-blow actions, deliberate and controlled. His eyes swept from one side of the room to the other, glaring at the richness of the oak-panelled walls hung with valuable paintings and various trophies acquired over the years. He thought of other holdings, shares, bonds, ware-houses and mills representing the sweat and scheming of what seemed a lifetime. The more he dwelt on the threat that Rick would bring that Bedford woman into it – that bloody guttersnipe of a guttersnipe father – the more his thoughts grew dark with his intention that never, not while he had a breath left in him, would he allow such a thing.

Strange as it seemed, he was at first surprised by the vehemence he felt towards this woman, whom he had disliked from the moment he had learned of her ident-ity. That dislike had ballooned into hate when he'd seen how brazenly she'd gone after Rick and now it had become such a loathing that he trembled whenever he heard her name. But it wasn't so surprising, he reminded himself. Not when he cast his mind back, as he often did, to that day almost thirty years ago now when Rita had confessed to loving George Kenney, admitting that he had bedded her more than once, and that in her belly was growing a child. Not her husband's child, oh no! Never *his* child, for it seemed he was not man enough to make one. The child was put there by George Kenney! And much as he himself had tried to forget the means by which that offspring had been conceived, much as he had strived and prayed to put it from his mind for Rita's sake, especially when the boy child had been tragically taken, he had not been able to. He had managed to keep his real feelings from Rita, whom he'd loved and depended on, but in doing so he had only driven those same feelings deep within him to a dark seething corner where they had festered and caused him an almost unbearable measure of pain.

There would be no daughter of George Kenney's in *this* house to live in luxury and be relied upon to produce an heir to the Marsden fortunes – *his* fortunes, which had cost him toil and blood. Never! And the minute Snowdon came up with the information he wanted, a torrent of activity would sweep away that creature together with any mischief she had planned. This very day, he had set off ripples which would swell into a tide to carry him and his to safety and to wash away any danger of the past catching up to destroy them.

With this in mind, he became calmer and as he turned to leave the room, other possibilities began to creep into his industrious mind. That solicitor, Snowdon, now there was somebody with access to all manner of information, documents and the like. And why shouldn't he do his best when asked, eh! Wasn't he paid a considerable retainer?

It had proved to be no problem when a death certificate had to be produced in order to secure Rita's acceptance of her sister's demise. Happen a contrived birth certificate for Rick would be equally successful. This would show himself and Rita as being the parents of Rick, thereby eliminating the awful stigma of the real circumstances of his birth.

It was advantageous, however, to keep Rick under

the impression that he and Queenie Bedford were sister and brother. This would be easily done by deluding Rick into believing that George Kenney's name was simply omitted from his and Rita's lives, and consequently from the new-born's birth certificate. This had indeed been the case with George Kenney's true boy child born to Rita.

There was a further justification for such a document, for in spite of Rachel Winters' sophistication and considerable business acumen, he was not entirely blind to her lack of real substance. There was never any doubt in his mind that she *did* love Rick, but in a way that betokened more greed and possession than any *real* love of the heart. She, like himself, was well aware of the far-reaching rewards and prosperity that an amalgamation of the Marsden and Winters concerns could bring. But for all that, there was not the slightest doubt in Mr Marsden's mind that if she should ever learn she was considering marriage to the son of a convicted murderess she would be gone before the last word was spoken.

As he came into the hall, he forced his mind to the matter in hand – that of making his way to the infirmary and to Rick. For the moment, all other matters could be left simmering.

The journey to the infirmary was only a matter of twenty comfortable minutes inside the plush luxury of the black Daimler: Mr Marsden at the wheel of his pride and joy, his wife Rita in the back, seated alongside Rachel Winters. The two women had seemed to make a special effort with their appearance on this Saturday morning. Rachel Winters looked breathtakingly beautiful in a rich green silk dress with high buttoned front and A-line skirt, which reached down to just above her shapely knees and hugged the perfect contours of her figure. The matching jacket, nipped in at the waist, was a perfect complement to the dress. With her mass of titian-coloured hair brushed out freely she could not have appeared more alluring.

Rita Marsden had taken her thin fair hair into a bun which nestled attractively in the nape of her neck. She looked pale and tired, but the warm autumn-coloured blouse and deep burgundy two-piece she had chosen stopped her from looking altogether wan.

Throughout the short journey there was little talk; none at all from Mr Marsden, who was steeped in thought, and no more than an occasional remark from one or other of the women. Rachel Winters had discovered a not surprising lack of mutual interest between herself and Rick's mother. Rita Marsden, for her part, found her first impressions of this young lady to have borne true . . . she was basically of a cold disposition and gave the impression that she was merely tolerating Rick's mother for the sake of Rick and the prospect of marriage.

Once at the infirmary, the three of them lost little time in straight away making for the private wards and Rick.

The two women continued on into the small room at the far end of the corridor where Rick was recovering. Mr Marsden broke away some few steps earlier to enter the doctor's office.

After the briefest of exchange of greetings the doctor asked, 'Have you seen your son this morning, Mr Marsden?'

'Not yet. I'll be along there in but a minute . . . thought it best to come and hear what *you* have to say. How's he doing? I mean *really* doing?'

Dr Stevens lowered his head and regarded Mr Marsden from over the rims of his glasses. He hadn't taken a liking to this gentleman, not at all. He found the man a bit too authoritative and blunt for his own taste. The son, Richard, now *he* was a likeable sort, a friendly no-nonsense type who expected no more from others than he himself was prepared to give. But the doctor was quick to appreciate the anxiety of this man, and so he put on his kindest voice. 'Well now, Mr Marsden, taking into account the extent of your son's injuries he's doing remarkably well as I've said before.'

'How's remarkably well?'

'The leg seems to have set well; no need for traction as I at first anticipated. The fracture in his skull is hairline and causing no real problem and fortunately there has been no intracranial haemorrhage or damage to brain tissue, apart from initial bruising, but there is no further danger of unconsciousness or vomiting. There's little to be done about the fractured ribs, I'm afraid, except to strap his chest round and give him painkillers. It takes a while, but they will knit by themselves. On the whole, we've done what we can, Mr Marsden. The rest is up to Mother Nature, but your son is on the mend, I can assure you.'

'When can he be taken home? If, as you say, you've done all you can, would he not be as well at home now? I'll appoint a nurse – he'll want for nothing!'

At this the doctor smiled. From the attitude of Richard Marsden to being, as he himself had put it, 'molly-coddled', he might well have some say in his father's intention to appoint a nurse. 'There's a lot in what you say, Mr Marsden,' he conceded, 'but if you take my considered advice, you'll allow your son at least another week under our observation. As I say, there appear to be no complications, but it's always advisable to be on the safe side.'

So it was settled. The last thing Mr Marsden wanted was to place Rick's full and quick recovery in jeopardy. He would stay at the infirmary for another week, after which the situation would again be reviewed.

Coming into Rick's room, Mr Marsden found Rita seated at one side of the bed and Rachel Winters at the other, holding Rick's hand and leaning over him. Rita came to her husband and quietly asked, 'Is everything all right?'

At his nod, she smiled freely, her face breaking in relief. Then, walking to the window, she glanced at Rick, then again at her husband, afterwards concentrating her attention on the forecourt outside, where a line of ambulances stood parked like little white soldiers on parade.

'All right, son?' Mr Marsden had taken up his wife's seat. Now, at his address, Rachel Winters released Rick's hand but as she leaned away her gaze never left his face until Mr Marsden then turned to her and asked, 'Do you think you could take Rita in search of a cup of tea? She looks as though she could do wi' one . . . give me five minutes!'

Judging by the look on Rachel Winters' face, Mr Marsden's request had not been well received; but when he took the trouble to repeat it, both Rachel Winters and Rita made themselves scarce.

When the door had closed behind them Mr Marsden

returned his attention to Rick, grieving to see his son in such a predicament. From beneath the bandages swathing the upper part of his head there ran a long and jagged cut, deep and angry-looking. His face bore marks and bruises from the falling timber; underneath a wire cage below the clothes his leg lay still and cumbersome, mummified in a heavy cast of off-white plaster.

Now, as Rick spoke, his face appeared stiff and his eyes of a less deep colour than usual, 'Dad . . . get me out of this place. I'm going crazy lying here!'

'All right son. I've already spoken to Dr Stevens and you'll be out of here soon enough, I promise. But not for another week at least.'

'Hell! All I need is a pair of crutches. I can get myself about if only they'd let me!' His eyes had suddenly darkened, and now they rolled upwards in frustration. He *had* to get out of this bloody bed! He had things to do, things which had been brought to a halt with the saving of that child. So close! He'd been so close to finding Queenie. 'They've got me trussed up here, so's I can't move! I won't stay here another week – not another day I'm telling you!' The burst of anger had caused Rick to strain from the bed tightening the bandages round his chest and irritating the ribs beneath. He fell back now, his face a grimace of pain and the beads of sweat standing out on those parts of his temples which were visible below the head bandage.

'I know you're disappointed, son, but it's best to be guided by them as know what they're doing.' In spite of Rick's obvious distress, Mr Marsden still intended to put forward certain information which could only increase his anxiety. It had to be said, for all that it was a blatant lie. Besides, he knew that Rick was already in possession of this particular knowledge, but it served a purpose for him to make Rick more strongly aware of it and so he went on, 'There's summat I think you ought to be told, Rick, summat I should have confided to you long ago. Oh, I know it makes little difference now . . . but the shock of your accident brought home to me how you've a *right* to know . . .' Here he broke off, a clever ploy to portray regret and unsettling emotion. The feeling was not entirely manufactured, for he was telling him a truth which in other circumstances he would not have done, that Rick was *not* his son. It was a painful thing, but bearing in mind the threat of the Bedford woman being brought into the family he could see no alternative. Apart from disowning Rick. And that would have been tantamount to cutting off his own right arm; so he continued, 'It's the matter of your birth, son . . .'

With a protest of 'No! Don't, father . . .' Rick attempted to head off what he sensed to be the beginning of a painful revelation. But with a determined shake of his head Mr Marsden went on, 'I should have told you long ago. You've a right to know . . .'

It was obvious to Rick that the past had reached out its long strangling tentacle once more. He was about to be told that George Kenney was his real father. He did not want to hear it; he didn't want those words to be spoken out in the open, after which they would lie like a great open wound between himself and this man who had been to him everything a father could be.

'There's no need to say it. I know! I've known for some time now. George Kenney himself gave me the information . . .' His voice had fallen below a whisper.

There was nothing to be gained should his mother suddenly return and overhear talk of something which she had rightly buried in the past.

At Rick's words, Mr Marsden feigned a look of surprise. 'You *knew*!' he said, not losing the opportunity to remind Rick of the very reason for this matter having been broached. 'So you're fully aware that Queenie Bedford is your sister – your own flesh and blood?' He watched as Rick winced and turned away. But he had to follow through. 'At one time, I thought you and she . . . well, thank God I was wrong. Such a thing would kill your mother. I'd rather she didn't know of this conversation, son . . . best to let it lie. Only I thought I owed you the truth. You don't think harshly of me for it, do you? I've loved you like my own. You *are* my own in every other respect!' This much at least was true, and when he reached out to grasp Rick by the hand, his eyes searching for reassurance, Rick caught the anxiety in his gaze and clutched the other man's hand as he told him, 'I know of no other father, nor do I want to. Don't concern yourself about mother. The matter's closed!' As far as anyone else was concerned, the matter *was* closed as it had been these past years. But in Rick's own heart, the pain was re-awakened, and it seemed that much sharper now, because of the fact that it had been openly broached and admitted at last.

'I'm sorry, son,' murmured Mr Marsden. But he was *not* . . . for the mischief he had sought to cause, the guilt he had strived to create in Rick blazed clear and painful in Rick's eyes.

Later, as he and Rita departed the infirmary, leaving Rachel Winters by Rick's side, Mr Marsden had the feeling of a job well done. The rest was up to Rick and Rachel now, for they were both well aware of his and Rita's expectations for their marriage. He told himself with some satisfaction that it would not be far off. Sooner than ever, once he had taken care of Queenie Bedford. Without her mixing into things, the way would be that much smoother and no mistake. All he awaited now was that particular information from Snowdon. Once in receipt of it, he would waste no time in making a move.

As it was, Mr Snowdon did better than expected. At midday on Tuesday he reported to Mr Marsden's office, armed with even more than the information requested.

He reported that the infamous Mrs Bedford Senior lived a dangerous and exciting life. The word was she bought and sold stolen goods, kept criminals for friends and was held in fear and high esteem by a regular fraternity of rogues. It was no secret that even *before* her son's untimely death she had long skirted the law in a small way. But losing Mike, first to the girl, Queenie, then to the wheels of a lorry, had deeply unsettled her, sent her right off the rails some said. For months afterwards she had searched high and low for the girl who had married her son, bitterly blaming Queenie for his death, her heart black with revenge.

When every avenue led to a dead end, the frustrated creature had vehemently launched herself into a full life of crime; being regularly brought before the courts, fined, and on at least one occasion sent down for a period of nine months.

Mr Marsden was delighted at such colourful news.

It was exactly as he had hoped. The woman *did* have a score to settle with her daughter-in-law as was. And by the sounds of it, she had the means of a useful 'reprimand' at her beckoning. Oh yes! Just as he had hoped!

'Her address, man! You have the woman's address?'

'I have!' Mr Snowdon reached inside his waistcoat pocket for a folded piece of paper which he straight away handed to the impatient fellow, saying with a cynical smile and a nodding of the head, 'And *there's* a turn up, eh? A *very* pleasant abode . . . situated in one of the better areas of town. Who says crime doesn't pay?'

Mr Marsden had snatched the paper. 'Ah! Preston New Road, eh?' He rammed the paper into his jacket pocket, at once lapsing into deep thought, only his puffy hand stroking against the drooping jowls of his face betraying his excitement.

In a moment he turned to address the other man. 'You've done well, Snowdon. I'll see you all right. Now be off!' He waved his hand in a gesture of impatience. 'If I've further need of you, I'll be in touch.'

Mr Snowdon, though surprised at such a swift dismissal, smoothed his snow-white hair, put on his trilby, gave a short nod and in the next instant was gone from the room, leaving Mr Marsden to contemplate a certain telephone number and decide what he might say to a certain person.

It was nine forty-five when the black Daimler drew up at the kerbside along Preston New Road some discreet way down from number 20 and from the Daimler stepped the unmistakable bulky figure of Mr Marsden.

Darkness had superseded the unusual dullness of a June day and now the rain was pouring from the heavens with a vengeance, lashed by a forceful wind.

Muttering 'Damned weather!' to himself Mr Marsden reached into the back of the car, taking from the seat a light grey raincoat and a trilby. After ramming the trilby down on his balding head he impatiently shrugged himself into the raincoat, which he buttoned and belted tight about his body. That done, he locked the car door, double-checking that it was secure. Then he thrust his hands deep into his pockets, lowered his head as a shield against the driving rain, and lost no time in making his way along Preston New Road, past the half-dozen houses on his right. In a matter of minutes he was standing at the door of number 20; where, being what his workers termed a man of belt and braces, he both rattled his fists against the door and rang the bell.

After what had seemed an endless age to the wet and miserable Mr Marsden a woman flung open the door to yell, 'What's yer bloody game then? Trying to waken the bloody dead, is it?' She was small but thick-set like a bulldog, he thought. Her face was bloated and the razor-short cut of her hair gave her the curious appearance of a man. Now, beneath the rather hostile glare from those small speckled eyes, Mr Marsden thought: better this woman was Queenie's enemy, than his!

'I said, what's yer game?' She leaned forward to peer more closely at the stranger. 'Is it Marsden then?'

'That's right. I telephoned . . .'

'You did! That you did! Brought me news of an old "friend" 'ave you not?' Stepping aside, she opened wider the door. 'Best get yersel' inside,' she told him.

Once inside the narrow hallway, which was empty of furniture save for the glass-topped rectangular telephone table over which was a wooden bar drilled with empty coat-hooks, Mr Marsden followed the woman past the open stairway and into the first door on the right. Here he found himself in a long narrow room, tastelessly furnished with nondescript rubbishy articles in laminated wood of a bright sickly hue. There were a number of wooden-armed chairs with thin little legs and upholstery of unattractive grey texture. Immediately by the door stood a long narrow settee which matched the ugly chairs. The woman pointed to it after telling her visitor, 'Sit yersel' down. What's yer poison, eh? Whisky is it? You look like a whisky man to me!'

Mr Marsden had already removed his hat, which he now held by his side. Running his free hand along both sides of his head where the thin clutches of hair were protruding bedraggled, he refused a drink, protesting that it *was* late and his business rather urgent.

At this the woman shrugged her thick shoulders before crossing to the sideboard where she poured out a healthy measure of whisky diluted with soda water. Taking a gulp, she at once turned about to face the watching man. 'You're a bastard! You an' your bloody kind . . . yer all the same! I'm not blind to the part your son played in plunging my lad's marriage down 'ill . . .' she accused him.

'You're wrong, Mrs Bedford!' At this point Mr Marsden felt the necessity to protest. 'My son was as much an innocent victim as was yours! Queenie Bedford kept them *both* eating out of her hand . . .'

'Aye! 'Appen yer right! Played one off agin the

other? Aye! That would be 'er style right enough.'
Tipping the glass to her mouth, she took another great
gulp of the warming liquid. 'An' don't call me "Mrs
Bedford"! These days I'm just "Bedford". That way
I'm given the choice o' surprising folk as don't know
whether they're dealing wi' man or woman.' Here she
gave a loud cackle. 'There's times when being one
serves a better purpose than being another, if you tek
me meaning?'

He didn't. But Mr Marsden thought it best to get on
and out of this place before she became rolling drunk.
'So what about your daughter-in-law, as was?' he
prompted her.

'Ah now!' Mrs Bedford returned her glass to the
sideboard top, her mood having quickly changed to
one of seriousness. Grabbing the back of a chair she
swung it to a position facing Mr Marsden. In an instant
she was seated in it and unnerving him by looking
straight into his eyes with such intensity that he was
convinced she could read every thought in his head.
'Yes! What *am* I going to do about the woman as
wrenched my lad away from me, drove 'im to an early
death then took to 'er bloody 'eels, leaving *me* to pick
up the pieces? Well now, in such like circumstances,
what would *you* do, I wonder?'

Not for a second did the hardness of her stare flinch.
For the first time Mr Marsden experienced an inkling
of regret for having contacted this woman. There was
considerable doubt in his mind that she was in full
control of herself. If it hadn't been for the fact that
she'd suspected his telephone call to be a possible trap
laid by the police, he would never have been persuaded
to set foot inside this house.

Now she was laughing, a dreadful chilling noise, forcing Mr Marsden to defend his presence there. 'I was given to believe . . . from various sources you understand . . . that you were for some long time seeking the whereabouts of the woman we speak of. As I said on the telephone such information came to my notice and I was of the impression that you might find it very useful . . .'

'I see! And as I don't expect a man of your standing to be looking for some sort of reward for this "information" I'm forced to ask mesel' why yer being so generous wi' the parting of it!' Here she paused, to scrutinize him for a moment, then a smile twisted her mouth as she said, 'And o' course, the answer presents itself. That woman . . . *that* bitch! Some'ow she's managed to trigger off the same hate in *you* as she 'as in me! Oh, an' it's easy to see why, eh? Back from wherever a divil teks itself, she's got fresh designs on your son! Oh aye! I'm right am I not? Yes, I can tell from yer face. I've 'it the bloody nail smack on the 'ead!' She had been smiling but now the smile fell from her face, and in its place there emerged a cold calculating expression. 'Want to be rid of 'er, do you? Aye! An' does it matter to you . . . a proud upstanding gentleman like yersel' . . .' She was sneering now, the hostility of which drew Mr Marsden to his feet as she finished, '. . . does it matter the length I might be forced to go?'

'What do you mean? Now look here, Mrs Bedford! I'll not be involved in anything extreme. But whichever manner you choose to teach the woman a lesson, so to speak, don't involve me! My visit . . . the telephone call . . . none of it took place. You don't know me, and you've had no dealings with me! That much *must* be made clear!'

'But you want her out of the way? Well, so do I, Mr Marsden, so do I!' At this point she thrust out her hand, and when Mr Marsden had placed a piece of folded paper into it she enclosed the paper with her fist, gripping it with such force that it drove her finger-nails into the palm of her hand to draw blood. 'Thank you,' she said, her eyes still fixed on his face. Then throwing back her head, she laughed aloud. 'So I don't know you, eh? Never met you nor spoken to you in me life, eh? That's just like your sort, putting the world to rights from be'ind a bloody desk! Yer all the sodding same – yer let loose the tigers, then run for yer bloody lives!'

Dropping her gaze she opened her hand to look at the paper. Then, after glancing at the address of Kingsway she looked up again. In a firm voice, she said, 'Fair enough! As far as I'm concerned you don't exist. Now, as yer don't exist . . . it's 'appen a good idea to mek yersel' invisible! Goodnight, Mr Marsden.'

'Good*bye*. I'll see myself to the door.' Mr Marsden was convinced that the quicker he got out of that place, the better. And as he left the house, he couldn't help but think about those 'tigers' he'd let loose.

However, once in the privacy of his car and heading for the security of home, any likelihood of something 'extreme' being done against Queenie Bedford seemed positively unlikely. After all, even a woman such as the one he'd just left, who was nothing more than a small-time crook when it came down to it, wasn't fool-ish enough to do anything *really* criminal. On the other hand there would likely be a little 'accident' in the form of punishment for the loss of a son . . . and maybe an unforeseen drop in the guest-house business, thereby forcing a certain person to take herself off out of the area altogether. Of course, things could no doubt be made so very unpleasant that moving from a particular area might prove to be the best move for some.

Mr Marsden didn't know what that roguish creature had in mind to do and he didn't really care. He would now put the entire matter out of his mind, for there were other more pleasant plans to consider involving a wedding.

Mrs Bedford Senior had plans also. But they ran along very different lines. Once she was quite satisfied that her visitor had departed, she put in motion the first phase of her plans. This entailed dialling a familiar number, which in turn brought to the telephone a man of old acquaintance. To this man, she gave a name and an address. Her following instructions were very precise; the man was alerted to the urgency of her call when she told him in a low, even voice, 'There's a "package" I want collected and taken to the "warehouse"! No slip-up, mind! This is a *particular* package. And it needs careful 'andling! Understand, do yer?'

After obtaining an affirmative answer she replaced the receiver, and in a soft voice said, 'It's time, Queenie, gel! Time to pay the piper!'

Chapter Ten

Thursday morning in the guest-house brought uproarious laughter. It all started in the dining room at breakfast time, with one Mrs Swift, a quiet and retiring woman of middle age who had been a regular paying guest at Kingsway over the past two years. This week made her third visit in all.

Queenie had just delivered a fresh pot of coffee to the couple by the window when out of the corner of her eye she caught sight of Mrs Swift, shyly beckoning to Queenie and looking uncomfortably embarrassed. At once, Queenie wove her way in and about the tables until she had brought herself to stand before the dear soul.

'What is it, Mrs Swift?' asked Queenie, lowering her voice as seemed to be in keeping with the situation.

With a quick nervous glance around the room, the woman gave a polite little cough, and leaning forward she crooked a finger to persuade Queenie nearer. Then, after Queenie had obliged by bending towards her, she murmured, 'I'm very sorry, but you see . . . there's no toilet-paper . . .'

Queenie lifted her head and fetched her gaze into the woman's now bright pink face, 'No toilet-paper, did you say? What exactly do you mean, dear? If you mean there isn't any in the toilet on your landing, you must be mistaken. I put one in there myself at six o'clock this morning,' she whispered.

'I'm sorry . . . but you couldn't have,' came the whispered rejoinder. 'You see, I was obliged to go first thing when I woke this morning . . , and . . . well, it was fortunate I always take my handbag with me . . . I'm never without a supply of tissues . . .' At this point, her face was suffused with a rush of bright crimson and she could say no more.

'She's right, you know!' The voice, loud and intrusive, belonged to a woman at a table nearby. 'An' what's more, so are you!' Mrs Fisher had twisted round in her chair and was addressing both Mrs Swift and Queenie, her arms waving about to take everyone through her actions that morning. It was to her delight, and poor Mrs Swift's obvious distress, that she found herself the centre of attention. Being a raucous big-hearted woman, the possessor of a raw Lancastrian tongue, misshapen from the bearing of too many children, she put Queenie in mind of Maisie Thorogood.

Queenie straightened up, and paid mind, for she too was interested in what Mrs Fisher might have to say about the missing toilet-roll. '*You* were right, dear,' Mrs Fisher pointed at Queenie, 'because there *was* a spanking new toilet-roll in the lavvy on the upstairs landing!' Now, she was pointing at poor Mrs Swift, who had visibly squirmed into the seat of her chair. 'But *she* was right an' all when she said it were gone a little time later!'

Queenie was intrigued, and by the cessation of clattering knives and forks, together with a collection of curious faces all turned in one direction, the guests were equally inquisitive.

'What's the explanation, then?' asked Queenie. 'There *is* one, I take it?' The situation was becoming increasingly funny and Queenie was finding it hard not to laugh.

'Simple! I crept upstairs an' *pinched* the bloody toilet-roll, cause there weren't any in the *downstairs* lavvy!' Of a sudden the big woman threw out her arms and legs and exploded in a great gush of laughter, her ample form shaking and shivering as all eyes grew wider at the sight. Then, amidst gasps of reviving air and fresh attacks of giggling, she screamed out, 'Coming to summat innit, eh? When we're robbed o' paper to wipe us sodding arses on!'

And at such a truthful observation, however crudely put, even the most genteel of Queenie's guests were forced to burst out laughing, Queenie along with them.

But later, when the laughter was spent and all quiet, Queenie drew Nancy on one side of the kitchen and gently chastised her. Guests' comfort must be placed above all else, which included remembering something as mundane as a plentiful supply of toilet-paper. All the while she was reminding Nancy of this observation, Queenie kept a straight serious face. But the minute Nancy had sullenly swept from the kitchen to replenish the stock of toilet-rolls Queenie fell against the door in a fit of helpless laughter, her mind alive with desperate folk creeping up and down stairs in search of a roll of toilet-paper.

Regaining her composure, Queenie reminded herself that there was no more time for laughter. Today being Thursday, it was now two weeks since she had written to Mr Snowdon, seemingly to no avail. She had even telephoned the prison governor, asking whether the letter had in fact been posted out to the solicitor.

Queenie had been assured that yes, the letter *had* been posted as promised and no, there was no reason that he knew of why she had not received a reply. Queenie thanked him and would have put the telephone down, but there ensued a very curious conversation, during which the governor informed Queenie of Hannah Jason's poorly condition, and asked that out of consideration for the woman, Queenie should not entertain any further notions of visiting her. After all, she was not a relative, now was she?

Queenie was not deterred, thinking her visits might well do Hannah a measure of good. She told the governor as much, but his response was curt and dismissive. 'I'm sorry but I really must insist. You will *not* be allowed a visitor's pass to see Hannah Jason!' He said nothing to Queenie of the sharp and reproachful letter which he had received from the eminent Mr Snowdon, reminding him of his trustworthy position, and pointing out the folly of his adopted role as 'mediator' which had encouraged him into forwarding a letter from a woman of what kind! A woman who was known to associate with undesirable characters such as the prisoner Bannion, a convicted prostitute and procurer of prostitutes! And the matter the woman had dared to raise in her letter, was of a private and confidential nature, not open to discussion.

All the while he had been talking, Queenie sensed there was something very odd about the governor's attitude. Yet, when she replaced the receiver and thought about it further, the only prominent recollection was that she had been denied a visitor's pass to see old Hannah. This much, together with her failure so far to contact Mr Snowdon, she would have to report to Sheila today who in turn would relay the news to Hannah.

But all was not lost, because this very morning, Queenie had got certain information from consulting the telephone directory.

She discovered that there were no fewer than fifteen entries under the name of Snowdon, four of them solicitors. Having secured this knowledge, Queenie had straight away taken down the four names and telephone numbers in order, then contacted the first one to secure an appointment for this Friday morning . . . tomorrow. If this particular 'Snowdon' was not the 'legal gent' to whom Hannah had referred, then Queenie would go on through the list until she either located him or saw that her enquiries must spread a broader net. Either way she had taken on the task, and she would certainly find him, for poor Hannah's sake. After that she would have to go with the tide, depending on what circumstances were revealed when this 'legal gent' was found. It might turn out that Hannah's purpose was not best served by pursuing her son.

'We shall have to see!' Queenie murmured, putting away the last of the breakfast things and going from the kitchen to the guests' lounge, a large square room with an east-facing window, through which the sun flooded in the morning. There were three large settees in this room, covered in cottagey floral material. Nearby stood four deep and comfortable armchairs covered in the same pattern. Dotted about among the seating were three large, low rectangular tables in richest polished wood. The heavy velour curtains matched the burgundy shade of the carpet. There was a cumbersome sideboard against the wall by the door, and a small square table in the corner on which stood a television. Various prints and framed embroidery adorned the four walls, all the pictures dating from many years back.

As Queenie busied herself about the lounge, polishing and vacuuming, the sound of music wafted in through the open window, perhaps from the radio of a parked car or someone playing a record in a neighbouring house. Stopping to listen, Queenie recognized the song 'Send me the Pillow that you Dream On'. It was not a new song, but one which Queenie had liked from its release some eighteen months back. She let her heart soak in the words which spoke of love between man and woman.

Her lips moved in a wry little smile. The song was indicative of the current loving, sentimental mood of the nation. Flower people proclaimed their message of peace and hope in music which spoke of joy, friendship and love. Oh, there were those who looked sourly on such things, but wouldn't that always be so, thought Queenie.

She stayed still, listening to the song, her mind on a certain man she would probably never see again. She felt nostalgic and sad; cheated. Abruptly the song came to an end. Just as abruptly, Queenie thrust the memory of it from her mind, forcing herself to concentrate on the work in hand.

She had finished the work and was just straightening the magazines on the coffee table when the telephone rang.

'All right!' The voice of Maud sailed up the hallway from the kitchen. 'I'll answer it!' Then, almost immediately, she showed her face round the door of the lounge, 'It's for you,' she told Queenie.

The caller was Katy. And the news was bad. Queenie listened horrified while Katy relayed the facts of the matter. Did Queenie recall the young man who had risked his life saving a little lass from the sea? Well, the young man was Rick!

As Queenie started her questioning, Katy broke in 'Now, don't worry, lass . . . because he's out of danger and on the mend. I'm only able to tell you about it now because I've not long been in possession of the news mesel! Father Riley, in 'is God-given wisdom, thought it best to keep me in the dark. Did you ever! I might be whizzing up to eighty at an alarming rate, but like I telled 'im, they don't come tougher than old Katy Forest!'

'He's all right, Katy? You're *sure* he's all right?' It had been quite a shock for Queenie and the first thought that sprang to mind was that she must go to him straight away.

'O' course I'm sure, lass, else I'd say so!' Here Katy paused, before going on in a more subdued tone, 'But 'ere now, there's summat else, lass . . .'

'Katy, I *must* go and see him!' interrupted Queenie, fearful that Katy was keeping something from her.

'I think so too, lass, but just 'ear me out. As I say, there's summat else. It seems Rick's preparing to wed a woman by the name o' Rachel Winters, comes from 'igh-rolling background by all accounts . . .'

As Katy talked on, Queenie's thoughts fell away, returning to the day of Mr Marsden's visit. He had said then that Rick would shortly wed. This woman Katy talked of now was the same one he had mentioned.

In a matter of seconds Queenie had been shocked, fearful and relieved in turn. Now, she felt empty and lost for words. He was gone from her now: Rick was to be married. Strange, she thought, how all these years she had tried desperately to shut him out of her mind and out of her heart. But she had never really been able to do that; and now it was as though Rick himself was drawing away from her, in too painful and final a way for her to easily accept – even though she had thought herself prepared.

'Queenie! Queenie, lass, *will* you go an' see Rick?'

'You're telling me the truth, Katy? Rick *is* on the mend?' Queenie had postponed an answer to Katy's question by asking a question herself. And only when Katy once again assured her of Rick's progress did she reply, 'Well then, Katy. In the circumstances it's best if I stay away.'

'If you don't seek 'im out, you'll lose 'im, Queenie, you'll lose Rick for good!'

'Katy, tell me one thing. This . . . Rachel Winters . . . does she love him? Does she?'

It was a moment before the reply came back. When it did, however reluctant, it only confirmed to Queenie what Mr Marsden had told her.

'Aye, well, if I'm truthful lass I 'ave to say that Father Riley thinks she's a good woman . . . in love, yes . . . and that the two of 'em will mek a perfect match.' And here, Katy's voice rose on a protest, 'But then *'e* doesn't know . . .'

'Thank you, Katy. That's all *I* need to know.'

'Aw, lass! Don't you think you owe it to Rick an'

yersel to ask 'im such questions to 'is face? You're giving 'im no chance at all! Look 'ere, lass, tek a day or two to think it o'er, I'll not worry you or sway you in one direction or another, but think on it, promise?'

Queenie gave her word, for she *would* think on it, day and night. And above all else, she would pray for Rick to regain his health and strength. She wished that his marriage would be equally healthy and that it would be a source of contentment and happiness to him. God help her, but there was nothing else she could do!

In the next hour Queenie left everything in order at the guest-house and walked to the bus stop to board the bus to the prison. After the usual procedures she was now sitting opposite Sheila. The strange thing was, Queenie could remember very little either of the journey or of the rigmarole involved in being brought into the visitors' room.

'What's up wi' yer, Queenie gel? Anybody'd think they'd fetched yer in 'ere an' thrown away the bloody key!' Sheila gave a raucous laugh which momentarily disturbed the buzz of talk filling the room, and brought a chilling stare from the officer on door duty.

Sheila stared back at one and all, at the same time murmuring from beneath her breath, 'Aw, arseholes, the sodding lot on yer! Miserable buggers!'

As always, Sheila's forthright manner and colourful turn of phrase brought a laugh to Queenie's heart, shutting out the pain and causing Queenie to feel ashamed that Sheila had so easily perceived her despair. After all, wasn't *she* the visitor, purporting to bring good cheer to her friend?

'Oh, Sheila, I'm sorry. Just got a few things on my mind, that's all.'

'Aye, well! Don't you let the buggers drag yer down, my gel! Now then, do I get me ciggies today, or what?' She leaned across the table, her eyes following Queenie's every move as the packet of cigarettes was fetched out of Queenie's handbag and put into Sheila's outstretched palm.

Eagerly taking one from the packet and lighting it up, Sheila relaxed into her chair; alternately puffing on the cigarette, sipping the tea Queenie had bought earlier from the counter and having a word or two to say about everything and everybody.

'Now then, gel. What's the news on Hannah's business, eh?'

As briefly and in as graphic a manner as possible, Queenie related every step of how she had followed up the whole thing. Not only had this Mr Snowdon seemingly ignored her letter, though the governor *had* assured her that the letter had been sent; she now had an appointment with the first solicitor named Snowdon on her list of four. Oh, and she'd been refused permission to visit Hannah again. Now, what did Sheila think to that! Wasn't it strange?'

'Strange! It's sodding diabolical, that's what it is!' Sheila was so outraged that she put the cigarette in her mouth and puffed at it with such zeal that Queenie could hardly see her face at all. What she saw was the cigarette going up and down in a peculiar angle from Sheila's mouth as she poured out her contempt for these 'bastards in authority'.

'Sheila, take that blessed fag out of your mouth and *listen* to me!' Queenie was acutely aware of Sheila's contempt for authority, and aware also of the way her volatile emotions were carrying that penetrating voice of hers across the room. Any minute now, Queenie was convinced the officer patrolling the room would close in and pluck Sheila right out of that chair. 'You've to take a hold of yourself this minute! I don't want you carted off and punished. Now just calm down, else you'll make me sorry I told you anything at all.'

'Hmph! Yer a bossy bugger, Queenie gel!' Sheila protested, taking the cigarette out of her mouth all the same, *and*, to Queenie's surprise and delight, stubbing it lifeless in the ashtray.

'And you're a *noisy* bugger, Sheila gel!' retorted Queenie. At which, the two of them burst out laughing and kept on laughing and giggling until Queenie felt an easing of the tension which had coiled itself up in her right from Katy's phone call that morning.

Of a sudden she felt a desperate urge to confide certain things in Sheila, who had settled into a calmer mood and seemed somehow to have sensed Queenie's restlessness. After quietly studying her friend's face a while, Sheila blurted out, 'Look 'ere, Queenie! I *know* there's summat ailing yer. Now, if yer can't tell an old friend as went to school with yer – grew up with yer! – then who the bloody 'ell *can* yer tell, eh? Come on, out with it, unless yer want me screaming an' 'ollering fit to wakken the dead!' She set herself hard in the chair; threatening any minute to test the strength of the building and the folk in it. Then, when Queenie put on her best smile and tried to change the subject, first assuring Sheila that there really was nothing at all ailing her, Sheila took quiet stock of her, then leaned forward, and wrapped her sizeable fist over Queenie's hand. 'Look, gel, there is summat, I know there is. We've known each other what, twenty years? Too long

anyroad, for you to 'ide owt from a nosey bugger like
me. Is it 'cause you've not been able to 'elp old
Hannah? Aw . . . yer will, gel! An' she *knows* yer will.'

'No, it's not that, Sheila.' The urge in Queenie had
pushed itself too near the surface now to be denied.
Queenie regretted that she hadn't been able to bring
herself to share a particular burden with old Katy.
Since learning that Rick was in the infirmary, there
had been like a lead weight lying in Queenie's stomach.
She could think of little except that Rick was badly,
happen more badly than Katy had admitted.

Oh, thought Queenie, it *would* be wonderful to talk
about things to Sheila; to explain the whole dreadful
business regarding herself and Rick and George
Kenney as was. Sheila wasn't as brazen as she sometimes liked to appear either, and she could be as level-
headed as the next one if she'd a mind. And mebbe
Sheila would see something that she herself couldn't?
No, that wasn't possible. Nobody had examined the
situation like she had from every imaginable angle. It
was a close-end situation with no hope of ever getting
out from it. But to confide her innermost thoughts and
fears? It *would* be a tonic for *her*, but what about
Sheila? Stuck in this place and then to have somebody
pour out *their* troubles . . . no, she wouldn't do it. Best
to keep things to herself, thought Queenie.

So, for the next half hour, in spite of Sheila's every
trick to drag Queenie's 'troubles' from her, no mention
of Rick emerged. But then, a curious thing happened.

Thinking on it afterwards, it had seemed to Queenie
that there had been *two* levels of communication taking
place between Sheila and herself. One was the verbal
conversation on the subjects of old Hannah, the guest-

house, and the 'sods who thrive on authority'.

The second and inexplicable mode of communication was an unconscious one, made up of emotions, senses, unspoken questions and answers. All these intangible things merged on their own accord, until forced to intrude with surprising suddenness.

It was just before the piercing sound of the bell signalling the end of visiting period when Sheila stopped in mid-sentence and with popping eyes, said in a breathless voice, 'It's Rick! It's Rick Marsden, innit?'

Taken aback by this sudden and remarkable supposition, Queenie found herself dropping her head in acknowledgement.

'What then? You've picked up with 'im agin . . . want ter get married, leave the guest-'ouse. What? For Gawd's sake, you'll *'ave* to tell me!'

And quickly, in the few moments left, Queenie told Sheila everything: of the way she and Rick loved each other, had always loved each other; how more recently he had been badly injured saving a child's life; and how very shortly he would be wed to a woman who by all accounts would make him a good wife.

'A good wife! *You'll* mek 'm a good bloody wife! Listen gel! Don't you concern yersel' about that sodding guest-'ouse! Shut the bugger up fer all *I* care, or leave them two women running it. They knows the business, don't they? Christ, gel! If yer let some posh cow mek away wi' Rick then yer not the crack o' woman *I've* allus took yer for! You tell that one to piss off!'

Queenie had not expected such an outburst from Sheila. Her own voice now sharp with impatience, she told her, 'Sheila! You don't understand . . .'

'Then *mek* me understand if yer can!' There was a look in Sheila's eyes that Queenie had never witnessed in her friend before, not all the years she'd known her. It was a strong look, challenging and angry. And there was something else too, hidden amongst the anger, but not so well that Queenie didn't sense it: there was a measure of fear. Queenie could relate to such fear, because hadn't she herself experienced it many times when her darling Auntie Biddy had been alive . . . and again on that dreadful night when George Kenney had maliciously wrecked Rick's peace of mind by shouting out that he himself was Rick's father?

Yes, she knew that look widening Sheila's eyes. It was not fear for a body's *own* happiness. It was a desperate, defensive fear born out of concern and love for somebody else's welfare.

Queenie lifted her head a little higher to meet that marvellous look in Sheila's eyes. As the two women looked each into the other, the years rolled away and they were small scruffy children, sitting on the kerb-edge and playing with one of Maisie Thorogood's yo-yo's with Auntie Biddy looking on and Maisie's colourful cart in the road, surrounded by excited children. Then they were tender teenagers, each yearning for a particular boy, Rick Marsden, Sheila with a roving eye for the moment, Queenie with a great love in her heart that she had carried over the years till now. A love which had sometimes been a reservoir of joy and sometimes a searing pain.

Queenie thanked her lucky stars for such a friend. Now, her own eyes misted over with love, with gratitude, and the knowledge that however much Sheila might want to move the world on her behalf, there was not a thing she could do that would change the truth of the situation.

So, Queenie began to explain. And when her voice broke out, it was from somewhere deep inside her body. 'It's a long way back to the beginning of it all, Sheila, but there'll be time enough later for us to sit and talk of it.' Sheila saw how hard this was for Queenie, but saying nothing, she merely nodded her head for Queenie to go on. 'What it all comes down to is that Rick and I have no right to love each other – not in *that* way. We're . . . we're brother and sister.' There it was said. Having said it, Queenie fell back into the chair, every ounce of strength seeming to have been sucked out of her.

The words had melted away, even the monotonous buzz of conversation previously emanating from around the room and permeating the air was stilled in that small space between Sheila and Queenie. The only disturbance came from the muffled ticking of the clock on the wall immediately beside them, the long-drawn-out gasp from Sheila, and the reverberation of what Queenie had said.

After what seemed an age Sheila spoke, her voice soft and enquiring. 'You and Rick . . . *how?* I don't understand. I don't!' It was at this point the bell sounded. And visibly recovering from the shock she had received at Queenie's words, Sheila spoke again, this time with firmness and urgency. 'Look 'ere, Queenie gel! I don't know what ter mek of all this . . . I need ter sleep on it. But 'ere's summat yer can be thinking on! Rick's badly, ain't 'e? Asking fer yer if I knows owt. Yer love each other, wrong or right. But

I'll tell yer summat gel! What if 'e dies, eh? What then, an' you've not gone to 'im?'

'He'll *not* die, Sheila. Katy says he's on the mend.' All the same, Queenie was fearful.

'But yer *don't know* that fer sure.'

The room was being cleared and there was no more time. They quickly hugged each other; Sheila saying as they parted, 'Yer love 'im, Queenie. Bugger *everything* else an' run to 'im, quick as yer can, eh?' Then she was gone.

All the way back to Kingsway and for the rest of the day into the evening, Sheila's words had burned in Queenie's mind. Queenie knew in her heart that Sheila was right, for hadn't she herself long wrestled with the very same arguments? Hadn't she told herself time and time again that life was short and if happiness was to be bought, then there were sacrifices to be made! Then came the other side of such an argument, the side which dictated to Queenie that happiness bought at *any* price would bring its own special brand of heartache.

It was nine-thirty pm. Nancy was serving suppertime drinks to the three elderly guests who had returned tired from a long exacting day along the Golden Mile. Queenie had escaped into the privacy of her own little sitting-room. Taking time to collect her thoughts, Queenie dwelt on recent events concerning Hannah and Rick. Both brought disquieting news. She recalled a saying of Auntie Biddy's: 'Bad news allus comes in threes!' Well, if that was the case, fate wasn't finished with her yet.

At this point, driven by a need to question Katy at greater length, Queenie got from the bed where she had been lying and began to make her way into the hall. It was just as she extended her hand to the telephone that the front doorbell rang out, shattering the hitherto peaceful atmosphere.

Calling to Nancy that she would see to it, Queenie went out into the vestibule and cautiously opened the door. It seemed late for holiday-makers to be looking for bed and breakfast.

However, one look at the man told Queenie that here was no holiday-maker. He was of medium height with a small dark moustache and a trilby. He had on a full-length brown mackintosh and carried about him an air of authority.

'I'd like to talk to the woman of the house, a Mrs Bedford, I understand?' His eyes were wide and enquiring, his smile charming 'It's a matter of extreme urgency.' Here, the man paused slightly, cursing himself for not recalling Bedford's explicit instructions. There had been something else – a name he was to mention. A name which had brought a devious smile to Bedford's lips on the uttering of it. Oh yes! Marsden, that was it. 'I've been sent to fetch you at once! Mr Marsden . . .'

'Marsden? *Rick* . . .' This was the trigger to set Queenie off. There were no more doubts, no more questions; he had sent for her, *needed* her. And she was ready. Of a sudden, nothing else in the world held any importance. She was going to him, and he would get better for her. He must! 'I'll get my coat!' she shouted, already on her way back into the hall. 'Nancy! Nancy, hurry,' she called, struggling to unhook a long green jacket from the peg. Then, when Nancy at once appeared, Queenie explained that she had been called

161

to a sick friend, in the infirmary after an accident. 'Now, you'll be all right, won't you, Nancy? If I'm not back tonight, then you'll need to get Maud in.' While she'd been talking Queenie had struggled into her jacket, and now she was at the door. The man had gone, but there was a car waiting at the kerbside. It was to this car she hurried, calling to Nancy to make sure and lock up properly last thing.

Once in the back of the car travelling out of Lytham St Anne's, then along the main road which would take them through Blackburn and on to the infirmary, Queenie's mind was in turmoil. Several times she had questioned the man at the wheel in front, but none of his brief answers really told her anything. Now, impatient and unable to relax, she looked out of the car window. It was pitch black and apart from the standard lamps illuminating the road ahead, there was really nothing to see.

What about Rick? Oh God! Please let him be all right. Don't let him die, please don't let him die! At one point the tears rolled down her face. She thought on Sheila, wondered whether Katy would be waiting at the infirmary; and in her mind's eye, she saw Mr and Mrs Marsden together with an attractive woman, Rachel Winters. She would not be well received by the latter, Queenie knew that. But of a sudden, it didn't matter. Rick had sent for her and she was on her way.

The subconscious is a curious thing, raising persistent questions and pushing them to the fore, until in a splintering moment they burst into the mind and demand recognition. Such a thing was happening right now to Queenie.

The road had been vaguely familiar. Then Queenie wondered whether the man at the wheel knew of a shorter route, this unbeknown to her. All at once, they were back in familiar surroundings. They had come round by Blackburn Market Square, through the cobbled back alleys, and of a sudden, to Queenie's surprise and confusion, the car was pulling into Parkinson Street.

Queenie's eyes widened. *Parkinson Street!* It *was* Parkinson Street. There was Farradays' shop, all boarded up, and the same with the houses opposite. Her thoughts whirled as she struggled to make sense of her realization.

'Hey! What's going on?' she cried out, leaning forward and grabbing the driver by the collar, which she proceeded to thrust back and forth against his neck. Something was very wrong, she knew that now, knew it in the marrow of her bones! If she had only paid attention to her instincts a while back, she would have realized *then*.

She knew they were close to George Kenney's old house, that little house which had been her life when Auntie Biddy was alive but which had later grown into a tomb.

Queenie dared not let herself look at that house. She was crying bitterly now and both her fists were beating at the driver. She couldn't get from the car, because she'd tried, and the doors were secure. She couldn't budge them! So in her panic she continued to beat and tear at the driver, first entreating then demanding, 'Let me out of here! What's going on? Who in God's name are you?'

When his arm came up and swung viciously back at

her, Queenie saw only the slightest movement; a dark shape rising, a carved silhouette against the windscreen, then a sound like a muffled sledge-hammer hitting the window and shattering the glass. Queenie knew nothing; except a stabbing of excruciating pain and an engulfing blackness. The last words to penetrate her brain were, 'You little bastard! I'd as soon deliver you lifeless as breathing!'

Chapter Eleven

'What do you mean, Queenie's been gone two days?'
Father Riley took a long hard look at Katy, his eyes
chastizing. 'So you *have* known where Queenie's been
all along! I suspected as much and so, I think, did
Rick! Now then, calm yourself! Tell me what it is
you're trying to say and take your time.'

'Oh, bless us!' Katy hopped from one foot to the
other, sweeping her pinnie up to her face, where she
nervously wiped it across her eyes, then twisted it
round and round between her fists as she hurried to
and fro across the library floor. 'She's gone, they say!
Just tekken off . . .'

'Gone *where*, Katy? *Who* says she's gone?' Coming
away from the fireplace, where he'd just emptied the
cold remains of his pipe, Father Riley took a moment
to light the fresh wadge of tobacco and solemnly draw
on it. Then he halted the frantic Katy in her tracks,
got hold of her by the shoulders, and gently pushed
her into his favourite armchair. 'Now! From the beginning,' he told her.

Calmer now, Katy related everything told her by
Nancy, who had taken it upon herself to look in
Queenie's little book kept in a drawer by the telephone

165

and containing Katy's name and number.

Well, it seemed that Queenie was fetched away from the guest-house late on Thursday night by some gentleman in a car. Queenie had been frantic, telling Nancy that she'd been called to a sick friend in the infirmary, and asking Nancy to get Maud in to help with the work as she might not be back till Friday.

'And 'ere it is, eleven o'clock of a *Saturday*, and she's still not turned up?' Katy would have got to her feet again, had Father Riley not put a hand on her shoulder and pressed her back into the chair. 'There's a lot I'll be asking you later, you old fox!' he said, not unkindly, 'but for now, Katy, what else did this Nancy say? Did she see the man? Or notice the car number? Did Queenie mention who this sick friend was? Or *which* infirmary she was going to?'

'No! No! I've already asked all them questions. Nancy says she's told us all she knows! Oh, Father Riley, where is the lass? What's become of 'er?'

'Now look, Katy! We don't *know* anything's "become of her". Her friend might be very ill . . . even dying. And if so, it's gone right out of her mind to let folk know where she is and when she'll be back.'

'No! You're wrong! Queenie's got no friends except me, and that blessed Sheila in the prison!' Catching sight of Father Riley's astonished expression and his movement to ask a question, Katy put him off with, 'I'll tell yer later all about that, and other things. For now, what are we to do? There's summat strange, I *know* there is! The only "sick friend" in the infirmary that Queenie knows about is Rick. And she's *not* been there . . . I've telephoned. Since Thursday morning, the only visitors to Rick's bedside have been Mr and

Mrs Marsden and that Rachel Winters. Anyroad, Rick's coming out this afternoon, they tell me. See 'ere, Father Riley, yer know I've a level 'ead on me shoulders. I'm not one to panic or jump the gun but I feel it in me bones. There's some'at bad going on 'ere, an' I can't fathom it out.'

'All right, Katy. As you say, you're not one to panic and you seem to know a heck of a lot more than *I* do. So you think it's a matter for the police?'

'I do! Oh, I do!' There was no doubt at all in Katy's mind. And what was more, she was of the decided opinion that Rick Marsden ought to know.

'Hmm . . . if you're so sure, Katy. But first, I think you and I will go and see this Nancy, have a proper talk with her. After all, we don't want to go rushing off to the police, not until we're sure that Queenie really *is* missing. Go on then, get your hat and coat. We'll go this minute. I've a feeling you're not prepared to do anything else till this is cleared up, am I right?' he asked. Judging by the way Katy got up out of that chair and made off towards the scullery, he could only conclude that Katy was desperately worried. And, as she had so rightly reminded him, in all of these thirty years and more he'd known her, Katy Forest had *never* been one to panic.

In a matter of minutes, the two of them were in the car and looking at each other; Katy impatient to be off and irritated that Father Riley appeared to be sitting there wasting precious time, 'Come on! Come on! Put yer foot on that confounded 'celerator thing and let's be off!' she shouted in her most authoritative voice.

'You've forgotten something, you bossy old tyrant . . .'

'I never 'ave!'

'Oh yes you have . . . You've forgotten to tell me which way I'm supposed to be headed!' His voice and smile were both gentle, designed to placate this dear concerned old lady who had worked herself up to a pitch not beneficial to a body of her considerable years.

'Oh, silly ol' fool that I am!' Katy declared, pink of face and feeling foolish. 'Mek fer the Blackpool road; I'll direct you as we go along.'

'Blackpool! You mean Queenie's been as near as that? And you saying nary a word! You really *are* a wily old fox. Now then, we've time enough on the journey for you to fill me in on what's been going on. And I want the *whole* story, mind!'

Katy was relieved to get the whole story off her chest even though, in confiding matters of Queenie, George Kenney and that unfortunate child in the churchyard, she was betraying a promise to Queenie. She sensed that the lass was in bad trouble. Queenie was not the sort to just disappear without leaving word. Look at when she'd gone from Blackburn those years back, with the weight of the world on her narrow young shoulders, she'd thought then to leave a message behind fer them as cared. Whatever it was that 'ad whipped Queenie away and out o' sight an' whoever that man was as Nancy knew little of, it were all pointing to the fact that Queenie were in some sort o' difficulties . . . an' if the tightening knot in that pit o' Katy's churning stomach were owt to go by, it were bad. In the back of her mind, Katy couldn't help but wonder whether the whole thing didn't have something to do with that blessed Sheila and the live stench left behind in that guest-house by yon Maisie

Thorogood . . . Lord rest 'er soul, whatever she's done!

Aye, there were men – and women an' all, who might bear an evil grudge o'er the shutting down of a den o' thieves an' prostitutes like that! Could'a got it in fer Queenie . . . Could'a been biding their time, she wouldn't be surprised. There was a core o' badness in Lancashire same as anywhere else an' like as not, Queenie might 'ave unwittingly touched upon it.

All of these fears and more she revealed to Father Riley, who had lapsed into silence at the onset of Katy's revelations and who now drove the car like a man in a trance. So! George Kenney had violated his own flesh and blood! His own innocent daughter? He found it hard to believe; and yet it was not so surprising after all, because if ever he had seen a man stand aside the devil, it was that one. And the child which Queenie had carried – thought to be Mike Bedford's – that child was the outcome of a deed of unspeakable badness. Lord forgive the sins of the children, yes! But forgive also the sins of the father!

And what of Queenie? Forced to run from a life of fear and drudgery and her no more than a child herself at the time. Now she had been back two years and more answering a friend's call and diving in with sleeves rolled up, to make a better world for that same friend to come home to. *That* was a woman of some character, indeed it was.

Katy's voice filtered in through Father Riley's thoughts, and he too realized her fears that Queenie might have become innocently enmeshed in some manner of revenge or other. He might be a man of God but in his dealings with the troubled folk, he had become only too aware of the creatures elbow deep in the devil's work. As to whether Queenie had fallen foul of such creatures, they would have to see.

Turning to Katy, his manner more serious now, he assured her, 'Take heart, Katy, lass! Let's be sure Nancy hasn't left anything out of what she saw Thursday night, then we'll see about the police. We'll find your Queenie. And you have my word: there'll be no stone left unturned!'

Chapter Twelve

Outside, the sun had risen brilliant in a clear June sky, and at six o'clock of a Sunday morning there were already sights and sounds of life down Parkinson Street.

The milkman's cart rumbled over the cobbles, waking the cats who uncurled lazily to saunter from various doorways in hopeful anticipation of licking up a spill of milk, or dipping a tongue into an open bottle-top after the thieving birds had taken their fill. But there was no hurry, for even at this early hour the close humid atmosphere heralded what promised to be a long and sultry day. For now though, the sun had warmed the cobbles and was beaming its early rays into corners made unkempt and dark by neglect.

There was one such corner, however, where the sun could not penetrate, for here it was forbidden access beyond the heavy threadbare curtains firmly drawn across the narrow windows of a particular house in Parkinson Street. This house was the one-time abode of Mike Bedford and his mother, and situated no more than a few steps from where Queenie had grown from child to woman, surviving one day at a time with George Kenney and Auntie Biddy.

These past years, the Bedford house had been used for two purposes. It made a home of sorts for the rough and ready Blodwin Torrid, the boozy kind-hearted and long-suffering mother of Queenie's kidnapper, Raith. This neglected and sorry house also served as a warehouse; of which Blodwin Torrid was appointed keeper, sustained by a plentiful supply of booze and food. In these matters of reward her son, Raith, was considered to be a good provider for so long as his old Irish mammy was vigilant in her role as caretaker to the numerous goods which found their way in and out of the upstairs back bedroom at an alarming rate, and at some considerable profit to the woman Bedford.

But none had given that woman more satisfaction than the particular package delivered here on Thursday evening – albeit in a torn and damaged condition!

For two and a half days, Queenie had lived in a twilight world of pain and darkness, carried on a shifting tide between total unconsciousness and fleeting half-awareness until all sense of identity or belonging was lost.

Now, something had probed the darkness of her mind – some sound or smell stirred her senses and in the stirring had come the sharp awareness of extreme discomfort; this in turn becoming an agony that stretched from her toes through her entire body, until it grew to unbearable pressure inside her head: a pressure that threatened to explode at any second. The groan forced itself from her lips of its own accord. Queenie would have moved in an effort to ease her distress, but something prevented her. Her body felt torn in every direction and all of them alien to the one she wanted.

In spite of this terrifying sense of despair, her body violently trembling first with cold then with pain, Queenie's searching thoughts struggled to assemble. Into her mind came dancing and grotesque images . . . of a dark-eyed and moustached man . . . of rough hands descending on her, and of angry shouting voices.

Slowly her head came upright on her shoulders and the weight of her eyelids was forced upwards. At this moment two particular things assailed Queenie. Her eyes were wide open now but she might as well be blind, for there was nothing visible in the total blackness. Then there was the smell . . . a thick, suffocating stench like that of raw fish, which impregnated the air and assaulted her nostrils until she was forced to keck.

Of a sudden the door was flung open to reveal the stark silhouette of a man, tall as the door frame and with a military bearing. The unexpected burst of light both surprised and pained Queenie, and in that instant, when she would have shielded her sore eyes with the palm of her hand, it came to her that she was secured fast in an awkward sitting position which tested every screaming nerve in her body. Then just as swiftly as the door had been flung open, it was slammed shut; the angry sound echoing round inside her head until she thought it must break.

Now, into the darkness, came a rush of movement . . . the heavy thud of footsteps negotiating a steep stairway; then voices . . . first rumbling then whispering, now at the door as it was inched open.

'She's awake *proper* this time, is she? Yer sure?' Though gruff, the voice was unmistakably that of a woman. Somewhere in the reaches of her memory, Queenie recalled such a hostile, probing voice. But whose? Whose voice? The question uttered itself in her brain and in attempting to move her lips in a shaping of the question, Queenie found them inhibited by a binding tape stretched tight and cruel across the lower half of her face.

In a moment the two figures had entered the room; then came the click of a switch. The bright light dazzled Queenie's eyes, temporarily blinding her.

With her head turned to one side and sorry eyes downcast, Queenie tried to voice the questions in her mind. 'Who are you? What do you want with me? *Please* help me . . . help me!' But these desperate enquiries emerged as mere muffled sounds only adding to her frustration.

Slowly her eyes became accustomed to the light, and blinking against it, Queenie lifted her head and brought her questioning gaze to bear on the two figures who loomed before her, standing quite still and looking down at the pitiful sight she made.

Having been half-carried, half-dragged from the car on Thursday night, Queenie was brought straight away to the upstairs back bedroom in the old Bedford house in Parkinson Street. Here, she was thrown into the deep settee chair and firmly anchored by thin leather straps which reached from the castor stubs on the chair to encircle her ankles. The same method had been employed to secure her arms, wrenched backwards and pulled round the chair by means of a strong twine rope which was then tightly knotted at the centre.

On the night she was taken, Queenie had been wearing a cream cotton dress. This was now shredded at both shoulders, leaving a pattern as though long tearing nails had ripped through the delicate material and left

deep scarring bruises reaching from neck to collar-bone
in the flesh beneath. As far as could be seen, every
button on the dress had been torn asunder; Queenie's
green jacket, thrown over the lower half of her body,
concealed any further damage.

'Looks a bit the worse fer wear, wouldn't yer say,
Torrid eh?' The woman's voice was cruel and showed
the delight she was taking in Queenie's predicament.
Now, with a small laugh, she gently dug the man in
the side with what appeared to be some sort of horse-
whip as she came forward, at the same time flicking
out this peculiar instrument to wedge the end beneath
Queenie's chin, forcing Queenie's head upwards so
that her frightened eyes could look nowhere else but
into the woman's face. With a little shock of horror,
Queenie realized that she did indeed know the voice
and the face. But such was the pained confusion in her
mind that try as she might she could not give identity
either to the voice or to the leering features! More
than that, a far more terrifying realization dawned . . .
she could not give name to her *own* identity.

As Queenie struggled to remember, she looked at
the woman, taking in every detail and finding a greater
confusion in what she saw. No ordinary woman this,
for she was set in a solid square frame, squat in appearance, with trousers and shirt more suited to a man,
and the hair on her head cut to within an inch of her
scalp. With the smoking cigarette dangling from the
corner of her thin spiteful mouth she looked almost
comical, in a sinister way.

But now, as she bore down on Queenie, bringing
her face to within an inch of her victim, it was fearfully
plain to Queenie that there was nothing 'comical' about

the woman's bulbous and staring eyes. Queenie did not flinch. Instead, she made herself stare deep into the woman's face, all the while striving to remember.

Of a sudden, as their eyes met and Queenie felt the hatred swallowing her whole, some deeper instinct seemed to paralyse her. Who *was* this woman? What did she want of her? Where were they, and why? But there came no answers, only a terrible gripping fear and an almighty sense of loneliness. Then, as the woman's face hovered so close she could feel the warmth of her breath, Queenie recoiled in horror, her hands and feet writhing to be free, and small unintelligible noises issuing from her mouth. In that instant she thought whatever her identity, she must be a Christian, because in her frantic mind she offered up a prayer.

Now the woman straightened up and moved backwards, her eyes continuing to bore into Queenie's face and a smile wreathing her features. Turning to the man, who had not moved, she laughed out loud, 'This is the beautiful and exquisite woman who can toy with a man's affections and drive him crazy, don't yer know!' Now, her laughter stopped and she snapped her attention back to Queenie as she added sneeringly, 'Tek a good look at 'er, Torrid . . . she ain't so "exquisite" now, is she, eh?' She glanced at the man, seemingly eager that he too should savour this pathetic creature, stripped of her dignity, emptied of her pride and desperately afeared! It gave her pleasure to display Queenie in such a manner.

Raith Torrid cast his dark eyes over Queenie's bruised and mangled body. He surveyed the marks stretching from her temple to her ear. The were splattered in pattern, like the window of the car. Mingling with the gashes was the strong-smelling application of iodine, its yellow tinge creating a ghastly painting amidst the dishevelled hair and congealed blood. This humane touch had been the handiwork of his mother, Blodwin, who had crept up here to bathe this creature's wounds and to apply the iodine, whose smell had deteriorated to the like of rotting fish. She had done so in spite of his strict instructions to stay well away from the creature . . . for in all truth, he cared not whether she lived or died.

But as he continued to stare at Queenie, at the same time touching his fingers against his own face and neck where the marks made by Queenie's nails were beginning to fade, his distinct impression of the captive was far removed from the one Bedford would have him enjoy.

In spite of the ragged clothes and torn skin, and in spite of the rope and leather which bound her, this creature was *not* humbled. Afraid, yes; that much was in her wide staring eyes. But more than that, she was proud, defiant even . . . and possessed of remarkable dignity. He wondered in what way this proud beauty had crossed the woman Bedford. Well, whatever it was, she'd pay for it now, for the woman Bedford was hard and heartless, made that way, so it was said, by the untimely and cruel demise of her only son, on whom she doted. As for himself, he had learned to draw a thick strong line between conscience and profit. He was paid well for his part in any 'underhand' dealings, and had been extremely well rewarded for his discreet handling of *this* particular affair. Apart from the profits made, none of this was his concern. He had long enjoyed the rewards earned by turning a blind

eye, and he saw no reason to discontinue such a policy.
Yet what he saw now sorely tried him.

Riddled with pain and all manner of disturbing
emotions raging through her, Queenie focused on the
movement as the woman again approached her. As
though through a tortured mist, she followed her cap-
tor's leering face, saw the mouth shape itself into a
thin cruel line and the words came to her ears in a
muffled murmur. 'Like 'er, do yer, Torrid? Want 'er
do yer?' Then a laugh, low and devious, and a hand
before her face, clutching a knife, with a grip so fierce
that it trembled. 'Well, if yer *still* want 'er when I'm
finished yer can 'ave 'er! Use 'er as teks yer fancy!'

At that moment, Queenie was convinced that she
would die here in this dark and frightening place, not
knowing who she was, or what terrible thing she had
done to evoke such hatred and revenge. Turning her
head now, she closed her weeping eyes and waited for
the worst.

In an instant her head was snapped back, rough
hands pushing it this way and that while the pain in
her temples throbbed like a thunderous echo inside her
brain.

For a while, the man stood in his place, making no
move. He was held fascinated as the woman tugged
and pulled at the braids of hair on her helpless captive
until they had come loose and the hair cascaded over
her shoulders like a glorious mantle of waves reaching
almost to the floor.

The woman Bedford took a step back and swinging
her face about, she asked, 'Ever seen the likes before,
'ave yer, Torrid? Like silk it is! Silky as fresh-fallen
rainwater.'

The man made no move and gave no answer. And the woman returned her crazed eyes to gaze on Queenie, who was now trembling uncontrollably. Then, lunging forward, she was on her again, and Queenie felt the vicious wrenching on her hair as the knife came down again and again in a frenzied hacking motion, gashing her neck and splitting off great hanks of her hair, which fell away against the bare skin of her legs before tumbling to the floor where they settled in a sorry, misshapen pile.

Done at last, the woman Bedford stood back a pace, admiring the results of her handiwork like an artist might review a painting. She swept her eyes over Queenie's terrified face, noted the brutally short, uneven raggedness of her hair, and the little runnels of blood trickling down her neck. And she was pleased. But not yet fully satisfied! For this creature now at her mercy . . . this creature with her stunning beauty and captivating ways had enticed away her one and only offspring, her boy, her Mike, who had once been so full of life. Her pride and joy with whom her every day started and ended. Now, he was gone, driven to drink and crushed to death. And all because of this one! Well, now it was *her* turn. Oh, how she had prayed for this very moment! And now it was here she would relish it. When she felt that Mike had been avenged, and *only* then, would the moment be over. Only then could the past be laid to rest with him. But she wouldn't do away with this one. Oh no: there were *worse* fates to be dealt with.

Once or twice, she walked round the chair which held Queenie fast. She savoured every step, delighted in every look at the helplessness of her distraught captive, who by now was emitting smothered noises like broken sobs.

Of a sudden she came to a halt, and turning sharply to the man near the door, she snapped, 'Out, Torrid! Get out and *don't* fetch yerself back to this room no matter what you 'ear! Understand? No matter *what*!'

He understood right enough! He understood that she was like a woman demented! And he didn't doubt for a moment that if he didn't do as she bid, like as not that knife could just as easily embed itself in his heart.

Hurrying downstairs, Raith Torrid came into the little front parlour, a small depressing room filled, he thought, with equally depressing items of ill-matched furniture; a cumbersome bow-fronted sideboard of dark wood with cupboards either side and a run of brass-handled drawers down the middle. In the centre of the parlour, dominating it, stood a large bulbous-legged table of light oak covered with a green cord tablecloth decorated with tassels, around which were arranged four ladder-back stand-chairs of similar wood to the table. Nearest the doorway there stood two uncomfortable black horse-hair armchairs which had been given to Blodwin Torrid by her old Irish daddy and had since taken pride of place wherever the Torrids had found a home. Worn coconut-matting squares covered the floor, while the wallpaper of blue forget-me-nots had long since faded.

Many times it had crossed Raith Torrid's mind to find his old Irish mammy a better abode although certainly not with him at his comfortable home in Pleasington, got with proceeds from dealings with the woman Bedford, and from his house of pleasure in Mill Hill, Blackburn, which fronted as a night-club and was known as 'Garrett's Place'. Anyway, for the time being it was convenient to keep his mammy here in Parkinson Street.

Nowadays, with half the houses empty and boarded up, there were few nosey-parkers to witness certain comings and goings. But, with Parkinson Street set to be pulled down shortly, he would have to put his mind to finding a place somewhere else, some other little out-of-the-way place, with no one to ask questions.

He looked at his mammy now, slumped in the armchair to the right of the blackened grate and oven-range, covered in that familiar grubby flowered pinnie, and clutching a half-empty glass of gin. Not much company for a man, he thought. And not much use to anybody. Still, she served a purpose and she came to no harm.

What a stark contrast with that creature upstairs, he thought, the young woman he'd fetched from Lytham St Anne's, the 'parcel' he'd been handsomely paid to deliver. By! But she had a look about her, that one, and something else besides. Something that few men ever got their hands on, a kind of inbred quality that had nothing at all to do with figure or beauty although she did indeed possess a figure like a dream, and a special sort of beauty. And what kind o' man was *he* to stand by while all that was being devastated?

Crossing to the sideboard, he fished out a bottle and glass, which he filled and took a swig from. What kind of man? A cautious man, that's what! And he was no fool to put his nose where it didn't belong. The woman Bedford had made it clear he was not wanted up there. So he intended to stay right where he was until sent for.

As always, when the drink went to Blodwin Torrid,

the singing came out and today was no exception. The song came softly at first, emanating from the chair where his mammy had stirred now and then to replenish her flagging spirits with a 'drop o' the ol' stuff'.

Now dragging herself up to a sitting position, she wiped the wisps of grey hair from her eyes and unceremoniously tucked them behind her ears. As Raith Torrid turned to look at her and their eyes met, her face became wreathed in a wide toothless smile, and she launched into a surprisingly beautiful rendering of one of his favourite songs,

> 'Oi'll take you home again, Kathleen,
> Across the ocean wild and wide
> To where your heart has ever been
> Since forst you were moi bonny bride'

Upstairs, the plaintive voice felt its way into every corner. On the woman whose hatred and unbearable grief had driven her to unspeakable things, the song had a surprising effect.

She had been standing with her back to the door, the knife still in her hand and her bitter eyes surveying the naked Queenie. It was a pitifully grotesque picture, covered from neck to thigh in a criss-cross of small red, weeping slits, carefully patterned with the tip of the knife blade.

Mercifully, Queenie had not been made to endure the pain of this particular ordeal, for when the woman Bedford had torn away the tape from her mouth, Queenie's pleading had brought out the worst in her. The answers she gave to Queenie's fraught and fearful questions were a series of spiteful blows to the head and face and which rendered Queenie deeply unconscious.

Now with old Blodwin's song filling the room and waking Bedford from the frenzy of her deed, she let the knife slip from her grasp and in a moment she was on her knees, head in her hands and bitterly weeping away that terrible loathing which had swollen and festered in her these past empty years.

After a while she got to her feet and stood resting her eyes on Queenie's seemingly lifeless form. For long moments she made not a movement. Then, her crying spent, she picked up Queenie's crumpled coat and she threw it with some contempt across Queenie's nakedness. When the sudden thrust of material against her broken skin caused Queenie to stir and moan Bedford smiled, saying sneeringly, 'So! I'll not be 'ad fer murder after all!'

She turned out the light and made her way downstairs, where Blodwin Torrid was sleeping happily and Raith was on his third helping of liquid courage. He turned now, silent and serious as he received further commands, 'Leave 'er be for the night. Then get yer mam ter clean 'er up as best she can! Then get 'er over to Garrett's Place. There's allus room fer another slag there. An' I know you'll soon deal with 'er if she tries to jump the net!' Now, she was smiling as she told him, ''Ave yer own way with 'er first . . . if you've a mind. After that, I never want to 'ear of 'er agin! Suffice to know she'll be put to good purpose . . . an mekkin' 'erself useful, lining worthy folks' pockets! An' you keep yer mouth shut o' my part in this! My business is me own, an' not fer others to prey on . . . understand?' Then, as he nodded, 'Yes, I'm sure yer do!

Well think on! When she's ready, put 'er to workin' . . . an' watch 'er like a 'awk!' Having made clear her instructions, she took herself speedily from the house and got into the back of the car parked outside with Raith Torrid hurrying behind, to drive her back to Preston New Road.

It was nigh on two months later when Queenie got from the narrow bed where Blodwin Torrid and her son had carried her; both horrified at the sight of her, and both of the opinion that she was nearing her last.

With old Blodwin tending to the wounds inflicted on her body, Queenie's physical scars slowly began to fade. But the pounding to her head and the deep shock in her mind was not something which could so easily be erased. As old Blodwin told her son on one of his fleeting visits, 'It's an evil harlot that did this! The lass's lost 'er memory – but if ye ask me, it's only thanks be to Jaysus she's not lost 'er mind!'

Chapter Thirteen

At ten-fifteen on a bitingly crisp Monday morning in January 1968, Rick Marsden eased his car into the one remaining parking-place outside Blackburn central police station. Losing no time, he got from the car and strode through the main doors, then after introducing himself to the receptionist and confirming his appointment with Detective Inspector Culworth, he made his way through the familiar corridors which he had frequented more times than he cared to remember over the past months, since his full recovery.

After presenting himself to the secretary, Rick was asked to wait a moment.

After a while of pacing to and fro, during which time he became more and more agitated, Rick sat on one of the four chairs surrounding an oblong occasional table and picked up the morning's newspaper; promptly throwing it down again on seeing yet more coverage concerning the American space programme.

Rick had things on his mind which were of far more importance to him than a race to the moon between the two great powers. In his desperate concern for Queenie, he would rather have seen the national press crying out for her whereabouts.

Recently his temperament had not been improved by dogged efforts on the part of his father to push him and Rachel Winters up the aisle. Last night however Rick had left them all in no doubt as to his feelings on *that* particular score. Now that Rachel had been left in no doubt that a wedding was the very last thing on his mind, he had a sneaking suspicion that she would very quickly disappear from the scene. He certainly hoped so, for any affection he might have held towards her had been irrevocably eroded by his father's interfering and by Rachel's own childish impatience and self-gratification.

Rick made himself relax into the chair, maybe he *had* been a bit too outspoken last night . . . but these days he had little patience with anything, and so much had seemed to go hopelessly wrong. Because of saving that child, which in itself he had never regretted for a single moment, fate had cheated him yet again out of finding Queenie. Then there had been Queenie's curious disappearance and old Katy Forest convinced beyond doubt that something untoward had happened. She had worked herself up into such a poorly state about it that things were being kept from her for the present.

These months since Queenie's abduction – for he himself was convinced that there could be no other explanation – he had stayed one step ahead of the police. He had questioned all in authority who might listen and who in his opinion were kicking their heels. He had questioned the two women at Kingsway guest-house. He had interrogated the neighbours regarding the car which had taken Queenie away on that dark night; he had conveyed to them what useless amount

of description Nancy had given him concerning the
man. And not one person was able to add anything
with regard to either.

Then, from what little information Katy could give
him, he had gone to the governor at Rirkham open
prison. Here, he had asked to see Sheila Bannion,
going to great lengths to explain the utmost importance
of his enquiries into the disappearance of Queenie
Bedford.

At the mention of Queenie's name the governor had
appeared to grow restless, and Rick, not knowing how
Queenie's quest for old Hannah's son had become a
thorn in the governor's side, took it that the governor
was a man of mean mood, and unfortunately the two
of them got off on the wrong foot. The only information Rick could elicit was a brief and sharp warning
that the prisoner, Bannion, had been despatched to a
closed prison of greater security, following a series of
upsets and attempts at escape. On the last occasion
there had been a violent and unprovoked attack on a
warden, who as a result was admitted to hospital.

Unfortunately for Rick's purpose, the governor
omitted to reveal that since the Saturday when Queenie
was due to visit and did not, Sheila Bannion had grown
increasingly irritable. Then, when she had written to
Queenie, asking whether she was ill, and the letter had
been sent back with 'not here' written on it, there was
no holding her. Convinced that Queenie would never
leave in such an underhand way, Sheila had concluded
that it all had to do with her search for old Hannah's
son. And she said as much to everyone who stood still
long enough to listen, forcing them to pay attention if
they seemed reluctant. In doing so, she lost all of her

privileges: letter-writing, visitors and leisure activities. When none of this succeeded in calming her down, she had found herself delivered in shame to the governor's office, where she poured out all her suspicions in a torrent, bringing up the business of old Hannah, and throwing out the name of that legal gent, Mr Snowdon. 'There's more to this than meets the bloody eye!' she had commented knowingly.

So Sheila Bannion was now restrained in a closed prison, under punishment, forbidden *any* visitors and facing fresh charges which were sure to lengthen her sentence.

All of this had been a source of great frustration to Rick who would have liked to talk to her. And now this very morning he had received a telephone call from the station, which had so enraged him that he had insisted on an immediate appointment to see the man in charge of Queenie's case.

Hardly able to contain himself at being kept waiting, Rick paced to and fro until finally he came to stand by the window which overlooked the car-park to the front of the building.

The snow had been falling all night and was still emptying from the bright laden sky with a vengeance, beginning now to heap layer upon layer.

'Like life itself,' he mused, a fresh layer of living covering up the one before . . . burying it beneath. Oh, but that wasn't true of *life*! How *could* it be, when his craving for Queenie ran through every layer like a thread of steel becoming stronger all the while? He knew that nothing had changed. By the very coincidence of their birth, he and Queenie could never be man and wife. How could he put that devastating fact to one side, when it haunted his every waking moment? But so help him, even that bitter knowledge was not enough for him to shut Queenie from his life. Because, somewhere deep down inside, beyond mere conscious knowledge and in spite of all the odds, there was a sensation, a voice, driving him towards his Queenie, his life and his future – a future which could only exist if Queenie was a part of it.

Now, she was gone. Like Katy, he could only believe that it was *not* of her own free will, for there were unsettling things which led him to believe that Queenie had gone from Kingsway that night with every intention of returning. First and foremost, the treasured picture of her Auntie Biddy was left standing on the dresser in Queenie's private quarters. Nothing and no one would have induced her to leave that picture behind. Then there was Sheila Bannion. She had leaned on Queenie for a crutch, and he was certain that Queenie would not willingly have deserted her unfortunate friend. And what of the fact that there had been no note left for Katy, and Queenie loving that dear old soul like she was her own.

All these things and more had convinced Rick that Queenie must be traced at all cost. This much he had related tirelessly again and again to the Detective Inspector. The purpose of his being here this morning was to impress upon that man yet again that here was no ordinary case of a young woman taking herself off.

Unfortunately the Detective Inspector was not of the same opinion, and neither apparently were his seniors. Shifting uncomfortably in his seat behind the safety of his desk, he grabbed at his tie to loosen the knot. His whole face suddenly less pink because of it, he leaned back in his chair to say, 'I'm sorry, Mr Marsden, but we've followed every single lead possible, and *nothing*! We've seen it all before, you know, the self-same pattern. A woman borne down by all manner of responsibilities and worries . . . she takes it for so long, then one day in a fit, she decides to leave it all behind and some of them are never heard from again. Believe me, it's not so unusual. And *this* young woman had taken on a great deal of other folks' responsibilities, don't you think?' As he looked at Rick, there was an almost pitiful look on his large-boned and homely face, but his voice lacked conviction.

From his place at the other side of the desk Rick regarded this man, this figure of authority, this stranger who knew nothing at all of Queenie, of her warm generous heart, her determination and her admirable qualities. If he had, his perception of the situation might be tinged with a greater degree of urgency.

Rick thought the man appeared capable enough; not a man to easily fall into complacency, and truth be told he *had* followed up what slim leads had existed.

Now, Rick was only half listening while the Detective Inspector went on at great lengths to explain how there was nothing else for them to do now but to deduce that Queenie Bedford had absconded voluntarily for her own good reasons. After all, he pointed out, hadn't she done the self-same thing once before?

Up till now Rick had not been paying full attention, because some curious and irksome thought was nagging at him, causing his mind to tick over at a furious rate. There was something, some small but vital thing he must have overlooked! There *had* to be, else why had everything come to a full stop?

Of a sudden he was on his feet and demanding of the man before him, 'Are you telling me that you're giving up? Dropping all investigations? Is *that* what you're taking so bloody long to tell me? Damn you – is it?' At this the Detective Inspector got to his feet and leaned across the desk, his large ungainly hands spread at just the right degree to prop his leaning weight comfortably, and on his tired face an expression that told Rick he was ready to fend off any argument.

'I'm sorry, Mr Marsden. I do know how worrying these things can be . . . but we've spent a deal of manpower on this one, and it all comes down to a simple case of gone missing under her own free will!'

'You're wrong, *wrong* I tell you! Look at the facts, man . . .'

'We have looked at the facts . . . all of them. And our enquiries have turned up nothing that's sinister, and nothing that warrants further time, effort *or* manpower on our part. She had a gentleman caller, she put on her coat and told one of her helpers that it was likely she would not be back that night . . .'

'She *also* said she'd been *fetched* to go to a sick friend, who did not exist . . .'

'Ah! We don't know that! And nine times out of ten, if they're discovered making an exit, these runaways will give out *any* excuse.' An expression of sympathy crossed the large homely face, belying the slight irritation in his voice as he told Rick, 'Look, she'll turn up; a lot of 'em do, y'know. There's nothing you can do . . . and *we've* done all we could.'

'No, you haven't!' *Now* Rick knew what had been bothering him all along. That small vital link he'd missed. It *had* to be Sheila! All other sources had dried up, offering nothing at all that could help. But Sheila Bannion was the one person he had not been able to get to. If anything had been preying on Queenie's mind, Rick was sure that she would have confided in her old and best friend. According to Nancy, Queenie had gone visiting that very day.

Now his mind was fixed fast on the idea that Sheila must surely know something that could throw some light on the situation, he would stay with it, come what may. He had questioned the Detective Inspector before concerning Sheila Bannion, because she had been an obvious lead to follow.

But now, his determination renewed, he launched into a series of new questions, more demanding, more probing, convinced that he hadn't been told all. 'Detective Inspector Culworth, you say you questioned Sheila Bannion, and that she was unable to help in any way?'

'That's right. She knew nothing – in fact we couldn't make head nor tail of *any*thing she said.'

'What did she say? Tell me, exactly, in her words.'

'Look, Mr Marsden, you're clutching at straws. That woman is not far short of being a maniac; even more reason for me to suppose your young woman was driven to running off. Sheila Bannion is extremely aggressive, violent! And totally incapable of holding a normal conversation. She has a fixation against *anyone* in authority . . .'

'Please! Just tell me what she said, word for word.'
Rick didn't doubt that Sheila had no love of authority . . . she never had. But violent? And incapable of holding a conversation? That didn't sound like the Sheila he remembered. What had happened, he wondered, to make her like that? He suspected she

was tough enough to take prison life. Could it have been something Queenie might have confided?

Now, the Detective Inspector was speaking again, and Rick was all attentive. 'Well, as you know, Queenie Bedford and the prisoner were old friends who grew up together and when Sheila Bannion was put inside, your young woman came to run Kingsway as a guest-house . . .'

'Yes, yes, I *know* all that! What I want to know *now* is, what sort of questions did you put to Sheila Bannion, and what manner of answers did you get?'

At this the Detective Inspector made a curious noise, something between a laugh and a snort. 'Questions and answers! Oh, it didn't work out like that, not at all! I began by explaining her friend's "disappearance" and asking whether Queenie Bedford had said anything at all that might help us in our enquiries. And all hell was let loose! She actually *went* for one of my officers! Screaming abuse and telling us we were "all in it" and that we'd "all pay"! And as for what she thought of the governor at Rirkham open prison! . . . well, I won't repeat it.'

'And that's all? *Think*, man! Was there anything else . . . a name . . . anything?' Rick had no intention of leaving it there.

'No, nothing, I'm afraid. She was led out, still screaming and shouting. Oh! She babbled out some garbled intention of finding a certain "legal gent" . . . Poor bugger! I expect she feels she's entitled to some sort of legal representation when she's brought before the bench.'

'Legal gent? That's all? You're absolutely certain?' Rick waited, and it did appear as though the other man was searching his thoughts. Then, when the reply came back, that he was certain there had been nothing more, Rick played another hand. 'Get *me* to see her! She'll talk to me, I know she will.'

Now the look of patience was wiped from the face of the Detective Inspector. Straightening himself up, he walked straight past Rick and stood by the door with his fist wrapped about the doorknob as he said in a tight voice, 'I can't do that, Mr Marsden, not even if you were a relative! Sheila Bannion is in solitary confinement inside a high-security prison, put there, I might add, by her *own* actions. You'd be surprised at the lengthy and complicated procedure this department had to undergo, just to get me access to question her, and I've already outlined the disastrous result of *that* useless little episode!' He swung open the door and nodded towards Rick. 'Now, if you'll excuse me, Mr Marsden. As I say, I've told you all I know and I'm afraid that as far as we're concerned, the matter has been closed!'

It was painfully obvious to Rick that he could gain nothing more by pursuing the matter here. So, without another word, he swept out of the room and out of the building.

In no time at all he was seated in his car, where he stayed immobile for some long moments, thoughtfully bumping his clenched hand against the steering wheel and carefully sifting through every word which the Detective Inspector had uttered with regard to Sheila Bannion.

Two particular things did stand out in his recollections. These were the apparent vehemence with which Sheila had accused the police officers of being involved in some sort of conspiracy, stressing her special loathing for the governor at Rirkham open prison. This Rick *could* sympathize with, for he too had found this man obnoxious in manner and decidedly unhelpful.

Then, there had been Sheila's avowed intention to seek out a certain 'legal gent'. That in itself seemed an odd sort of thing for her to be dwelling on. Even more curious that she should be engaged in thoughts of defending herself when in the very same moment she was throwing such fits and rages that would guarantee her further punishment.

The more Rick mulled over these facts the more curious they seemed to him. Such was his growing excitement that he spoke out loud to himself. 'Katy! She's the one to talk this little lot over with!' Without further reflection, he started the engine into life and headed straight away for Cherry Tree and the vicarage.

The journey from Blackburn to the outskirts of Cherry Tree was not a difficult one, and in normal circumstances Rick would have covered the few miles in a matter of fifteen minutes.

As it was, it took him that length of time just to leave behind the streets of Blackburn, choked as they were with the heavy fall of snow and the 'dozers working flat out to clear a two-way passage for motorists and traders. It was Rick's misfortune to get hemmed in behind the 'dozer going his way.

Once out on a cleared open route towards Cherry Tree however, he had every reason to be thankful for such great cumbersome machines. Within ten minutes he had left behind the town centre, come along the main road which ran parallel with vast open fields, whose boundary hedges and low undergrowth had been swallowed up by the furious deposit of snow, and now he was turning into the drive which would take him up to the vicarage. Here he was obliged to slow his speed down to a crawl, for by the look of it his was the first vehicle up there that morning and his car was increasingly pulling in opposite directions as he steered it by instinct along the track.

Drawing up by the front entrance Rick was relieved to see that the snow had stopped falling. As he crossed to the front door he followed a snow-free path, smiling to himself at the image of Father Riley out there first thing to shovel a clearway about the house, and not even allowed the privilege and comfort of giving it a good cursing.

Lifting his hand up to pull the bell-chain, his smile broadened on hearing Katy's unmistakable tones. 'Now Father Riley! I'm a long way from meeting me maker just yet. Look, I'm as full o' fettle as I've *ever* been!' With great majesty, her indignation sailed out through the window which, in spite of the bitter weather, was partway opened. This was not in the least surprising to Rick, who knew only too well of Katy's fiendish fondness for fresh air.

On the way here Rick had felt somewhat apprehensive at his intention to discuss this last business with Katy. After all, Father Riley had suggested that because of Katy's poorly state of health it might be wiser not to purposely offer information concerning Queenie.

Rick, too, had been concerned with Katy's health. But now, by the sounds of it, she was in a fighting mood and back to her old self. Indeed, in a moment, Katy herself appeared, threw her arms about him and practically dragged him through the door. 'Well I never!' she kept saying, as she all but frog-marched him across the hall where the delicious aroma of bacon and onion dumpling assailed Rick's nostrils, reminding him that he had not eaten for nigh on two days. Yet he had no inclinations towards food. His energies must presently be employed elsewhere.

Katy had drawn Rick into the library where Father Riley stood with his back to a blazing fire and his familiar worn pipe clenched in his teeth. 'Well I never, Rick Marsden!' Katy repeated. 'You'd best be bringing me news o' yon lass else I'll want to know the reason why!' She pointed to a leather armchair by the fire. 'Sit yersel' down an' tell us what's on yer mind!'

Rick eased himself into the chair, taking pleasure in the warmth emanating from the great coal-fire which intensified as Father Riley stepped away to seat himself on the settee beside Katy.

At this point Rick looked into Father Riley's face, searching for some sign that it was not against his wishes for Katy to hear news regarding Queenie. But if *his* glance was surreptitious, Katy's was quicker.

''Ere! Don't you two gurt men go treating me like no infant! If you've summat to say, say it at once!' she ordered.

'It's no use, Rick!' laughed Father Riley. 'I don't know which is the worst of two evils – having Katy in her sick-bed where I can bully *her* or having her well, where she can bully *me*!' His brown eyes twinkling, he took the pipe from his mouth and relaxed his hand against the arm of the chair. Then his face grew more serious as he asked of Katy, 'Have you forgotten what the doctor told you?'

'Aye, well! Bugger the doctor!' Katy retorted.

Father Riley was so astonished that he sat upright, mouth agape and eyes bursting from his head, 'Katy Forest!' he gasped, in a tone more of shock than condemnation. Rick found it necessary to look away, for fear that he wouldn't be able to keep a straight face.

'Ooh! Lord forgive me,' Katy quickly added, hurriedly making the sign of the cross upon herself. Then just as quickly, and with her chin set firmly into her neck the way she was wont to do when being cantankerous, she sullenly declared, 'But bugger 'im all the same!'

In his best diplomatic attitude Father Riley took the course of leaving well alone, and instead asked Rick, 'Has anything new turned up with regard to Queenie?'

At once Rick revealed the futility of his visit to the police station that very morning. He went on to tell them how the case had been closed and how it was now registered as a matter of Queenie 'gone missing of her own free will'. All of this was greeted with some amazement and a good measure of anger by both Katy and Father Riley.

'What's your father's opinion of it all?' Father Riley asked, only too well aware of how strained the relationship was between Mr Marsden and his son. He didn't like to see such a thing and hoped that matters might have improved of late.

Rick's answer, however, promptly shattered any illusions Father Riley might have on *that* score. 'I haven't discussed it with him to any great extent. He and I have little in common these days, I'm afraid!'

As to the business of Sheila Bannion and the particular conclusions he had reached, Rick was delighted to find that he was not the only one to perceive the whole matter as very curious to say the least.

The three of them talked round it for a while, throwing up first one idea to be chewed over, then another. *None* of them made any real headway until of a sudden, Katy jumped to her feet. 'Look 'ere!' she cried, at once greatly agitated and full of impatience. 'To my mind, there's only one thing to do!' Gathering up her voluminous skirt she picked her way over Father Riley's large outstretched feet, then hurried to the door. 'Move yersel' then, Rick Marsden!' she called out behind her. 'Father Riley can't be coming wi' us, 'cause there's confession services in fifteen minutes. An' it's allus busy on a Monday after a weekend o' boozing an' fighting.'

'Katy! Calm yourself. Where is it you want to be running off to? You're not making sense at all, woman! And it's not for you to pass judgement on my parishioners, Katy Forest!'

'Away wi' you! On a Monday morning, week in week out wi'out fail, there's a stream o' folk waiting their turn in that confessional box . . . an' nary a one wi'out a painful 'angover or a colourful prize to sport from a weekend o' tipping the ol' bottle!'

Father Riley's condemnation of her had caused Katy to stop and turn at the door. Now, with a shake of her head, she concluded her retort, 'An' well you know it, Father Riley!'

That said, and Father Riley left without an answer, she returned her attention to Rick. 'Come on then, let's be 'aving yer!' she called out, before disappearing away into the hall.

Father Riley had long grown used to old Katy's eccentricity and forthright manner, so he made no attempt to move, choosing instead to spend the few minutes before confessional warming his shins against the fire and sucking comfort from his pipe.

Rick, however, was on his feet and already going after Katy, explaining to the bemused priest, 'Whatever Katy's got in mind, it has to be worth following up!'

And what Katy had in mind was much akin to a particular idea which had occupied Rick's thoughts intermittently all the way over here. So, in no time at all, the two of them were in the car heading towards Blackpool.

There was little traffic on the road and Rick was thankful for that. He was thankful, too, that Katy had enough presence of mind to have secured old Maud's address for future reference.

'Keep to the Promenade,' Katy was presently instructing, 'we'll find the turning some short way past the Tower, I'll tell yer when!'

Rick had no great love for Blackpool in the heart of winter. Today, with the pier closed, the broad promenade empty and little sign of life anywhere, it seemed too much as though everything and everybody had gone into hibernation, as it were suspended between the illuminations in autumn when a colourful extravaganza attracted droves of worshippers, and that long period throughout spring and summer when the whole place came alive and holidaymakers arrived by every mode of transport available, spilling out in their thousands to enjoy all the fun and entertainment which Blackpool had to offer. After all that noise and laughter, after the squeals and screams of ecstasy which echoed from the great pleasure fair from morning to dusk, when the mingled smells of candy-floss, meat and tatty pies and toffee-apples had all melted away with the funmakers, Blackpool seemed to fall into a restless sleep, impatient to be woken again at the first opportunity.

Today, with heaped-up snow lying against the kerbs where the 'dozers had pushed it, and with the sea in a turbulent angry mood, Rick thought he couldn't remember a time when this place looked quite so bleak. Or perhaps it's my own mood and my impatience to find Queenie which only makes it seem so, he thought.

"Ere we are, Rick!' Katy shouted. 'West Street. Now! Turn now!'

Number 40 and Maud were quickly found, and just as quickly the key to Kingsway was secured.

'Mind you fetch it back, Mrs Forest,' Maud had said, not too eager to let the key out of her safe-keeping. 'I'm responsible for it, you understand . . . *entrusted* with it till Mrs Bannion herself relieves me of it!' She had held the key tight in her fist until hearing Katy's firm reassurance that the key would most certainly be returned within a couple of hours at the outside.

Maud was not one for inviting folk into the privacy of her home, and during the few minutes which Katy had spent on the doorstep of the modest little terraced dwelling she had been subjected to the closest scrutiny by the anxious Maud. In but a moment, though, the anxiety had been swiftly replaced by a cautious smile. Then, after reminding Katy yet again that she was imparting a trust, the key was given over and as the car left the street, carrying Katy and Rick to Kingsway, Maud could be seen watching them right out of sight.

Katy had made the comment that she could easily see why Queenie had taken on such a loyal and conscientious lady.

The strangest of feelings came over Rick as he pushed open the door to Kingsway and stepped inside. It wasn't like the last time he'd been here, the one and only time, when he had talked to Nancy and Maud at great length and to no avail. Then the house was catering for a number of guests and what with the police presence and Nancy's excitable state of mind over Queenie's disappearance, the atmosphere had been one of chaos and confusion.

Today there were no people apart from himself and Katy. In the silent, almost brooding house, Queenie seemed a living presence. She was alive in the carpets, in the furniture, in the walls and in the very air he was breathing; she was vibrant in his mind and in his heart. Then, when he felt Katy's hand on his arm and heard her breathless murmur, 'Lord bless us!', Rick knew that she too had sensed Queenie's presence, and it seemed almost to be trying to touch them, to be asking for help.

The whole emotional experience had shaken Rick to the roots of his being, raising up in him three great tides of emotion: his deep abiding love for Queenie, his instinctive fear for her safety, and the urgency of his errand. 'Come on, Katy!' he cried, at once striding forward into the inner hall, 'there has to be *something* . . . some inconspicuous thing that's been missed, and that can give us a clue. We must find it! Even if we have to search inch by inch!'

For the next hour and a half, search inch by inch

was exactly what they did! There wasn't a room, a cupboard or a drawer left untouched. Katy and Rick were meticulous in their search. They scanned ledgers, shopping lists, guests' registers and any paper or book they found; but nothing gave up any indication as to what might have happened or where Queenie might have hurried off to on that particular night.

In a forlorn mood, Rick had come to stand with his back to the window in the kitchen and his weight leaning heavily against the polished worktop. He felt utterly dejected, his thoughts racing ahead to question the next move. What now? he asked himself, satisfied that here in this house there was nothing more to do, nothing to be found that could help in any way. He looked across to where Katy had slumped into one of the stand-chairs by the small table. Seeing that she was exhausted and close to tears, he went to her, put his arm about her shoulders, and said quietly and with more conviction than he felt. 'We'll find her, Katy. I promise you that.'

All the while he was talking Rick's mind had continued to question, to search. And of a sudden, his thoughts were pulled up by something which had crossed his mind not two minutes earlier. He and Katy had been well-organized and methodical in their search, but there was *no one* better organized or more methodical than Queenie herself. That had been proved over and over again, in the neat and meticulous keeping of every ledger and every register he and Katy had come across this day. What was more, the manner and upkeep of the large appointments book kept by Queenie in a drawer in the hallway dresser would put any first-class secretary to shame.

Now he was stooping to look into Katy's face, his two hands on her shoulders and his eyes reflecting the excitement in his voice as he cried, 'Katy! Think! Did Queenie keep a smaller appointment book, or a diary?'

At once Katy was upright, enthused by Rick's eagerness, and after a moment's thought she was on her feet. 'Yes . . . she *did* keep a little pocket-book of sorts . . .'twas a blue colour! She kept my phone-number in it, an' Sheila's prison visiting times . . . things o' the like! Oh, Rick, Rick, d'yer think she took it wi' 'er that night?'

'No, Katy! Judging by what Nancy told me, Queenie was in too much of a hurry that particular night to stop for anything!' Rick was already on his way out of the kitchen and making hurriedly for Queenie's private quarters. Katy was hard on his heels and calling out, 'It *can't* be in there! We've looked into *every*thing!'

'Then we'll look *again*! It has to be there, Katy!'

In Queenie's bright little bedroom, Katy was again given the delicate task of going through every item in every drawer while Rick examined the wardrobe top, the window-sill, the shoe-boxes and even lifted the carpet all round to search underneath; each time when he felt sure there must be a small blue-coloured pocket-book, there was nothing vaguely resembling it.

Now, all else exhausted, he and Katy were both going through the items in the wardrobe. They had searched the wardrobe before, but this time, Rick took out every single garment and laid it across the bed, where for the first time he and Katy shook the garments one by one before delving in every pocket.

All but two of the items had been replaced into the wardrobe and Rick was letting his hands linger lovingly over Queenie's green cord two-piece, when Katy's voice rose shrill and jubilant across the room. 'Lord love us! I've found it, Rick. In her dressing-gown. 'Tis Queenie's pocket-book!' She raised a small blue book into the air, and with her free hand grabbed a hanky from her pocket. In the swift movement it took for Rick to reach her, Katy had thrown herself into a nearby chair and with her head buried into the hanky she was crying tears of relief. When Rick gently collected the book from her shaking hand, she told him, 'Find summat to 'elp us in there, won't yer?'

The beautifully-written entries in the pocket-book were more or less as Katy had described: her own phone-number, the prison postal address and the times when Queenie visited; together with entries of moderate payments made on a regular basis to a Mr Bartholomew. There was also a most curious entry, dated the very day before Queenie had gone missing, and the same day that she had been to see Sheila at the prison. It read: 'Seeing the solicitor tomorrow – first on the list. I hope to hear something favourable for old Hannah.'

Katy explained that the 'Mr Bartholomew' mentioned in Queenie's pocket-book was the old parishioner who kept up the resting-places in the churchyard of George Kenney, Auntie Biddy, and Queenie's child. Such information was given by Katy with a measure of pain. It was received by Rick with the same degree of sadness, but at the mention of George Kenney there came into his heart a dreadful rage, not only because of the way this man had cheated Queenie and himself of happiness, but because of the bestial and inhumane crime he had committed against his own daughter; the tragic consequences of which was lying beside him in that churchyard. Yet there was a measure of peace in the churchyard and their ordeal was over. But what of Queenie, what of *her* peace? What of the anguish which she must carry in her heart for all of her life! Rick had been brought up a Christian, but he could find no compassion or forgiveness in him for the devil who had fathered Queenie and him and in doing so had destroyed all their hopes. Yet, by acknowledging the circumstances of his birth, an admission which filled him with bitterness and loathing as it shattered his dreams so ferociously, Rick had finally burned up these punishing emotions and now was filled with a stern determination. This determination at this very moment was shaping the one purpose in his life. The purpose was Queenie. Day or night, there was no other.

As he looked at Katy now, Rick's dark eyes were narrowed in concentration. 'Hannah,' he repeated, 'who is Hannah? Do *you* know, Katy?'

By now, Katy was newly composed, her eyes still bright from tears and the hankie carefully thrust back in her coat-pocket. She had to disappoint Rick, for she could throw no light on the situation at all. 'Y'know, I do 'ave a feeling that I've 'eard Queenie mention that name . . . but fer the life of me, I can't think on it more.'

'All right Katy. Don't fret yourself. There must be other ways of finding out. And what about this "solicitor" being the "first on the list"? Odd that . . . most odd!' Rick resisted the impulse to question Katy further, only too well aware of her recent illness and of her present exhaustion. He speculated silently to himself. Was the solicitor written in Queenie's pocket-book anything to do with the 'legal gent' mentioned by the prison governor to the police, and sought by Sheila Bannion? Were these two men of legal profession one and the same? Rick felt sure they were because with Queenie and Sheila seeing each other on a regular basis, talking of matters known only to themselves, it couldn't be pure coincidence that Sheila had intentions of locating a 'legal gent' and Queenie had made an appointment with one. It was the logical conclusion to assume that the two were indeed linked. Rick could only deduce that the link was the 'old Hannah' mentioned by Queenie in her pocket-book. And who *was* this Hannah? Was she a friend of Sheila Bannion's or a friend of Queenie's? Surely, if she had been a friend of Queenie's, Katy would certainly recollect? Oh, it was all very perplexing!

'Rick, are we any nearer?' Katy was standing before Rick now, her hands on her hips and her overall stance suggesting that she, like Rick, thought that at last they were onto something.

'Yes, Katy! We *are* a little nearer I feel. But there's a way to go yet.' He got to his feet and began to pace slowly back and forth across the bedroom, an exercise he always found useful when gathering his thoughts. 'You remember what I told you, about how Sheila Bannion was taken away screaming something about finding a certain "legal gent"?' He paused to look hard at Katy, and when she nodded, he came to stand before her, waving Queenie's pocket-book and continuing, 'Well, that "legal gent" and Queenie's solicitor – they've *got* to be one and the same!'

'O' course! Aye, o' course they 'ave!' Unable to control her joy, Katy was hopping from one foot to the other, as she was prone to do on such occasions. 'An' this ol' Hannah, she must be an acquaintance o' Sheila's or 'appen somebody as knew o' Maisie Thorogood, eh? Maud should know. We'll mek tracks to West Street an' ask Maud!' In an instant, Katy was out of the room and off down the hall.

Rick was not of the same opinion as Katy in her belief that Maud could enlighten them with regard to this Hannah person, for he felt certain that had she known, it would have come up on the last occasion of his talking to her. Lord knows he had dug deep enough to turn over even the *slightest* snippet of information! Something else was nagging at his senses also. That was the business of a list – 'first on the list', Queenie had written. First? On *what* kind of list? Could there be a list of business people? Relatives? He probed and probed at the question until his head began to spin.

Realizing that he would need to turn all these things over in greater detail and in a quieter mood, Rick followed Katy out of the house, and after locking the front door he climbed into the car beside Katy and headed back to West Street and Maud, Katy encouraged by their findings and excitedly chattering all the way.

But it was as Rick suspected. Maud was not able to identify Hannah. 'Naw, Mrs Bedford never mentioned such a person! Not to me, nor to Nancy, else I would have learned of it from her. I'm sorry . . .'fraid I can't do you no good at all!'

Rick and Katy thanked her kindly and departed, Rick not too surprised and Katy's face down in her boots.

'Aw, come on, Katy!' he told her, with a great deal

more cheer than he was feeling, 'we're that near to finding her, you must be able to feel it in your bones, eh?'

This brought a wide open smile to Katy's face, as she replied 'D'yer know Rick! Come to think on it, yer right! Yes! I do believe 'appen yer right!'

Rick returned the smile and told her she was not to worry. Afterwards the both of them lapsed into silence, Katy saying a little prayer to herself and Rick yet again sifting the facts through in his mind. But the more he dwelt on certain things, the more like a broken-up jigsaw it all seemed. The thought occurred to him that fate alone must hold the master cards in the game of life; fate, which played with people's emotions like they were so many numbers on a dice, to be flung first one way then another. Fate! Which seemed to take sadistic pleasure in throwing obstacles down time upon time. From the very first, it was as though his life and Queenie's were inter-locked, yet cruelly kept just that far apart for them to be taunted almost beyond endurance. There had grown in him a deep and painful bitterness because of it. Before he first clapped eyes on Queenie there had been little meaning or direction in his life. Then when he had come to know and love her, there was room in his heart for nothing else and over the years only his love for Queenie had stayed warm and alive. His heart, though, had hardened. So too had his determination to defy the tide of destiny and to follow that inexplicable belief that somehow, somewhere, happiness was waiting for him and his Queenie. But for now, there were puzzles to be solved and more questions to be asked if he was to find her.

Rick conceded that in the final event, it just might

require a far more analytical mind than he himself possessed; an investigative mind, or a *legal* one. Thinking on these lines brought Rick to recollect his father's long-standing business colleague and legal adviser; a man with whom the shrewd and discerning Mr Marsden had kept confidence for a great number of years. It followed that the man must be unusually capable in his field.

Should Rick himself be unable to get to the bottom of who this Hannah was, and why Queenie had become so concerned for her that she had arranged to see a solicitor on the woman's behalf, Rick thought he might do worse than to make use of his father's legal representative.

For the moment though, in view of the possibility that Queenie's pocket-book might lead to the identity of Hannah, and consequently the discovery of what *did* happen on the night Queenie left the house, Rick had two more immediate calls to make. One to Detective Inspector Culworth . . . the other to the prison governor!

Chapter Fourteen

'For God's sake, man! We've given her too much. I've warned you time and time again, you can't fool about with *this* drug!'

Ron Garrett was the front man at Garrett's Place, the man who took care of Raith Torrid's pleasure palace and bore the consequences when things went amiss. He was a man of many achievements; the highest being considerable recognition in the medical profession, the lowest a surreptitious and dangerous abuse of his position of trust, for which he had been struck from the list of recognized and legal practitioners. He was also a man of startling contradictions. For all his high qualifications and insatiable taste for the very finest of material luxuries, for all his expensively tailored suits and patent shoes, and in spite of his select cigars, Ron Garrett's vast burly figure, colourless rough-featured face and black larded-down hair told a very different tale. He could so easily have been mistaken for an ex-boxer or one of those commendable souls who eked a living in the coal-pits hereabouts. His large square hands were certainly capable of crunching a man's face, or tearing a wedge of coal from the earth in that place beneath God's green valleys where the daylight gave no relief from the thick blackness which was forever night, forbidding and unwelcoming.

Tonight was such a night, oppressive and cloaked by a thick grey layer of fog. Raith Torrid had chosen both the hour and his lowly companion well. It was the first evening of February, in that interlude when the darkest of nights hung suspended between day's end and daybreak. On such an evening, Raith Torrid and Ron Garrett were on an errand of shame.

The streets and alleyways around Mill Hill were quiet and unlit. Decent folks were abed these past hours and the drunks had rolled into their hidey-holes long ago.

This area of Mill Hill had once contained a thriving industry of cotton mills and busy warehouses where every weekday morning the cobbled roads would echo beneath the wheels of carts, the hooves of horses, and the comings and goings of commerce. The air would be rent by early morning hooters screeching out another start to yet another working day. The pavement would come alive with hurrying feet clattering along in clogs and boots, all carrying the chattering laughing mill-hands to their daily grind.

But now, the few rows of tenement houses that had straggled round the great Victorian mills near Peel Street were all but disappeared . . . felled beneath that relentless axe called 'progress'. All those gaunt Victorian monstrosities, which had produced countless millions of tons of best quality cotton for home and the world, made lifelong friends for many, and had provided all with roofs over their heads, clothes on their backs and meals on their tables; they too were silenced. Many were firmly secured against vandalism, some were let out in smaller units for various activities, and there was even talk of preserving one or two as museums and places of curiosity for visiting tourists. Others had been sold to private enterprise for the provision of sport and leisure facilities.

The small mill on Peel Street had been snapped up by Raith Torrid for a ridiculously small sum, and it was here in this converted cotton-mill that he had created a vast money-spinner, pandering to the quirks and needs of men and women alike. This was Garrett's Place, a warren of small useful bedrooms upstairs and a complex of games rooms, gymnasium, night-club and gambling dens downstairs.

Because of the nature of his particular business this night, Raith Torrid had chosen a time early in the week, at an hour when all would be quiet.

All the same, he was anxious that Queenie should be quickly despatched upstairs into the rooms which had been especially prepared for the old Irish and her charge; rooms which he himself had chosen as being pleasant enough to house the two women over the next few weeks. However, he did have certain misgivings concerning his ability to persuade Queenie that she was as much a part of Garrett's Place as were any of the girls who got a living from catering to the sordid desires of all kinds of men who frequented his seedy establishment. Some of his girls were tasty enough for any man. They had the looks and presence, and they knew how to make a man happy. One or two of them might even be described as classy. But Raith Torrid didn't fool himself when comparing the very best of them to Queenie because there was no doubt that weak and unglamorous as she was right now, there was about her a unique and striking quality that he had not previously encountered in any woman. If his own taste had run in that direction, he would have moved heaven and earth to possess her. As it was, his own inclinations were more favourable towards his own sex . . . the younger and more tender, the better. It was the way he was made. And there wasn't a thing he could do about it!

Impatient at the disgruntled mutterings emanating from the other man, Raith Torrid got from the now stationary car and in a low forced whisper which carried more ferocity than a bellowing shout, he said, 'Stow the bloody moaning, Garrett! Knowing your record, I wouldn't a' figured *you* for squeamish! I've told you, turn a blind eye. That's *all* you need to know! As for the girl, she's made o' strong stuff an' it suits me for now to keep 'er mind pliable.'

'But I was led to understand that she's forgotten everything . . . who she is, where she's from, even her own name till you told her. I would have thought you couldn't have her mind more pliable than *that*!'

'That might be true enough if she was a run o' the mill sort, but she's a fighter, a thinker! An' she's nobody's fool. Now enough o' this! Wake the old Irish an' grab a hold o' this one's legs. Sooner we've got 'em upstairs and outa sight, better I'll feel!'

Quickly now, the two men bundled the limp figure of Queenie out of the car and after Raith Torrid fumbled open the front door they took her on up the red-carpeted stairs and into a set of rooms situated away from easy access at the far end of a long straight passage, with a number of plum-coloured doors on either side. Raith Torrid would have preferred to leave off the lights and feel their way down but imagining the almighty fracas the old Irish was likely to stir up if asked to grope her way in the dark, he decided that switching on the lights was the lesser of the two evils. As it was, there were enough complaining noises coming from his old Irish mammy as she brought up the rear.

Some few moments later Blodwin Torrid was lying flat on her bed, out to the world and snoring off the booze, Ron Garrett had spirited himself away to a room further up the corridor, where he was sure to find a warm welcome, and Raith Torrid was gazing down on Queenie's unconscious form, gently laid on top of the narrow bed and covered over by a green candlewick spread.

For a long moment in the half-light from the shaded bulb on the cabinet, he stood very silent and very still, his black devious eyes searching Queenie's face. In his mind's eye, he could see that dark grey and gently smouldering gaze which had so often moved him of late. On an impulse he reached out his hand, and with the lightest of touches he stroked his fingertips into her matted hair. Something like a stir of conscience swept over him as he recalled the way he had stood by while the woman Bedford had reduced this one to within an inch of her life. He felt no real pride either in his own part played these last weeks . . . keeping Queenie subdued by underhand methods, but precautionary and necessary methods nevertheless. It was as he'd told Garrett: she might have lost all track of time and memory, but it suited him that way, for now she had come to rely on him and his old Irish mammy. She had not yet learned to know them or to trust them, but all in time! All in good time! And he would make it his business to see that she came to no harm at Garrett's; so long as she kept his clients happy, there would be no problems. A couple more weeks should do it, then he would make her a first introduction. He had just the man in mind, a respectable sort who had never been known to play rough with any of the girls here. It pleased his vanity to add sophistication and an element of quality to his establishment. And the word was bound to spread, to attract a better class of clientele which in turn would swell his wallet.

In a way, he was beholden to the woman Bedford; though it would take wild horses to drag this admission from him. It had not taken too much puzzling on his behalf to realize that this one had been married to the son of that desperate woman and held grimly responsible for the young man's tragic end. *There* was the reason for such hate, such terrible and venomous loathing as it had been his own lucky lot to escape. Well, that was all water under the bridge now. Queenie Bedford was in his care and under the ever-watchful eye of his old Irish mammy, until such a time as he had persuaded the lovely and exquisite creature that she was made to give pleasure and that she had been thus employed for as long as he had known her.

Raith Torrid crept from the room and away down to the bar, where he helped himself to a hefty measure of brandy. Taking his time over the drinking of it, he made himself comfortable in one of the red leather club-chairs, thoughtfully contemplating the future.

As the brandy warmed him through and imbued him with a deep feeling of contentment, he grew more and more pleased with himself. He hadn't forgotten a certain hue and cry in the weeks following Queenie's disappearance from Lytham St Anne's. It was plain to see why a young woman of Queenie's calibre would be easily missed. But the fuss had died down, and what with Queenie's memory gone and no one else to identify her, the road ahead ran straight and clear. Queenie was a prize he wasn't ever likely to come across again. And she belonged to him! He did not anticipate any difficulties in wooing her into a certain way of life; for there were ways and means of persuading even the wildest and strong-minded of creatures to become like putty in his hands.

Part Three

February 1968

Tomorrow is another day

. . . I dream to see
His voice of silent thought,
His form mirrored in me.
Spenser

Chapter Fifteen

'Jesus, Mary and Joseph! Is me own son trying to finish me off or what?'

Blodwin Torrid was in a highly agitated state, evinced not only in her anguished cry, but in the perpetual rolling of those small pink eyes all but lost in the bulbous rises of her face. After some moments of shaking her grey head from side to side releasing hanks of hair from their hairpins, she looked an almighty pitiful sight.

When the agitation in her became so great that she could not bear even another minute in that chair, she wrestled her ample shapeless form into a standing position, straightened the brown garment which hung about her like a sack and launched into a further volley of abuse against her son as she waddled across the room towards a closed door in the far wall. She made no move to enter, but pressing her ear to the door, she called, 'Are ye awake in there?' There came no answer, so she pushed the door ajar. With her toothless mouth wide open and her eyes screwed up to focus on Queenie's figure prostrate in the bed, she leaned inside the room and called out again, 'Look here, colleen, yer wouldn't be knowing where that bloody son o'mine's stowed me gin-bottle, would ye?'

When again there came no answer, she snapped tight her mouth, shut the door and returned to the rocking chair, where she took to abusing all and sundry; until in an instant she was back on her feet tottering up and down the room. 'Ye varmint . . . ye're a varmint to hide yer ol' Irish mammy's lifesblood. But I'll find it, sure I will . . . I'll find it!' Fetching herself to an abrupt halt, she took up guard in the middle of the room, her ears alert for the opening of the door which might admit her son, Raith, and her little pink eyes raking the room.

On the other side of the door which led into the bedroom, Queenie lay perfectly still and silent for yet a few more moments after the old Irish had withdrawn, closing the door behind her. She dare not move, nor show any sign that she was awake, for fear that the door might suddenly swing open and bring in unwelcome visitors. And there had been many of those – a man with larded-down black hair and great clumsy hands which gripped her arm and injected it with needles until the darkness came on her again was the one who frightened her most. Then there was the other dark-haired man with black eyes and a soothing voice, whom Queenie remembered from somewhere; but like many other disturbing sensations his image came and went in waves of grey and hazy recollections, none of which ever came together in one complete picture.

There were women too. One slight and blonde and smelling of a sickly perfume. And the other vaguely familiar, cumbersome, reeking of gin and forever singing. These women and the two men all sat by her bed at one time and another, none speaking directly to her or answering the unspoken questions in her troubled mind, all of them unknown to her.

In those all too brief and spasmodic moments when she felt herself more alert to the strange surroundings, Queenie searched within herself for an explanation of what was happening, for even in her half-conscious state she sensed a very real danger from the strangers who came in and out like so many guards at her bedside. But try as she might, the answers just would not come. The pictures in her mind teased and tormented until every waking thought became like a torture she was helpless to stop. Fragments of memory yielded weird and hazy shapes, showing a dark night, with the black-eyed man at her door, and she following him; there were other disjointed and unfinished pictures of yet another man, this one of striking build, with fair hair and eyes of love . . . then there was a room filled with people and patrolled by uniformed officers bearing serious faces, forcing Queenie to wonder whether she was in a prison. Was that it? she asked her self time and time again. Was she a criminal, locked away because of some terrible deed she had committed? And were these 'strangers' appointed to watch over her? She didn't know! Dear God, how *could* she know? Whenever her senses began to grow sharper the man with the larded-down hair and big hands came yet again into the room and in a moment had diffused all of her gathering thoughts.

Queenie was mortally afraid. What in God's name had she done to warrant such treatment? Why were her frantic questions ignored and left unanswered? Where was she? How long had she been here and, most important of all, *who* was she?

Queenie was only certain of her determination to discover the truth of it all. Recently, desperation making her artful, Queenie would lie prone when she might have begged for answers, thus betraying the fact of her waking. When spoken to she learned to remain silent, and when that door came open, as it had done just now, she would push herself deeper into the bed, close tight her eyes and make not the slightest move.

As a result, she was rewarded of late by a sharper wit and the formulation of a devious plan which might get her out of this room past the strangers to learn more about her predicament. The more artful she became at playing this game, the more revelations came to her. She had a name now to put to the image of that fair-haired man with eyes that spoke of love. His name was Rick! How many times since learning it had she whispered that name to herself and derived the greatest comfort from it? How often she had drifted into a fitful sleep, only to be startled from it by gyrating figures in her mind and the name of 'Rick' on her lips.

Daring for a moment to lift her head from the pillow, Queenie listened, her large grey eyes wide open and more alert than they had been for many a day. From the outer room there came frantic noises of drawers being yanked open and after a moment, slammed shut again, and now came the voice which Queenie recognized as belonging to the grey-haired Irish woman. Usually that voice would be full of drink and singing. Now, however, the voice was raised high, spitting out the foulest of language as it heaped hell and damnation on 'the varmint who's hidden away me lifesblood!'

To Queenie's ears, the noise outside her door rose to a deafening climax, seemingly not a single soul escaping the wrath of the old Irish.

Of a sudden, the door burst open and falling in with it came the misshapen form of Queenie's gaoler, a torrent of abuse issuing from her toothless mouth as she made straight for the bed and Queenie.

'Ye little sod! Sure yer playing the jinks wi' a poor ol' woman so ye are! Fer shame on ye!'

In a minute the old Irish was at the bedside. In another minute she would have had Queenie by the throat as she yelled, 'I fetched an' carried fer ye, so I did! Fetched an' carried an' nursed ye fro' the brink! An' what's me reward, I'm askin'? What's me reward, eh? Fer ye to tek me bloody drink, that's what!'

Above the fury of the old Irish, Queenie's protests went unheard. When another voice projected itself above the din, that too went unheard until all at once the old Irish was wrenched away from the bed and swung away to face one of Garrett's more successful pleasure-girls. She excelled at her job, and was passionately fond of it. She prided herself on her appearance and on the ability to keep herself ready for any man, at any time of the day or night.

At this particular moment, however, neither the girl's appearance nor her readiness for pleasure was evident. With features unattractively distorted, she yelled at the old Irish.

'You silly ol' cow, you! I've a gentleman friend next door an' what with all this racket 'e's likely to take to 'is 'eels an' never come back!' Throwing a cursory glance towards Queenie, she grasped the old Irish by the shoulders and roughly propelled her towards the outer room, at the same time demanding,

'How in the name o' commonsense d'you fancy *she's*

pinched yer bloody booze? Y'know well enough who's confiscated it, an' y'know well enough *why*! Now get away out of 'ere – an' fer Christ's sake, be quiet! It's lucky it were only *me* as 'eard yer carryings-on, an' not Garrett! Y'know what a pig *that* one can be.'

'Yer *all* pigs, sure ye are!' returned the swift and cutting retort as the old Irish viciously punched the air with one clenched fist, and with the other fought to release herself from the girl's hold. ''S right! – *all* pigs, an' all as wicked as the black divil isself!'

During the few moments it took for the girl to man-handle the old Irish out of the door and into the other room, Queenie took quiet measure of her. She was of slim attractive build, with tawny hair piled up on the top of her head. Her thin features were of clean sharp line with large and perfectly-rounded eyes, more unnerving than attractive. Protruding from her small painted mouth was a long tortoise-shell cigarette holder which appeared curiously stuck to her lip as it bobbed up and down with her every word, now and then emitting a small puff of dark grey smoke. Her bright red dress was painfully short, with a plunging neckline which revealed a nicely-rounded chest.

It had occurred to Queenie that here might be an ally. But when a moment later the girl came back into the room Queenie thought better of seeking her help. For what she said to Queenie was, 'Can't 'ave the old bugger finding 'er drink can we, eh? What! Garrett an' Torrid would tear 'er throat out if she was to let you escape! I wouldn't like to see 'er given a leathering, 'cause when all's said an' done, she ain't a bad ol' trout!' For the briefest instant, her voice softened as she continued to talk through the small even teeth that still gripped the cigarette holder. 'Oh, you poor little cow, you! Don't know what's 'appening do you, eh? Well, let me tell you there's worse places than *this*. An' until you come round to their way o' thinking, you'll be kept confined in this room, an' subdued by that divilish-'andsome Garrett for as long as it takes!' Now, her voice had resumed its grating hardness. But when she suddenly peered deep into Queenie's half-closed eyes, it was as though she felt a degree of compassion for this girl not many years older than herself, for stroking her fingers over Queenie's mangled hair, she murmured, 'The trouble wi' you, my gal – you've too much spunk, else they'd never 'a done this! Of all the girls they've brought 'ere afore you, there's not been one as took so long to know where they're better off. There's a deal o' brass to be earned 'ere y'know!' She waited, as though that particular snippet of information might warrant Queenie's attention. But when there was no response she snatched away her hand from Queenie's hair, and stepping back a pace, her voice hard, she added, 'There's only one girl as comes to mind afore you, who proved to be a bit of a problem – an' that were April! A pretty little thing at one time, but she put up such an argument that they'd no choice but to increase 'er "medicine". Our April's a junkie now. Silly little trollop! If she'd only known what's good for 'er, she'd a' done all right.'

A shrug of impatience lifted her narrow shoulders, and only now did she remove the cigarette-holder, as with a disgruntled glance at Queenie she remarked with a certain callousness, 'You're a fool! You can only hold out so long – then you'll either go the way of our April, or you'll be glad to do what you should 'ave done in the first place! Either way you'll end up as one o' Garrett's girls!'

This said, she gave a small snort, then ceremoniously replacing the cigarette-holder between her teeth, she turned and left; throwing a few cautionary words at the old Irish on her way out.

Queenie gave a sigh of relief at the girl's departure. Having heard what lay in store, her instincts were even stronger to get away from there.

She sorely regretted the fact that someone had seen fit to hide the old Irish's gin-bottle, for the finding of it would surely make her own escape that much easier.

Lifting her head, she strained to hear what the old Irish might be up to. It was quickly obvious that the need for her booze overrode the fear of a 'leathering' for the furtive noises and muttered abuse were again beginning to swell into pandemonium.

Of a sudden, the noises outside Queenie's room ceased. For a while the silence seemed to Queenie almost as unnerving as was the screeching. But then, in a moment, the air filled with laughter and singing, and Queenie deduced that the old Irish had found her elusive treasured comfort.

Queenie decided that if she was to make a move, it must be now. *Now*, before the man returned to put her to sleep and before the next stranger appeared to sit by her bed, watching, watching and waiting.

But if Queenie's intention was strong, her body was pitifully weak, as she discovered when gingerly raising herself out of the blankets to sit on the edge of the bed with her feet touching the floor.

The floor was covered with linoleum and it was cold. *She* was cold, trembling in fact. Even as she sat there, resolute and determined, her head felt like a stone weight on her shoulders and the room was spinning about her as though she was adrift on board ship in a vast ocean tossing about like so much driftwood.

The floor was coming up to meet her and the furniture had taken to the air. That tall brown wardrobe in the corner, her narrow bed and the similar one beside it, the paintings on the wall, both showing the same Victorian lady in different poses, the kidney-shaped dressing table, its matching stool and the rocking chair against the wall . . . all were airborne and merging one into the other, until Queenie's reeling senses took flight with them, rendering her helpless as a new-born babe.

Undaunted, Queenie spread her arms out behind her and stretched the palms of her hands across the bedspread till she felt her sense of balance gradually restore itself. 'Easy, girl!' she told herself. 'Slowly does it.'

Gasping at the air, she drew in a number of deep reviving breaths. Then slowly, very slowly, she inched towards the brass bed-head, and using it for leverage, she pulled herself up to a standing position. When the dizziness threatened to come on her again, she gripped the brass railings and closed her eyes for a moment. Mustering every last ounce of strength in her tired body, she let go the rail and with the greatest of care and trepidation shuffled her way to the dressing-table, each dragging footstep like a mile uphill. When, with a muttering of thanks she had reached her goal, Queenie dropped onto the stool and looked into the mirror before her, forcing herself to focus. At first she could see nothing through the pain in her eyes, but then she stared harder into the mirror. And what stared back at her was the face of a stranger. It was a face with some strength of character, showing a perfectly-shaped straight nose and high sculptured cheekbones, and looking back at her from within that kind oval face were large grey eyes with dark sweeping lashes, the depth of which for a moment startled her. It was a pleasing, beautiful face, a face to be proud of, a face of honesty; yet Queenie could take no pleasure in it, feeling as she did outside of it, a stranger looking at a stranger.

Only the eyes reflected those disturbing emotions deep within her. They were filled with a haunting, intangible kind of pain.

In stark contrast to these features the brown matted hair was ugly, unkempt and ragged; the sight of it caused Queenie to fetch a hand up to her mouth, stemming the cry of horror which broke from her. Beneath the hairline on the left temple an area of scarred tissue was visible, still angry and misshapen.

Queenie had no recollections of the Bedford woman's vicious attack on her. She knew nothing of how, in a frenzy, that creature had taken a knife to her hair, chopping and hacking to within an inch of the skull; in places yanking the hair out by its roots and scoring the scalp in torn, bloody trenches. So no amount of imagination on Queenie's part now could explain her awful appearance.

Because of the strange inexplicable circumstances of her being contained in this room, and now because of what she had seen in that mirror, all of which pointed to something evil and terrifying, Queenie's already aroused fears deepened. Every instinct in her racked body urged that she must never relax her guard, not for a single moment.

Just then, from the outer room, came the banging of a door, and the sound of men's voices, raised in anger. 'Damn and bugger it, Torrid! The old hag's sozzled – drunk out of her senses!'

'I'll thank you to remember that's my old woman you're talking on! Leave 'er to *me*! You get an' take care o' that one in there!'

Queenie was terror-struck. If they came in now, that would be the end.

'Oh, God!' she muttered, dragging herself from the stool and on tottering legs struggling her way across the room. 'Keep them out a while longer.'

How Queenie got from the dressing-table and into the bed, she would never know. But when the two men entered her room she was down beneath the covers feigning sleep, only her face visible and every inch of her body aching with cold, yet oozing warm sticky sweat.

The first voice to speak Queenie recognized as being that of the man called Torrid. 'Christ Almighty! You an' your bloody drugs! I reckon you've done for 'er, man! Three days she's been good for nowt, an' look at 'er now, wringing wi' sweat! Look 'ere Garrett, you'd best think on summat an' bloody quick! I don't want 'er dead, man. I want 'er alive an' earning!'

'And so you shall! So you shall, my friend. Up to now, I've withheld the *stronger* drug – we don't want another April on our hands, do we, eh? But then again, if you want this one receptive to the clients you've lined up for her, she'll need to be given just the right amount to dull her memory.' Here, he cast a quizzical frown at his companion. 'You know, the memory's a funny thing. It plays tricks. One minute it can be gone, an' the next it can be triggered by just a word, a scene,

a face! This beauty will need to be kept just this side
of that thin line, don't you see?' He suddenly smiled,
and cocking his head to one side, he said, 'She'll be all
right, I promise you. I might be guilty of certain . . .
irregularities but I've never lost a patient yet. Now
then, you go about your business with an easy mind,
an' leave *me* to do what I know best, eh?'

'I'm trusting you, Garrett! You'd best 'ave this one
ready for work in a few days – ready *and* willing!'

Not moving a muscle, Queenie followed the retreat-
ing footsteps, after which came the slamming of a door
and a furious exchange of words between the old Irish
and the man declared to be her son. Then came the
slamming of another door and a spate of singing, followed by a loud torrent of abuse, during which the old
Irish threatened that if she wasn't straightway given
back her bottle, she'd be off out in search of a friendly
drink, an' to hell wi' that one in there!

Queenie was in no doubt as to who 'that one in
there' was. In the greatest discomfort and waiting only
to seize her chance, she prayed for the man at her bed
to go and leave her be, as he had done on so many
other occasions. But this time it was not to be so.

For a long moment, the man, Garrett, continued to
stare down on Queenie, his features a study of conniving. He cared not that her face was turned away from
him, for this creature had the kind of eyes that could
strip a man's soul. And what was there at this moment
was not for anyone's eyes.

With the deftness born of practice, he began to
undress; hampered only by the obvious physical rise of
his great excitement. In a matter of seconds he was
stripped naked, his appetite for Queenie's body enor-

mously evident, his whole being trembling and his eyes narrowed and darkened by the passion raging through him till all that could be seen of them were slim opaque slits beneath the rim of his dark brows.

Aware that Garrett was still in the room, Queenie did not know what were his intentions, nor did she suspect the meaning of the quiet rustling and muffled sounds that disturbed the solitude of the room.

Wary as she now was, Queenie was totally unprepared for what happened next. She felt the bedcovers being gently lifted from her body, the ensuing draught making her shiver and forcing her to control herself in order not to move or to cry out. Now she felt a disturbing presence, warm breath on her neck and face, and the dry nauseating stench of stale cigar-smoke. Close to her ear a voice murmuring, 'You shouldn't be shared, pretty one. A body like yours should be kept for one man only . . . it would be a great pity for it to be mauled and spoilt.' The mouth closed on her ear in a gentle sucking movement, before wiping itself down her neck and against the bareness of her shoulder.

Of a sudden he was in the bed beside her, his nakedness stiff against her groin and his groping fingers sliding now across her arm, in a moment caressing her breast and toying with her nipple until she felt sure she must scream aloud and turn to rip out his eyes with her nails. God! She would not, could not allow this to happen, whatever the consequences! As the mouth sloped dangerously close to her own, and the trembling hand felt its way across her thigh and inwards, there came into Queenie's heart such searing revulsion that in but a moment she would have betrayed the fact that she was not as unconscious as he might think.

Queenie thought afterwards that God must have heard her prayers, for at that very instant when she would have been lost, when she must either throw herself or Garrett from the bed, the door opened. At once, the air was alive with the sound of the old Irish.

'So! Ye filthy wretch! What sort o' creature are ye to be interferin' wi' a helpless woman? Out! Out I tell ye! An' ye can be sure my boy'll hear o' this, so 'e will!'

In an instant, Queenie felt the weight of the man lifted from her, the bedclothes thrown over her body, and in another instant she heard the two intruders leaving her room, one swollen with indignation and issuing all manner of threats, the other, having hastily thrown on his clothes protesting that it wasn't at all what it seemed. And didn't she know that Torrid would skin him alive if she told? To which back came the considered opinion that, 'If ye can't take the consequences, well then ye shouldn't take the risk now, should you, eh?' Then quickly, the advantage of the situation must have dawned on the old Irish, because without further ado she stopped in her tracks and was heard by Queenie to remark that she had 'a tongue as knows how to be still – for a drop o' the ol' nectar!' At which point, there was a deal of giggling and the two of them hurried on out of the room.

After a while Queenie's ears were assailed by the familiar tones offering up an exquisite version of the song 'Danny Boy'. Smiling to herself, she said, 'Go on, my old darling, sing! Then when you've done with your singing and you've a need to sleep it all off, *that's* when I'll take my chance!'

But for now, drained by the effects of three days

without food and hindered by a crippling tiredness, she would rest quiet, close her eyes and gather her strength for what she had to do.

With her tired eyes growing heavy in her head and the silky tones of the old Irish washing over her, Queenie felt herself in grave danger of drifting into a deep sleep. With the stark realization she jerked open her eyes, drew herself up on one elbow, and vigorously shook her head from side to side as though to eject the weariness from it. Then she got to her feet, drew the blue towelling dressing-gown from the chair and after struggling into it, tied tight the belt and went on slow tiptoe to the window, where the watery noon-day sun filtered in. From here Queenie could see out across the road to where solid walls, eight feet high, skirted the pavement for as far away as the eye could see. Beyond these, the great sprawling cotton mills, whose chimneys were now silent, stood like magnificent sentries left to guard a deserted treasure. There was no sign of life out there, and none in the street below; although Queenie could see a number of cars parked directly in front of the place which to her had become a prison.

The singing had stopped now and as quickly as she could force herself, Queenie searched through the dressing-table drawers and looked inside the wardrobe. She had hoped to find outdoor clothes that might perhaps belong to her, garments which could make her less conspicuous than she would appear wandering about in dressing-gown and bare feet. But the drawers and wardrobe were totally empty, save for a pile of old newspapers in the bottom of the wardrobe and an empty spectacle case in one of the drawers. Gritting her teeth and prepared now to *fight* her way out if she had to, Queenie stood still for a moment, leaning against the wardrobe and sucking in long deep breaths of air, until she felt slightly stronger. Then she made her cautious way towards the door, her ears sharp, her heart thumping as if it might jump right out of her chest, and her throat so dry it was agony to swallow. Suddenly, hearing a scraping sound from the other side of the door, she stopped and listened, praying that no one would come bursting into the room and hoping that what she would find out there was only the old Irish, alone and out to the world.

Satisfied now that the noise she had heard was of no significance, Queenie proceeded to the door with the utmost caution. She wrapped her hand round the door-knob and laid her ear to the crack where the door met the jamb; all the while afraid to breathe, lest even the trembling softness of her breath should be perceived from beyond. But there came no sound, save for a low rumbling noise which Queenie took to be the snores of the old Irish.

By now Queenie was shaking uncontrollably, her legs had been reduced to jelly and rivulets of sweat were trickling down her back and face. She had to wipe away the sticky film from her hands on her dressing-gown before securing the doorknob in a firm grip. Now, as she turned it to feel the door released and starting to open towards her, Queenie prayed like she had never prayed before. 'Let it be all right . . . Please God, help me,' murmured over and over again.

When the door was wide enough ajar for Queenie to peep out, she ventured a step forward, apprehensively casting her eyes about the room. It was quite large, long and narrow, furnished with old black wooden furniture including a low squat sideboard and small rolltop desk. Among the chairs were two high-backed rocking chairs, one of which was occupied by the old Irish. Her full and shapeless form spilled out over the arms; with the exception of a rhythmic rising of the chest and the accompanying rumbling snores, she appeared lifeless.

From the calendar on the desk and the red rings which had been drawn round each day up to and including the fifth, Queenie took the date to be Thursday 6 February 1968. The pendulum clock hanging on the wall gave the hour as eleven forty-five am. With the acquisition of such information, Queenie felt more comfortable inside herself. She had a reference point and, of a sudden, a feeling of belonging.

Giving up silent thanks that the old Irish was indeed the only person in that room, Queenie lost no time in edging her way into the room. Crossing more quickly towards the far door, she discovered it led to a broad corridor with six heavily-panelled doors situated down both sides spaced evenly some four feet apart. Here the thing that struck Queenie the most was the gloomy darkness of this wide spacious corridor, surprising in view of the fact that it was nigh on the brightest hour of day. On looking closer, Queenie saw that there were no windows, not a single one, and the only scraping of day entered through a wide skylight up in the roof.

Queenie could see no stairway leading out of there and for a frantic moment panic began to set in. Then, in her most firm and chastising voice, she murmured, 'Calm yourself, girl! There has to be a stairway. It must be behind one of these doors!' Without further ado she moved forward, her ears alive to the various noises filtering from the rooms beyond; sounds of laughter, of people coughing and talking . . . and just now of low moaning as from someone in the deepest throes of the most horrific pain, or the most exquisite pleasure.

She had not the slightest idea what place this was, nor did she want to know. It was enough for her to feel captive here, in an environment which her every instinct told her was alien. A quick glance confirmed Queenie's suspicions that the stairway must be located behind one of the doors, for there was no opening anywhere, not even a fire-escape of sorts. There was nothing for it but to try one of the doors. Supposing she opened the wrong one? Oh Lord! Which one? Of a sudden, it came to her that the most logical thing would be for the stairway to run down from the *end* of the corridor. Then doubts trickled into her mind. Surely it would run from the centre, where the rooms fell away on either side, wouldn't it?

Fearfully aware that time was ticking away and that she could be discovered at any minute, Queenie decided to listen at each door, eliminating those where she heard sounds of occupation. Swiftly she did so, amazed and enlightened by what she heard, and by the time she had discounted three doors on either side Queenie was left in no doubt as to the activities going on in those rooms and the purpose of this building. The discovery intensified her determination to flee from that place.

There were just three doors left, one on the right and two on the left. Deducing that it had to be one of the end ones, Queenie opted for the one on the right which to her way of reckoning was on the same side as the room she had come from so must lead to the front of the building and the main entrance. With the greatest trepidation, Queenie inched open the door, her fears soaring to relief as she saw before her a wide winding stairway leading down to the floor below.

Quickly now, with her heart racing, she put forward one bare foot, her mind already ahead in the streets below, racing away to freedom and she knew not what.

When the voice boomed out Queenie recognized it at once. 'For Christ's sake! What the hell are you at?' Raith Torrid emerged from the room behind her, and now, with his shirt tails flapping and his face registering a range of expressions from surprise to shock, then black anger, he hurtled after Queenie who by now had taken flight down the stairway.

If determination and a nature of defiance had been enough to carry Queenie away from the man who bore down on her at every second, he would have found his quarry elusive and unattainable. As it was, ironically because of her own plan to fool these strangers who held her, Queenie had gone days without food; the debilitating effect of drug injections were still with her, and not yet fully recovered from the violent attack by the Bedford woman, she was at her lowest strength.

When two-thirds of the way down the stairs, Raith Torrid pounced on her, Queenie was close to collapse. And when, breathless and outraged, he dragged her back up the stairs and into the room from which he had come, Queenie's frail body was rent by terrible sobs not of pity or pain, but frustration and anger.

Some short time later she was tied to a chair in that same room where a boy of some twelve years cowered in the bed, his dark eyes large and afraid. Queenie knew now the depths of depravity to which creatures like her captors would sink!

In the room, with her hands and feet cruelly secured, and with her head being yanked back by Garrett, Queenie was forced to watch while Raith Torrid defiled the boy, his sadistic appetite whetted. All the while he made certain low promises to Queenie, including the assurance that her 'turn would come'.

When the boy's pained eyes caught hers, silently pleading and filled with a fear which Queenie could recognize, her heart went out to him and there rose in her a torrent of hatred and rage that she could not control. With super-human strength she bent her head back into the hands that gripped her, then spat fully into Garrett's excited and laughing face, arched her back and using her feet, weight and the element of surprise thrust the chair backwards into his solar-plexus. The impact caused him to let loose his grip and shout out in agony.

Immediately there followed a scuffle during which Queenie found herself lying on the floor, still strapped to the chair with her body twisted into an awkward position, the rage within her finding further outlet in the stream of abuse she poured out.

The last thing she heard was Raith Torrid shouting, 'Get the bitch out of 'ere! An' I don't care 'ow you shut 'er up.'

The last thing she felt was the chair and herself being yanked up, and a moment later the needle sliding into her arm.

For a long while, Queenie knew no more.

Chapter Sixteen

At four the following afternoon, a confrontation of another kind was taking place on the premises of Rirkham open prison.

'You do understand this is highly irregular! And that I'm allowing it only under the strongest of protests!' The prison governor thrust out a defiant chin and with bright angry eyes stared first at Detective Inspector Culworth then, more viciously, at Rick. 'Hannah Jason took a very bad turn not a half-hour since, and is this very moment being prepared for transfer to Blackburn infirmary. She's in too poorly a way for us to cope with her . . . we've no facilities for such events. And I'm insisting that you take full responsibility if you've still a mind to question her!'

'I'm not heartless, man! I do appreciate the poor woman's state of health,' replied the Detective Inspector, inclining his head to where Rick was standing grimfaced, 'as I'm sure does Mr Marsden here. But the fact still remains that there is every possibility that your Mrs Jason might be able to throw some light on the disappearance of Queenie Bedford. As I said the discovery of her pocket-book does lead me to believe after all that hers is a suspicious disappearance. If she had just run away, her pocket-book would most certainly have gone with her. *And* there's the question of a couple of puzzling entries, one, as I've already pointed out, involving Hannah Jason and another referring to an appointment with a gentleman of the "legal profession".' Here, his sharp eyes surveyed the face of the governor who, being somewhat unnerved by this latest development, was secretly commending himself on keeping guilty thoughts from being displayed across his face. 'You know, I can't help feeling you could have saved us all a great deal of time and trouble by pointing us in this unfortunate inmate's direction before now!'

'I'm sure I haven't the slightest notion of what you're trying to get at!' The prison governor dug his finger beneath the collar of his shirt and in an agitated movement, ran it round his reddening throat. To Rick, who all this time had said little, but had not once taken his dark brooding eyes from this man, the action only confirmed his inner dislike and suspicions of him, and his continuing protest served to endorse the feeling. 'I have most certainly given you and your officer *every* possible assistance in this matter! The fact that this Queenie Bedford made the occasional request for a visitor's pass in favour of Mrs Jason . . . well, I just didn't attach any great importance to it. And I'm sure there was none!'

'Hmh! That may be. But for future reference, you would do well to remember that it's for *us* to decide what importance should be attached to certain information. Now, if you please, I think we'd best see the lady in question. Don't concern yourself, she won't be subjected to more than a couple of simple questions.

It'll only take a few moments at the outside.'

At this, the prison governor flicked a hand towards the uniformed warden who was standing upright and alert at the door. 'All right! Take them down to the sick quarters . . . no more than five minutes you understand!'

With the exception of the governor, the men moved forward towards the door. Drawing his gaze from the three departing figures, the prison governor now slumped heavily into his chair, and flinging his arms across the desk, he absent-mindedly shuffled a batch of papers from one side to the other. Christ! he cursed at himself, what had possessed him? First he had been foolish enough to send Queenie Bradford's letter to Snowdon, knowing full well that the man was an eminent and influential representative of the legal profession *and* a very powerful, politically-motivated man. There was little doubt that such a man, if unwittingly dragged into a mess of this sort, could make life very difficult indeed! Particularly if it came to his notice that his discreet payments to ensure the very careful monitoring of the prisoner, Hannah Jason, had *not* secured the privacy which they were meant to purchase.

Considering himself all kinds of a fool, the prison governor would have given almost anything to turn the clock back. In his mind's eye, he could see the good and dedicated work of twenty years going out the window. And for what? A moment of weakness! His greed fuelled by the showing of a bunch of notes . . . payment for erasing a number of details from the records of a certain inmate, and for channelling all progress reports and information concerning that inmate to one person in particular. God Almighty! This was a pretty stinking kettle of fish! True, he *had* destroyed certain background details on the prisoner Jason . . . but in the doing had caught sight of the name of her only blood relative. That name was 'Marsden': the very same as the man now seen to be working hand in glove with the police! Yet the 'Marsden' mentioned in the files was a *woman* and, if he remembered correctly, Hannah Jason's *sister*! So, who was this man? Was the name just a coincidence? But if so, how strange it seemed that even now he was on his way to one particular prisoner out of *hundreds*! And what of Queenie Bedford? Disappeared under suspicious circumstances the police seemed to think, and she a link between this 'Marsden' and Hannah Jason? It was all very worrying, the more so because the whole business appeared to have taken its most suspicious turn following Queenie Bedford's contact with Snowdon . . . and through *him*! Oh, he daren't think on it, because the more he thought, the dirtier and more devious it seemed to get.

The three men had departed the room, Rick last of all, his eyes straying back to look at the face of the man in charge of this prison, a man with a frightening level of power, a worried man, and a man to whom Rick had taken an intense dislike. He was convinced that the prison governor's face had betrayed a measure of guilt, the possible cause of which intrigued him, as it had done on the occasion of their previous meeting.

It took some ten minutes to negotiate the distance from the office to the sick quarters. They went to the end of the corridor, down two flights of broad stone steps hemmed in by a run of off-white wrought-iron panels, then down yet another seemingly endless corridor, flanked on one side by green-painted walls and on the other by a series of equally dismal doors, the corridor closed off at both ends by tall spiked gates of steel. Finally the three men arrived at the thick double doors which led into the sick-ward. A grid of steel barred the way beyond the doors, but at a word from the officer it was promptly opened by the uniformed female guard on the other side.

'If you'll just hang on here a minute, I'll fetch the ward-orderly.' The prison officer who had escorted them this far directed the two men towards a row of armless leather seats situated against the wall to the left of the doors. 'I'll be right back,' he added.

Although Rick had no illusions concerning Her Majesty's prisons there came over him a feeling of despondency that people such as Hannah Jason should be locked away for the whole of their natural life and even when desperately ill were not allowed the dignity of lying in a sick-bed without it being secured between locked bars and guarded day and night by grim-faced officers in black uniforms. It was true that she had committed a heinous crime, that of murdering her own kin, and she with a child left to take the consequences. But what were the circumstances? he wondered. A woman driven to taking her husband's life, when she had a child to consider? If she was any woman at all, with a mother's love, then how she must have suffered for nigh on thirty years, with all of that terrible guilt on her mind.

Of a sudden, Rick pulled himself up short; turning over the possibility that she might be a cold-hearted calculating murderess with no sense of guilt or regret.

Then in the next instant he dismissed such speculation, because had that been so, his Queenie would never have befriended her. No, he was quite prepared to give this poor ill creature the benefit of the doubt . . . just as he knew Queenie must have done.

Looking around him now, Rick's searching gaze travelled from where the guard sat in his little windowed cubicle to the large office directly opposite with its closed door and into which the man who'd accompanied them had disappeared, then down to where there was yet another door, upon which was a sign saying simply 'ward'.

While Rick was looking about the Detective Inspector got to his feet. 'I don't know about you, Marsden, but I can't stand the smell in these places!' It was true. All about them hung a clinging odour of disinfectant, the sickliness of which seemed to match the pale green distemper on the walls.

Before Rick could make any comment, the door opposite was pushed open and through it came a large smiling woman, dressed in a dark uniform which resembled that of a nursing assistant. From the wide black belt around her waist hung a huge bunch of keys, and after requesting that Rick and the Inspector follow her, she selected a key and with it opened the door which led immediately onto the ward.

When they were all inside with the door locked behind them she looked more closely at Rick, who was little more than three feet away from her. Seeming to be taken aback, she drew her breath in with an audible gasp. 'Good Lord!' she exclaimed, for a moment forgetting the discipline she prided herself on, 'you could be *him*! The *image* of him, you are!'

Rick had been both surprised and embarrassed by her observation. But now, he was intrigued. 'Oh? And *who* could I be?'

Having by now fully composed herself, the orderly smiled in that particular way the prisoners had come to know and hate. Going to the front, she moved the party on, with the exception of the warden who had brought the two men down and who now positioned himself by the door to await their return. 'I'm sorry,' she continued, pausing again for a moment and eyeing Rick most severely, 'are you a relative of Hannah Jason's?' On hearing that he was not, she produced that smile again, saying, 'Really? I do apologize!' She walked on, this time with a degree more urgency, at the same time explaining, 'Hannah has no personal possessions, apart from a fading picture taken from a newspaper which reported the . . . crime . . . all those years go. She's treasured the picture ever since. Keeps it folded in her underwear and prays over it every night, poor demented soul! Normally, she won't let anybody touch it but she's so ill, she doesn't really know what's going on. I'm sending it to the infirmary with other information regarding her condition.'

'This picture, what is it of exactly?' Rick experienced an inexplicable sympathy with Hannah Jason, and he felt the need to know.

'Her husband – the man she stabbed to death. It's a reproduced photograph of him and her on their wedding day. You know how the newspapers like that sort of thing! Good for sales figures. Hannah Jason kept it tucked away where the light couldn't get at it. It's still remarkably clear, particularly good of the man. And believe me, after only a moment ago looking at it, the sight of *you* gave me quite a start! The face, the hair . . . even the build! That photograph could be *you*! Ah! here we are.' She had led the two men through a narrow passage, which had opened out to where the ward stretched before them. It was a remarkably small area, with four iron-framed beds on either side beneath barred windows. Half the beds were neatly made up and empty. The others, three on the right hand side and one on the left, were occupied. Down the centre of the ward stood two large tables, each with six upright chairs around them and in the middle a large potted plant.

'We're never very busy. It's not done to encourage prisoners into the sick-bay because we're not equipped for anything above emergencies of the less serious nature. We had hoped to send Hannah Jason back to the cells but her condition suddenly deteriorated early on today. She's in here.' Taking a step to the right, she quietly opened the only door and lowering her voice, she said, 'The ambulance should be on its way. I'm afraid I have to ask you to respect her condition . . . two minutes!'

'Thank you. It's to be regretted that I need to bother her at all,' replied the Inspector in equally reverent voice, 'but I promise we'll do nothing whatsoever to distress her.'

'Indeed you won't! I'll be right behind you' came the retort, upon which the orderly introduced Rick and the Inspector into the room, presently following them in and closing the door behind them.

In all of his life, Rick had never experienced emotion the like of which flowed through him now. And it was clear from the curious way he glanced at Rick, his brow furrowed and his mouth half-open, that the Inspector felt it too.

When Rick and the others had first set foot in the room it was clothed in oppressive gloom, broken only by the thin shaft of light coming in through the half-open curtains, and by the incessant moaning which filled every corner of the room with its eerie sadness. To Rick, it was as though the moaning was alive in its own right and had instantly wrapped itself around him like a desperate embrace until his very mind had seemed to be bathed in its essence. He sensed the agony in that pitiful voice, and he was deeply moved. For if ever there was a soul in torment, it was the soul in this room, in that bed which was a prison!

Quietly now, the orderly tiptoed to the window, and as she pulled back the curtains just a little, the room was brighter; but as Rick examined its every aspect he found it no more cheerful.

The opening of the curtains had revealed a high narrow window, barred and grimy. Directly beneath it there stood a pot handbasin and beside that two wooden shelves all securely fixed to the wall holding an enamel mug, various toiletries and a folded towel. Against the wall opposite was a small brown cupboard upon which stood a deep enamel bowl and large white jug. Some small distance from that stood the bed, narrow and flat without a headboard or foot. The walls were smooth and undressed as was the stone floor.

At this point the two men stepped forward and the orderly stepped sideways to place herself so that she could monitor the proceedings without being too much of a hindrance. 'Remember,' she murmured, 'just a few minutes!'

Rick's gaze had fallen on the tiny figure in the bed, his attention totally engrossed by it. But the Inspector acknowledged the orderly's warning with a curt nod of his head, placing himself at the head of the bed while Rick stood directly opposite. The two men looked at each other and on impulse Rick said in a whisper, 'I'm not so sure this is right . . .'

'She's the only real link we've got, Marsden,' replied the Inspector in equally quiet voice, 'we'll be quick as we can.' Shifting his gaze to where Hannah Jason's pale pinched face lay almost lost in a sea of pillow, he spoke out, 'Mrs Jason . . . Hannah! I'd like a word with you.' There was no response, except for the briefest moment the moaning ceased before starting up again, this time more pitiful and intense.

Disturbed and somewhat ashamed, Rick leaned over the bed, and gripping the Inspector's cuff, he told him, 'Leave her be. She can't help us, man, can't you see that!'

Rick had slightly raised his voice above the awful wailing, which by now was splitting his ears. So, when of a sudden it stopped the occupants of the room were startled and a silence more eerie than the pitiful moaning fell.

Still leaning across the bed, Rick perceived the slightest of movement beneath the clothes and on glancing down, he was surprised and shocked to be looking straight into Hannah's pale eyes, which were open wide and looking startled. Quickly Rick straightened up. As he did so, the eyes followed him, smiling now and sending all manner of emotions through him.

In frustration, he drew his gaze away from that tiny wizened face and he raised his eyes to the Inspector.

'Get on with it!' he pleaded, hating this whole sorry business, but always bearing in mind that it was for Queenie. 'Mrs Jason . . . Hannah . . . we're looking for Queenie Bedford . . .'

Before the Inspector could finish it seemed that something had triggered off a reaction in Hannah's mind, for now she had moved her head slightly towards the Inspector, and in a pained voice was murmuring over and over, 'Queenie . . . Queenie . . .' It was obvious that she knew the name and was becoming distressed.

The Inspector would have continued, but Rick raised a hand in protest. As he brought his fist down Hannah lifted her arm to rest the tips of her fingers on Rick's coat-sleeve. In a moment, she had interlocked her fingers with Rick's and was looking up at him with a direct and questioning expression.

The silence was unbearable. Almost afraid of the inexplicable feelings which deeply disturbed him, Rick was urged to speak. 'Hannah,' he said, his voice warm and tender, 'do you know Queenie? Do you know where we might find her?' He leaned forward, still holding tight those thin delicate fingers which had clasped his. 'Please, Hannah, try and remember. She may be in danger . . .'

Rick could see that his words were falling on deaf ears and he was desperate. He was also acutely aware that Hannah still had her gaze fixed on him. Even as he looked at her face, the expression which had at first been quizzical then confused, had melted into the most wonderful picture of love he had ever seen. Hannah's face held him entranced. It was growing more beautiful and youthful before his eyes, and in spite of the urge to pull away he was held to her by some deeper instinct he could not understand. There had risen in him an overwhelming affection towards this little deprived creature, an affection that was both tormenting and protective.

Hannah was crying now. The tears had misted those huge eyes, somehow making them richer in life and colour. The tears spilled over to run in streams across the withered jowls and onto the pillow, where they spread out in little damp circles. 'Oh son, son!' she cried out, unable to see but the blur of his face as the pent-up emotions of nigh on thirty years spilled out of her. 'You've come to me at last . . .' With her every ounce of strength, Hannah had drawn herself up in an effort to be closer to Rick. And he, seeing her dilemma, could not understand it and was unsure what he should do. It hurt him to see her in distress. He was aware also of the Inspector's face, and of the regret that he too must be experiencing. Then, just as he would have spoken to the Inspector to suggest they leave, the orderly came forward and said softly in Rick's ear, 'It's your uncanny resemblance to the man in the picture. Humour her . . . it will give her something . . . and cost you nothing.' With that, she moved away.

The next few moments were to stay with Rick for the rest of his life. Never for one single moment did he ever come to regret them. He took the woman, Hannah, into the loving strength of his arms, listening to her and whispering words of endearment, while she stroked his face and called him 'son'.

To the onlookers it was the strangest scene and they could not help but be moved by it. To see old Hannah in Rick's comforting arms, he whispering endearments to her for all the world as though he'd known her for years, was indeed a curious thing. Yet how much more curious should they be made to realize that what they were witnessing was indeed the emotional reunion of mother and son! Though Rick himself had no way of knowing this, except perhaps in the darkest depths of his infant memory, old Hannah knew. She knew, and with her dying breath she gave heartfelt thanks that at long last she could go from this cruel world into a safer and gentler place.

But for now, her sorry heart was filled with joy to be in the arms of her child, the son she had robbed all those years ago of a father, of a mother, and of the love she could have given him, but which instead she had been made to store throughout the long empty years of her imprisonment. This love now poured out on him as though to make up for all that lost time.

Hardly able to speak for the sobs which had drained her fast ebbing strength, Hannah drew away from Rick and smiling into his strong kindly face, she asked, 'Will you call me mother? Just once, please . . .'

All the while he had held this tender soul and spoken to her as a son might, Rick had fought to suppress the lump which had risen in his throat, and he had forced himself to be reminded of the other two people in the room. A few moments, he'd told himself, and we'll all be gone, leaving Hannah Jason to find her peace with God. But now he felt himself curiously drawn to this woman. Surprised and confused by the depth of his feelings, Rick wondered whether they were brought about by Hannah's very real and moving joy at the 'fact' that at long last she had found her son, and in his forgiving her, all her prayers had been answered? Then he thought that the emotions he was experiencing might be directly attributed to the deep and inner calling which he once had to serve in God's house as a priest, in which capacity he would have done his best to make Hannah Jason's passing a calm and peaceful one. All of these observations Rick put to himself, yet none of them gave him satisfaction. It was as though in her great distress and extreme joy this poor tormented soul, Hannah, had found in him a great reservoir of feeling so deeply hidden that until now he had not known it existed. It was true. She had awakened something in him, a need, an inexplicable sense of belonging, that was frightening in its enormity. Yet at the same time, he found it exhilarating beyond words. And if only time had been kind he would have done everything in his power to help Hannah Jason leave this place and to assist her in finding a new life.

But it was plain that Hannah Jason's life was fading fast. When she had called on him to say 'mother', he thought it little to ask and even less to give, and when he uttered that precious word it seemed also to give *him* a sense of peace.

'And you forgive me . . . say you do, son,' she was pleading, the brightness of tears sadly unable to disguise the dimming light in her eyes. 'Of course I forgive you . . . don't I love you, mother?' Rick replied in the softest of voices and with the tears he had hitherto suppressed now welling from his sad dark eyes. He felt emotionally drained. He was ready to leave now, for he could take no more. Gently distangling the little woman from his embrace, he let her back softly onto the pillow. As he straightened up, she caught his hand.

'Bless you,' she whispered, the faintest smile lighting her face. Then with that clarity of mind which often comes before darkness she added under her breath, 'And bless Mr Snowdon for finding you.' Then her eyes closed and she was at peace.

At that moment the orderly admitted two uniformed ambulancemen, one of whom crossed to the bed, where after careful examination he folded Hannah's arms beneath the blanket, drew it up to cover her face, and told his colleague, 'No hurry with this one.'

In the few minutes since Hannah's last words, the Inspector had entered into a conversation with the orderly regarding Hannah's reference to this 'Mr Snowdon'. And Rick had been rooted to the spot!

Snowdon! Hannah Jason had mentioned a Mr Snowdon! Rick could think of little else at that moment other than the name of Snowdon and Queenie's pocketbook entry! What was it she'd written?

'Seeing a solicitor tomorrow . . .

. . . hope to hear something favourable for old Hannah . . .'

So *that* was it! Queenie had somehow got herself involved in a search for Hannah's son. And she was going to see a solicitor. Just now, Hannah had said, 'Bless Mr Snowdon for finding you.' Could it be that the Snowdon who for many years had been his father's adviser and *Hannah's* Snowdon, were one and the same?

Going out of the sick-ward, along the corridors, then out of the building and into the fading brightness of late afternoon, Rick nodded his head and occasionally showed polite interest in the Inspector's speculation as to who this 'Snowdon' might be. But Rick's attention was elsewhere, his thoughts occupied by two matters. Part of him was back there in that prison with old Hannah. He had been greatly affected by that dear soul; the sorrow of it all still lingered. His heart felt sore and filled with alien emotion, something, he thought, akin to regret. It was a most uneasy feeling, and one which could only be subdued by the other matter on his mind, which was Queenie.

To this end his thoughts were busy sifting and assessing the information he possessed, both old and new. He began dismissing insignificant items and disregarding many of his previous possibilities; until finally he was left with three disquieting facts. First of all there was no doubt that Queenie, having taken Hannah as much to heart as he had himself, had been pursuing Mr Snowdon on Hannah's behalf in the search for her son; secondly, if this Snowdon *was* his father's legal adviser, then the whole sorry business did seem to be shifting uncomfortably close to home, for there were very few confidences that his father and Mr Snowdon did not closely share. All of this led inevitably to the *third* fact of the deep dislike Rick knew his father had for Queenie.

Outside the prison Rick thanked the Inspector, who assured him of his belief that Snowdon might be a private detective of sorts. This would be investigated at once. Indeed he was this very moment intending to go back inside the building, where he had a mind to speak to the prison governor who he thought had not been anywhere near as forthright as he might.

Rick made no mention of his own thoughts. There would be time enough, when he'd satisfied himself as regards any part his father might have played in all of this. He glanced at his watch. It was a quarter to five. By the time he had driven back to the house, his father would be home. These days his working hours got shorter and shorter; but it was just as well, because the things he had to say to his father were best said in the privacy of his own home. And by God, he had some strong questions to ask, some strong accusations to make. Clever as his father was at squirming out of a mess, there'd be no avoiding the issue *this* time. The more Rick thought about the possibility that his father knew of Snowdon's involvement with Hannah, and subsequently with Queenie, the more he grew convinced that there was a devious and loathsome side to the man. As God was his judge, if Queenie was harmed in *any* way, there would be no mercy shown . . . father or no father!

When Rick stormed into his father's house some fifteen minutes later there was a roaring in his heart which by now could only be placated by some honest and straightforward answers. He was now convinced of his father's part in all of this, because the deeper he had thought about it, the clearer it all became. His father's involvement would explain so many things. On the drive from Rirkham prison, all manner of niggling little incidents had come into focus in his mind, urging his recollections back over these recent years to examine the unusual difficulty he had encountered in his enquiries into Queenie's possible whereabouts; also the apparent incompetence of each and every private investigator he had employed. Then there was his father's active dislike of Queenie, whom he rarely referred to, except as 'that wretched Bedford person'!

Only once had he summoned the neck to say it in Rick's presence, after which a heated exchange had ensued, but Rick suspected that his mother was not excused from bearing witness to such ravings, even though she made no mention of it to him.

His father's vehement disapproval of Queenie had been a piercing thorn in Rick's side, and the only excuse he could find for it was that it surely stemmed from the past, from the love affair between his mother and Queenie's father, George Kenney. But if that really was the root of his father's hatred for Queenie why wasn't he himself subjected to the same hatred? For wasn't *he* the son of George Kenney, the bastard begot by that illicit affair . . . and thus a more painful reminder to Mr Marsden of his wife's betrayal all those years ago? Rick had long puzzled on this particular aspect, and in a way had admired his father's big-hearted capacity to love his wife's son as his own; but now, he was contemplating a far different side to his father's many-faceted nature. And he didn't like it! Take his father's over-zealous pursuit of an early marriage between Rachel Winters and himself. Questions of 'love' or 'happiness' did not come into it. The marriage of Winters to Marsden was a business proposition to his father, a huge commercial enterprise which would merge two of the most successful cotton empires in Lancashire. Well, as far as he was concerned, there was no danger of it. And there never had been.

When a time back Katy had asked him in a fearful voice whether 'summat bad' had happened to Queenie, Rick had been swift to offer reassurance that Queenie would come to no harm. Now, it was he who desperately needed that reassurance, for he sensed that there was indeed some mischief beneath all this business. When it came to being devious and cunning, the Mr Marsdens and Mr Snowdons of this world were a far superior race to innocent gentle folk like his Queenie. Rick had seen his father's cunning under the clever disguise of business acumen, and there was no doubting the lengths to which he would go in order to achieve his own ends. But if he had worked his mischief on Queenie then Rick swore that his father would be witness to a side of *him* that he'd not see before.

As he strode into the hall and made his way towards the drawing-room, Rick recalled his mother saying last evening that she would be on charity business most of today, and not to expect her until at least nine pm. He was glad of that, for he would not want her to be present when he put certain questions to his father.

When Mr Marsden heard Rick approaching, he took up position with his back to the fireplace, a cigar in his mouth and his hands behind him, shielding the lower half of his back from the heat of the roaring fire in the grate. He had on his flabby features the semblance of a smile. But on seeing Rick's stormy expression, the smile slid from his face and snatching the cigar out of his mouth he asked sharply, 'What is it, son? You look fit to fight the world!'

To this Rick gave no answer but quickened his pace until he was standing almost toe to toe with his father, his eyes, like his countenance, dark and threatening. 'I want straight answers!' he demanded. 'I want to know what putrid game you and Snowdon have been playing at! And I want to know where Queenie is.'

'Have you gone bloody mad or what!' Mr Marsden gave a half-laugh, his face stripped of bravado, his voice pathetic and just for the slightest second, his bottom lip trembling. The heat from the fire was intense on the backs of his legs; yet compared to the heat in his son's condemning eyes, it was bearable. He had been caught completely unawares by Rick's outright onslaught, and just for a moment there his cunning had deserted him. Now though he drew himself up, mentally preparing his defence and wondering how the hell Rick had made the connection between him, Snowdon, and Queenie Bedford? No matter! He'd got himself out of stickier situations than this one! You didn't stay on top in business without learning a trick or two. And there couldn't be any *proof* of his involvement here. He'd been far too careful for *that*, he felt sure!

'Look here!' he protested, the growing confidence of his own ability swelling to an expression of indignation, 'I've no idea what you're talking about! And what's more, I'll thank you to guard your words.'

'Oh, you'll thank me to guard my words will you, father?' Rick demanded icily, standing his ground and deriving a certain degree of satisfaction from his father's uncomfortable position, then, staring down into the other man's reddened face, he spoke out again, his voice clipped and hard. 'Well, in as few words as it takes, let me spell it out for you! I suspect that you know where Queenie is and know where she's been these past years. And while I've been doing everything in my power to find her you, and the equally conniving Mr Snowdon, have been blocking my every move! Oh, I don't know *how* exactly! But no doubt I'll find out in due time.'

At this point Mr Marsden opened his mouth to protest. Upon seeing no evidence that Rick's fury had in any way subsided, however, he set his face into a grim expression, closed his mouth and kept his narrow eyes fixed onto Rick's accusing glare, at the same time moving slightly sideways from the fire's heat in an effort to alleviate his extreme discomfort. The easing of his *mental* anxiety however, was not so readily achieved, for with his next words, Rick opened up a gaping snake-pit.

'Your cruel unwarranted meddling may well have gone unnoticed but for one thing! You taught me well, father . . . and when I want something badly enough, my tenacity at least is equal to yours. If you thought for one moment that I'd give up searching for Queenie – however long it took – then you don't know me!' Here, he paused. He moved a pace back, the disgust within him spilling into the glare still unwaveringly fixed on the other man's face. He was about to deliver his ace up the sleeve, and he watched carefully to gauge the reaction it might produce. 'I've just returned from a particular appointment with Inspector Culworth . . . the most revealing yet! I take it you're familiar with Rirkham open prison? You *and* your Mr Snowdon?' If Rick had expected a reaction of sorts, he was not disappointed. Mr Marsden's carefully calculated reserve crumbled. The high colour of his cheeks melted away into small mottled patches of pink before disappearing altogether and leaving him ashen-faced, with wide-open eyes and his every ounce of self-control being called upon to save his legs from buckling beneath him.

'So! It *is* true . . . all of it! Where is she? For God's sake, man, where's Queenie?'

By this time Mr Marsden had come to realize that the game was up, and that nothing in his power would stem the tide of events already overtaking him. As he crossed from the fireplace to the armchair, his shoulders were more stooped and his step weary. But when seated in the chair, and looking up at Rick who towered over him impatient for an answer, the glint of defiance had not gone completely from his eyes as he replied, 'I don't know *where* she is, I tell you . . .'

'Don't give me that! You know all right. And if you won't tell *me*, you can tell the police. You and Snowdon both! Somehow, it's all tied in: you, Snowdon, and Hannah Jason. We heard it from the poor woman's own mouth. Oh, you're involved all right . . . so . . .'

Rick stopped short as his father thrust out his arm and in a moment had grabbed Rick's jacket with a grip like steel. Leaning forward with a curious look on his face, he was asking, 'Hannah Jason? What do *you* know of Hannah Jason?'

At once Rick was aware of deeper issues here. He sensed the fear in his father, and his own curiosity was aroused. 'I know that Hannah Jason is imprisoned for life for the murder of her husband. I also know that she had a son who was taken from her and that Snowdon knew of it! And somehow, Queenie took it upon herself to help search for Hannah's son . . .'

At that moment there came a movement from the doorway. When the two men looked up, it was to see Rita Marsden standing there, her blue eyes shocked, and her two hands flattened over her mouth as though in an effort to stifle the words which now broke free. 'Hannah?' The name came as a whisper, but as she repeated it there was not only strength but an element

262

of disbelief. 'You spoke with *Hannah*?' The question was directed at Rick, but Rita's gaze encompassed both men as she cried, 'But Hannah's *dead* long ago. They told me!' Now, her eyes were riveted on the face of her husband. '*You* told me that Hannah was gone . . . *you* and Mr Snowdon . . .'

As Rick came swiftly to his mother's side, his immediate fury had vanished beneath an avalanche of other emotions, among which were concern for his shocked mother, confusion, and the deep sense of curiosity which had been aroused in him and was now burning to be satisfied. Above all, he had a strange murmuring anxiety in the pit of his stomach, which warned him of things fearful and secretive. Things which had lain dormant and which he in his search for Queenie had roused from their uneasy slumber.

As Rick gently took his mother and led her to the settee, a glance towards the armchair showed Mr Marsden to have slumped into its depths as though hiding from the probing eyes of his wife and son. His face was expressionless, the gaze vacantly falling onto the flames which leaped and crackled up the chimney-back. Rick felt no compassion for him, only bitterness and anger at the deception and trickery employed against him and Queenie, by this man he had once looked up to and loved with the worshipping heart of a son. But no more! Too much had passed between them, too many barriers had been erected. And it wasn't over yet, for Rick would not leave this room until he got what he came for.

His mother looked as though she was on the point of collapse. And this brought on by the mention of Hannah Jason! The whole thing was beyond understanding yet he felt instinctively that in some strange way both he and Queenie were involved, not just because of Queenie's name on Hannah's lips or because of the way in which that desperate little woman had been the thread by which his father, Snowdon and Queenie had all been drawn together.

All these revelations were disquieting on their own, but most disturbing of all was his mother's alarming reaction to the name of Hannah Jason.

Even more surprising was Rita Marsden's plea as she wrapped both her hands around his and drew him down to sit beside her. When she lifted her pale eyes to sweep his face, Rick saw in them such pain and bitterness that for a moment he was shocked.

'Please, Rick . . . you said you'd seen Hannah? Spoken with her . . . Is that true? She really *is* alive?' There was desperation in Rita Marden's voice.

Rick was at a loss. He'd no idea at all that his mother had known Hannah Jason. It occurred to him that the two had been brought together by his mother's charity work, but then he thought not, for if so why would his mother have been deliberately led to believe that Hannah Jason had passed away some time back. Yet *another* example of his father's genius for deception! What, he wondered, was behind it all?

As briefly as he could, bearing in mind that his mother had already suffered the news of Hannah's demise once and was about to learn that today it was indeed the truth, Rick told of how Queenie's pocketbook had inadvertently led them to Rirkham prison and consequently to Hannah Jason. Then, in response to more insistent questioning from his mother, Rick explained how it seemed that on her visits to Sheila

Bannion, Queenie had befriended old Hannah and had thereafter got caught up in efforts to trace Hannah's son, presumed to have been adopted at the time of her imprisonment and whom she had never since set eyes on, much to her great sorrow.

Rick kept nothing back, with just one exception. That was the taking of Hannah into his arms while she became convinced that he *was* the son she so desperately sought. In a curious way that part of the story seemed too private and emotional to be shared with anyone.

Now, with the story told, and the news of Hannah's peaceful passing given as tenderly as he knew how, Rick looked at his mother's face, and what he saw there was something akin to what he himself felt. He could understand how his mother might have come to be fond of old Hannah, for even though his own meeting with her had been all too brief, he also found her to be a very special person. This he related to his mother. And when in return she began to cry softly, he took her by the shoulders, and gently raising her to her feet, he added, 'I'll take you up to your room, mother.' Then, with a cursory glance at his father, 'After which, father and I have certain business to finish!'

Rick expected his mother to go with him, seemingly spent and distressed as she was. But then she surprised him by turning away and crossing determinedly to where Mr Marsden had sat all the while she and Rick had been discussing the matter of Queenie and Hannah Jason. Up to now he had not moved an inch, nor shown any signs of emotion. But on Rita Marsden's approach he got up from the chair, and like a man carrying the weight of the world on his shoulders he went to the fireplace, where he placed a hand on either corner of the mantelpiece. Then, with his body leaning towards the now quietly-burning embers, he gazed downwards into the grate, and in a strangled voice the like of which Rick had not heard before, he murmured, 'I swear I was doing it all for the best. Can you forgive me, Rita?'

Rita Marsden swung herself round and brought her gaze directly to bear on her husband's contrite face. Then, her eyes still glistening with tears and heavy with emotion, she told him in a quiet, accusing voice, 'One day I may be able to forgive you, but I will never, *never* forget what you did. To tell me that Hannah was dead, when she was still alive! Rotting in that prison and believing her own sister didn't even care enough to come and visit her. I can never forget that!'

'What are you saying, mother?' At this point Rick came forward, a look of incredulity on his face. 'Hannah Jason was your *sister*?' His voice was soft yet sharp, indicative of the shock he had just experienced on hearing his mother's words.

Now, visibly shaken at Rick's intervention, Rita Marsden realized the consequences of speaking out in his presence. She was suddenly afraid of losing him, yet in her heart she had long accepted that the time was imminent for Rick to be told the truth of his parentage. That time was here, in this moment, and there could be no postponing it. Rick was a man of strong will and admirable character. Though he might momentarily condemn her and her husband for the lies they had woven around him all these years, Rita Marsden had every hope that his capacity for forgiveness would prove greater than the contempt he must surely feel for them in but a moment. She prayed it would be so, because she loved him as though he had been born of her own body. In spite of the trickery and underhandedness employed by her husband, which she had silently condoned, he too loved Rick as fiercely as any father could love his son.

As Rita Marsden took a step towards Rick, Mr Marsden stood upright and gripped her by the wrist, saying in a quiet voice, 'No, Rita. You mustn't tell him . . . not before you've thought about it.' He had sensed her intention and was afraid. Afraid that he had gone too far, been too sadistic; and in the case of Queenie wicked beyond words. There was no question in his mind now but that Rick would turn from him in disgust if he knew the whole truth. And, dear God, who could blame him? Yet, sorry as he was at the extent of his own interference in Rick's life, Mr Marsden was still adamant that Queenie Bedford would never *never* be allowed under this roof. Not while he was master here . . . and not even after that, if it was in his power to deny it.

When Rita Marsden looked at her husband, felt his restraining hand on her arm and saw the appealing look in his eyes, she was not moved. For she saw in him something else also. She saw the corrosive influence of power and wealth on such as he; she saw how over a matter of years a man could be corrupted as much by love as by hatred. And she saw too that the loathing her husband had entertained towards the innocent and lovely daughter of George Kenney was still alive in him. It was there in his eyes and, she knew, in his heart.

Shaking off his hand, she stepped away from him. When he groaned like a man in great pain, pushing past her and lowering his face as he hurried by Rick and on out of the room, Rita Marsden sensed the coward in him, and after all she was not so surprised.

'Mother, what *is* all this about? You never mentioned Hannah. Why?' Rick would have followed his father from the room. But something in the man's downcast eyes as he departed, and that same fearful expression in his mother's eyes now, held him mesmerized. Of a sudden he too felt afraid, the rising anxiety in him urging him to ask, 'What in God's name *is* going on here? Why was I never told about Hannah? And what did father mean just now when he said you mustn't tell me . . . not before you've thought about it? Thought about what? What?'

Rita Marsden looked up at Rick's handsome face, and through its manly strength she saw the boyish features and remembered with heartrending affection that small lost child who for many weeks had sobbed for the mother from whom he had been wrenched. Never once had he cried for his murdered father; but his heart had nigh broken for the mother who had idolized him.

Rita Marsden had never forgotten the trauma of those first, long, distressing weeks, before her devotion and that of her husband had brought the child out of his pain and into the bosom of a family again. All that was a long time ago, and throughout the years the love that she and Mr Marsden had felt for Rick had grown even stronger.

She knew that their love had always been returned by Rick as a child, a growing boy, and now a man. It was on Rick's love that she was now counting, for what she was going to tell him would sorely test even the most devoted of sons. Strange, she thought, how all of their married life, she had seen her husband as the strong one. Yet in a moment he had gone, hidden himself away, while she was left here to shed the burden of a secret kept for close on thirty years, a *heavy* burden which would now bring its weight to bear on Rick. How she would have given the world to have spared him from it.

But she could not. From the moment Rita Marsden uttered the words 'Hannah was your mother,' *nothing* was spared. As the truth of his background unfolded, Rick found himself lost in a sea of turbulent moods. He struggled to come to terms with so many things. He learned of his father's philandering ways, of the cruel taunting which his gentle mother, Hannah, had suffered at her husband's hands, until the fateful day when she could take no more. When Hannah Jason was arrested, there were those who willed that she should rot in gaol, and there were those who expected the court to show her mercy in the wake of the provocation which had driven a mild and gentle creature to such a terrible thing. But it was not to be.

'The rest you know,' concluded Rita, the strain of her own ordeal showing on her tired and tearful face. 'Will you ever forgive us for not telling you?' she asked, her voice low and trembling. 'Please understand why we kept it from you as long as we could.'

Rick gave no answer, for, lost in thought, he had not heard her question. Getting up from the settee, where the two of them had sat these ten minutes or more, which to Rick had seemed like a lifetime, he went to the window from where he gazed out on a grey overcast evening. He felt as though in great pain, and yet he felt numb. He recalled over and over again all the things his mother had told him. Yes, he still regarded Rita Marsden as his mother, for he could remember no other. And what of Hannah, that tiny, wizened little creature whose child he had been. He thought of her, the loneliness she must have suffered these long years. And the tears flowed unashamedly down his face. He thanked God for the opportunity which had brought them together in her last hours, when she *had* recognized him as her own son, and she had made her peace. For that much Rick was grateful. And he hadn't known! Oh God! How *could* he have known? Mountainous and fierce emotions clawed at him . . . shame, regret, love . . . and a searing need to do the right thing in the light of it all. He must give Hannah a proper resting-place. It was a sad and terrible thing, but it was all he could do now.

Of a sudden it came to him that Rita Marsden was still seated on the settee, her head bowed into her hands and quietly sobbing.

In a moment he was beside her and had gathered her into his arms. No words were spoken between them, nor were any needed. After a while he drew her away from him and cradling her face between his hands, he looked down at her to say softly, 'Thank you for telling me, mother.' At this her eyes filled with a new tide of tears and her face became wreathed in the most wonderful of smiles. In a soft voice she asked, 'Will you go up and talk with . . . your father? Please.'

At once the warmth drained from Rick's face, and in its place came a look of hardened stone. When he spoke his voice was harsh, and to the woman listening, the words he spoke were terrible-sounding.

'Oh yes! I'll talk with him! I'll tell him what I think of the way he led you into believing your sister . . . my mother to be dead. I'll thank him for crippling my efforts to find Queenie and for the way he's always set himself against her. And yes, I *can* understand how he could have slipped into a hatred of George Kenney. But how can I forget how he's constantly battled to keep me and Queenie apart? And I haven't told you, mother, but I believe that he and Snowdon are up to even *more* trickery where Queenie's concerned . . .' Of a sudden, Rick was on his feet, almost blinded by the light which shone forth dazzlingly in his mind!

Wave after wave of shock surged through him, bringing the realization that swept all other thoughts clean away. Of course! Queenie and he were *not* brother and sister! They were *not*! They were *not*! And at any time these past years they had been free to marry! Oh, God, what waste! Years of waste and wanting, when all that time they *could* have been together. He could taste the bitterness of it all and the fury exploded in every corner of his being. Well, they were going to be together now, for he would move heaven and earth if needs be!

Watching Rick as he turned to storm out of the room, Rita Marsden conceded that it would take a long time, if ever, for peace to be restored between her husband and the only son they had known. With some shame she accepted her own passive part in the ostracizing of Queenie from Rick's life. She should have been stronger, more truthful and outspoken. And if the rift between her husband and Rick was so wide it was impossible to breach, then she too must accept a deal of blame.

The sound of raised and furious voices railed now

from behind a closed door upstairs, seeming to Rita Marsden to bounce off every wall and fill every room in the house; one demanding answers to questions regarding Queenie, and the other vehemently denying all knowledge of her present circumstances. It came as a total shock to Rita Marsden when it was revealed that Rick had long believed Queenie to be his sister.

When abruptly the voices were stilled and the door flung open Rita Marsden came into the hall, and from there her attention was drawn to where Rick was speeding down the stairway two steps at a time, his face like thunder and his mouth set so grim it could have been granite.

'Oh, Rick! Rick! Surely to God you don't *believe* the terrible things you accuse him of?'

The pain in Rita Marsden's voice and the distraught manner in which she twisted her hands together caused Rick to take her by the shoulders and to kiss her gently on the forehead. 'I'm afraid I *do* – because I know them to be true! I'm sorry, mother, but he's had every chance and I intend also to enlighten *others* as to Snowdon's part in all of this and to ask that they meet at his place as soon as possible. I'm going there the minute I've spoken to the police!'

'No! Look . . . I'm sure there's no need to do any such thing as call the police . . .'

'Let him call the bloody police!' Rick and Rita Marsden looked up to where Mr Marsden was staring down at them over the bannister, his face stripped white yet stubbornly defiant. 'They'll get the same from Snowdon as you got from me! We neither of us know nothing! Got that have you? Nothing!' And swinging away, he quickly disappeared back into the room from whence he'd come, viciously banging the door behind him.

Rita Marsden watched helplessly as Rick contacted the police. When he left, she returned to the drawing-room to watch him from the window as he drove away. And she wondered whether her husband really *was* capable of all that Rick had accused him of. Intending to confront him, she began making her way towards the hall, only to stop in her tracks when she heard Mr Marsden's voice speaking into the telephone. 'No . . . you stay at the club, Snowdon! If they can't find you they can't question you . . . and think on, man . . . you know nothing at all of Queenie Bedford. Or *any* Bedford come to that! Right! No, don't worry, there's not a thing they can do. Just remember what I've told you!'

There then followed a click as the receiver was replaced. By the time her husband had come into the room where, without acknowledging her presence, he began to pour himself a sizeable measure of whisky, Rita Marsden was no longer unsure. Rick *had* been right! This man whom she could not help but love was indeed capable of surprising cruelty. And if Rick, on whom he doted, had not been able to tap in him the love and compassion she knew was there, then how could she hope to? No, in all of this she was out of her depth.

But there was one thing she could and *would* do. And that was to help Rick and Queenie in their pursuit of happiness. She thought of Rick out there now, desperately looking for the young woman whom he had always loved, even when they were both little more than children, children torn apart by circumstances not of their own making. She thought of George Kenney, of the son she had borne him and later lost. And in her heart she saw how Rick and Queenie's heartache had taken root in the act of adultery committed by herself and George Kenney a lifetime ago. It was true that the sins of the fathers are visited on the children. But now she intended to play a part in putting things right.

Rita Marsden thought of Queenie, and hoped with all her heart that she had come to no harm. Oh, she prayed it was not too late!

Chapter Seventeen

'Blaggarts they are! Blaggarts all of 'em!'

Blodwin Torrid was in a sullen and vindictive mood and pausing only to hear the clock chime out the hour of three am, she continued to rock back and forth in her chair, frantic for a 'sup o' liquor', occasionally murmuring to herself and gingerly touching the bumps and bruises fast erupting on her face and shoulders. She ached from top to toe, but the ache from the physical battering she had received was as nothing compared to the aching desire she had to inflict the same treatment on Garrett and that no good son of hers!

'Ye buggers!' she moaned beneath her breath, the rocking of her chair growing more agitated with her desperate need for the drink she'd been deprived of as a punishment, and her frustration acutely aggravated by as bad a case of revenge as she'd known since the rozzers came to fetch the ol' fella one dark night. 'Rob a poor ol' soul of her lifesblood, would ye? Blame me for that one mekking off . . .' She jerked a thumb towards where Queenie was gagged and trussed in a chair by the bed, her eyes watching the old Irish's every move. 'Be the love o' God!' she went on. 'What sort o' son is it, that would stand by to see his own mammy get a thrashing? Oh, he'll be sorry, sure he will! They *both* will!' Of a sudden she stopped in her rocking, her eyes round and bright as pink marbles and a look of conniving on her face. 'Three o'clock of a morning!' she observed in a loud whisper, at the same time rising from the chair and stealing away to the door. Putting her ear against it, she gave a low throaty chuckle, then turned to Queenie and said, 'Music's finished! They've all gone from downstairs I expect . . . away whorin' and drinkin'! An' me wi'out a wet to me tongue! Ssh!!' She put a finger to her mouth, and rushing back to the chair, whispered to Queenie, 'Close your eyes! *Close 'em* I say!'

Ever since coming round to find herself still trussed up in that chair, Queenie had been watching the antics of the old Irish for some time and for the life of her she didn't know what to make of it. It was apparent that the old Irish, like herself, had taken a leathering; Queenie had gathered as much from her murmurings. And it did seem to follow that in order to escape Raith Torrid's wrath himself, Garrett had shifted all the blame onto Blodwin Torrid for letting the prisoner escape the room. Queenie felt sorry that the old Irish had suffered a beating on her account, but if she saw another chance to get out of here she would unhesitatingly take it.

But for now there were footsteps approaching, and the most sensible thing to do was to follow the old Irish's instructions and close her eyes. This she did. What Garrett saw when he came in from the corridor, through the outer room and into the bedroom, was Queenie seemingly still out of her senses and Blodwin Torrid sitting up, alert and watchful. Pleased, he pursed his lips in an attitude of concentration, nodded his head and before closing the door on his departure, he told the old Irish, 'Pity you can't do your duty well enough, without having to take a thrashin'. See you keep your eyes *open* this time!' Here he gave a leering smile as he added, 'I shan't be too far away. Got some . . . entertaining . . . to do!'

On the instant she heard the outer door close, Queenie saw the old Irish get from her chair. And indicating yet again for Queenie to stay quiet, she went stealthily from the room.

In the few moments she was left alone, Queenie made every effort to writhe free from the straps that secured her, but there was no budging them. There wasn't a square inch of her body that didn't hurt, above all the centre of her shoulder-blades, which felt as though they were being slowly wrenched apart. Sitting up as straight as she could, and taking deep breaths, seemed to help. These slow deep breaths also had the effect of clarifying her thoughts. In her mind, she had pieced together all manner of things. She knew her name was Queenie, and that for some reason not yet clear to her she was confined in this wicked place, a place where Queenie knew instinctively that she could never belong. And what of the man whose image kept emerging above all others . . . what of Rick?

Queenie would have continued to puzzle and to question, but just then the old Irish returned. As she approached her Queenie froze, for in one hand the old Irish was brandishing a bottle of gin from which she greedily took the occasional gulp and in the other hand she wielded a long pointed knife, which she was now waving an inch from Queenie's face and cackling,

'Ye're a bad un, colleen! 'Scapin' like that! You got me a doin' over, so ye did!' As she lunged forward, fetching the knife lower, Queenie set herself, waiting for it to plunge into her heart. When it didn't, and instead the ties which had secured her wrists broke away, Queenie was never more surprised.

'Here ye are, colleen . . .' The dry musty smell from the gin bottle now thrust under her nose caused Queenie to retch. 'Take a sip o' that, me darlin' . . . it'll give strength to yer legs, so it will!' When Queenie hesitated, not certain whether to trust the old Irish, the bottle was put to her lips and tipped up, sending the stringent liquid down her throat. Coughing and spluttering, Queenie pushed the bottle away from her.

'Jesus, Mary and Joseph . . . will ye look at her? After spillin' me bottle when I took the trouble to steal it from the bar!' cried the old Irish, swinging the knife towards the back of the chair in order to slash through the remaining straps.

Astonished, but not stopping to ask questions, Queenie at once began rubbing her wrists and ankles vigorously, encouraging the strangled circulation; at the same time wondering just what game the old Irish was playing. Now there were clothes being thrust at her; a loose green dress and a cardigan. 'There's no shoes, me beauty, but quick! Get the clothes on! When ye're out the front door, go right, then follow the back alleys to the main road. Ye'll see the kirk directly. Batter at the door! Ask for Father O'Donnelly, he's a good man, sure he is!' While she'd been giving out instructions, Blodwin Torrid had taken stock of this woman her son had meant to keep here and to fashion in the ways of the seedy underworld he'd wallowed in since the ol' fella was gone. Ah, but try as he might to introduce this one to whorin' an' fornication he would not succeed. Oh no! In spite o' the cruel loss o' that beautiful hair an' even in the sorry state she was, there was no denyin' this Queenie creature was a cut above the company her son was used to. This one would *never* buckle to his wishes . . . not in a million years.

While quickly dressing, it occurred to Queenie that there'd be hell to pay when it was discovered she was gone. When she said as much to the old Irish, back came a string of abuse concerning two particular men. 'Oh, the buggers'll be sorry, so they will! Leather a poor ol' thing like meself, would they? Well, be jabers! I'll gi' the varmints a reason now, won't I?' With half the bottle of gin emptied inside her the old Irish was ready for singing and giving a toothless smile she executed a small jig. 'Go on! Away with ye now! Afore the buggers poke their faces in here,' she commanded Queenie when she had stopped dancing.

Queenie didn't need telling twice. Pausing only to throw her arms about the old woman's neck in a hug and to say 'Bless you!' she went swiftly to the door, her heart beating like a mad thing and her sore body in an excited tremble.

It was as she had her hand on the doorknob ready to turn it that the door swung open to reveal Raith Torrid standing there. At the sight of Queenie, his eyes popped from his head as he roughly bundled her back inside, crying, 'Mam! You useless old cow, get out here!'

When the old Irish appeared and saw her son grappling with Queenie, she charged at him like a bull-elephant, first fetching the whole of her considerable

weight behind the flat of her hand, which she brought
crashing down about Raith Torrid's ear with a resounding clap. When, with a cry of pain, he let go of Queenie
and grasped his mother's shoulders, the old Irish
fetched her arm back yet again, this time releasing the
full force of it across her son's face, at the same time
shouting at Queenie, 'Away with ye! An' if ye've a
mind, fetch the bloody rozzers!' As Queenie sped out
of the door she could hear the old Irish laying in to
her son and yelling, 'It's a bit o' the leatherin' ye
ordered for me! An' be jabers, ye'll get as good as *I*
got, or me name's not Blodwin Torrid!'

Beneath the relentless battering from his old
mammy's large flailing fists, Raith Torrid was reduced
to protecting himself like a school bully who suddenly
finds the tables turned on him. The old Irish was giving
no quarter – the more he screamed and shouted, the
more she laid into him.

Whether it was the great torrent of gin flung down
her throat by the old Irish, Queenie couldn't be sure.
But of a sudden a desire to giggle bubbled up in her.
'Hell hath no fury like an old Irish deprived of her
drink,' she thought.

With all the hollering spilling out onto the landing,
it was inevitable that a few doors would be flung open.
At one there appeared a warped vision of manhood,
provocatively dressed in a flowing black gown, stiletto
heels, and wearing a flamboyant red wig which exactly
matched his beard. From the room next to him
emerged a man completely naked apart from the chains
thrown about his torso, and carrying a woman over his
arm. By the time Queenie had reached the stairs almost
every door along that landing was ajar. The sights
Queenie glimpsed through them might have stopped

her dead in her tracks were she not still in mortal fear of being dragged back and subdued by that needle which took away her senses.

Now came the cry behind her, 'Jesus! Torrid'll have my bloody hide if I let *you* go!' Glancing back, Queenie recognised the cumbersome figure of Garrett. In the few seconds it took for her to slam the stairs door in his face and to hide herself in the large cupboard beneath the stairs, it crossed her mind to compare Garrett and Raith Torrid to a couple of reptiles: the one handsome and poisonous as a cobra, the other big and slow like a turtle out of water.

From her hiding-place, she heard Garrett first rush down the stairs and out of the front entrance, then come hurrying back and up the stairs, all the while calling for Torrid.

Taking the opportunity, she crept away and was swiftly out of the building and following the directions given to her by the old Irish.

Even in broad daylight, the area would have been strange to Queenie. But in the pitch black it was eerie and forbidding, and around every corner Queenie almost expected to confront the most terrifying of monsters. She recalled the directions given her.

'Go right, then follow the back alleys to the main road. Ye'll see the kirk directly . . .' But the way seemed unusually long and her body screamed in agony. The back alleys were narrow and the cobbles brought blisters to her bare feet, yet she kept on. There was nowhere else for her to go, no other direction for her to take. Queenie knew beyond any doubt that Torrid would have men out searching for her in no time.

After blindly running through long winding ginnels

and litter-strewn narrow back alleys which chewed mercilessly at the soles of her feet and the palms of her hands when time and time again she stumbled, Queenie found herself breaking through an outlet which opened directly on to the broad flagstoned pavement of what looked to be a main road.

As Queenie took a moment to lean back against the wall and recover her breath, her eyes were drawn upwards to where the first break of dawn was creeping into the sky, its faint light streaking and splitting the darkness, bursting it asunder with thin daggers of brilliance. Silhouetted against the shards of light rose the tall graceful spires of the church immediately opposite where Queenie stood. Giving thanks, she hobbled to the kerb-edge, then across the road and in through the heavy arched doors which led straight into the church.

Once inside Queenie paused, her back to the doors and her gaze resting on the altar at the far end of the aisle, where the lit candles cast long trembling shadows high above the wall. There were three long arched windows of stained glass, the widest centre panel depicting Christ on the cross, the windows on either side abounding with bending flowers and spectacular doves with their wings stretched wide as though to encompass the suffering between them. Through all the windows, the dawning light of day had already begun to dissipate the gloomy atmosphere.

As Queenie lowered her eyes, she gave a small gasp at the sight of an unusually plain coffin on a chrome trestle placed directly before the altar. As she moved down the aisle towards it, Queenie recognized the age-old tradition of bringing a departed loved one into the house of God, where through the night it could be cradled in the blessed arms of the Lord, after which its physical remains would be laid to rest and its soul transported into paradise.

Of a sudden Queenie felt like an intruder, painfully lonely and overwhelmed by the tide of events which had brought her here. Wave upon wave of weariness and utter futility washed through her sorely-abused body until the last remaining ounce of strength drained away from her. Falling to her knees, she began to sob loud racking sobs over which she had no control and which rang through the church, shattering the hitherto peaceful tranquillity. 'Please help me,' Queenie pleaded, her stricken eyes lifted upwards to the face of Christ, 'dear God in heaven . . . if I've been wicked, I can't remember and I'm sorry! If in any way I've forsaken you, forgive me . . . but oh, I need your help now! Dear God, help me, please help me . . .' When all remained still, with only the sound of her own voice for comfort, Queenie's sobbing subsided and into her heart stole an uneasy calm. She must find Father O'Donnelly! His house must be adjacent to the church. She would rest a while and gather strength, after which she would seek him out. With great determination and with grit which belied the dragging weariness of her bones, Queenie managed to move herself into a pew. Here she stayed, her knees bent against the cold stone floor, her arms crossed one over the other on the hymn-book shelf. Bending her head forward, she cradled it into her arms as though on a pillow, then with a prayer on her lips she closed her eyes to rest.

Departing Garrett's Place in leaps and bounds, Rick quickly got into his car, leaving behind him a building blazing with lights, crawling with police constables, and alive with the abusive protests of its colourful inhabitants. The loudest and most offensive voice was that of Blodwin Torrid who, rolling with drink and worked up with indignation, was busy informing one and all that her own son was a pimp of the worst order, and that if his daddy was alive, sure wouldn't *he* have gi'n the little blaggart just the very same hidin'?

As Rick sped through the streets, his frantic thoughts ran ahead of him. Blodwin Torrid had been eager to report how she herself had 'set the young colleen free . . . told her to mek a run for it and head to the Kirk of the Sacred Heart!' So, leaving Inspector Culworth and his officers to deal with matters of fornication, prostitution and whatever else might be uncovered Rick was on his way to find Queenie, to take her in his arms and to tell her that after all they were free to marry, had been right from the first. Oh, how the very thought of it ground into him! What was unforgivable was the way his father had known all this time, known and twisted the situation to his own ends. What a low creature to do such a thing, all in the name of fatherly affection. Well, if by doing it he had thought to keep the love of a son, he couldn't have been more misguided, for till the end of his days Rick would never again set foot in that man's house. His mother he could forgive, bearing in mind that she had not long recovered from an illness and that she had little strength of character against such a strong-willed man as her husband; but the *master* of the Marsden household would never be welcome in Rick's sight again. And as for that skunk Snowdon, once pinned down he let go the whole sordid business, like the whimpering coward he was. Rick was under no illusions about the two men who had forged a certificate of death for Hannah; bribed prison officials; kept company with criminals such as the Bedford woman and consequently been party to the kidnapping of Queenie.

Shaking his head as he thought on these things and wondered how many more were hidden away from prying eyes, Rick was in no doubt whatsoever that neither his father nor Snowdon would be brought to answer for their dealings, because, as Snowdon's quick legal tongue had pointed out, these things must be proven in a court of law. When it came right down to it, Rick suspected that the further up the ladder you were, the less you'd be splattered by mud from below. It would likely be the old code of honour among thieves that would protect the likes of his father and Snowdon, probably encouraged by the promise of a bundle of notes in payment for a span of silence.

When Rick brought the car to a standstill outside the church doors, his heart was in his mouth. Queenie *had* to be in there. For if she were not, where next could he turn?

With some trepidation, he entered. He hadn't known *what* to expect, half thinking she wouldn't be here at all, but in the company of the priest in his house next door, half expecting to see Queenie perhaps kneeling in prayer at the altar. Judging by Blodwin Torrid's drunken ramblings about how Queenie had been beaten so badly by the Bedford woman that she had lost all sense of identity and of how she was kept sedated by Raith Torrid and Garrett, Rick should have been prepared for anything. But he was not. And when his searching eyes fell on the limp and broken figure collapsed across the hymn-book rack, he at first looked away, believing it to be some God-fearing drunk or lowly creature crept in the church to plead sanctuary. Having looked away, his eyes continued to scour the pews in search of Queenie. When he felt satisfied that she was not there he turned to leave, convinced that the priest must have her with him.

When his fingers were wrapped about the great iron ring which at a turn would loose the door, Rick made to leave. Then, of a sudden, his back stiffened and a band of cold steel gripped his heart! That slight and bedraggled figure on the bench, that bent and silent creature: surely to God it *wasn't* Queenie?

For a moment his mind refused to think, did not want to accept such a possibility . . . yet it *was* the possibility that turned him about and took him hesitantly to where the pitiful figure was slumped and making not even the slightest sound of breathing.

Even when but a hand's breadth away, Queenie was so changed from Rick's memory of her, so bruised and torn that it was only when he placed his hand beneath her chin and tenderly raised it that he saw. What he saw struck both relief and fear in him, for the small heart-shaped face with its delicate features told him that it *was* his Queenie. He had found his Queenie at last! Yet the dreadful fear in his heart as he gazed unbelievingly at her bruised and bleeding body, the shock of hair that lent an almost savage look to her, and the marble coldness of her figure in his arms, warned him that he might have found her only to have lost her forever.

Such thoughts, such a terrifying prospect he would *not* accept! Not now! Not when the world was opening its arms to them! Of a sudden, he tore the coat from his back and wrapped her in it. Grabbing her to him, he vigorously rocked her back and forth, calling out her name in anger and desperation, and infusing her with the warmth of his body. When after a while there came the lowest of moans from the limp figure in his arms, his voice took on a gentler tone. 'Queenie, oh Queenie,' he cried, the relief and gratitude swelling in his heart with unbearable pain and the tears running down his face. She was alive! Alive! And he was not ashamed to shed tears. He would shed blood if needs be for no man could love a woman more.

When Queenie opened her eyes, it was to see the face she had so often seen but did not know: Rick's face and, her heart told her, the face of the man she adored.

When she murmured his name and smiled up at him, Rick gazed into those soft and loving grey eyes. Drawing her to him, he showered her face with the gentlest of kisses, rocking her like one might a child, and murmuring, 'You'll be all right, my darling. Thank God. Oh, thank God!' In a moment he was on his feet, with Queenie still clasped tight in his arms, her head buried in his chest. 'I'll get help for you, my lovely,' he said. 'I won't leave you ever again. We can be married, my darling! Do you hear me? We *can* be married?'

Carrying his precious Queenie, feather-light in his arms yet a heavy wonderful burden in his heart, Rick walked quickly down the aisle and towards the door. When only a few steps from it the door swung open to admit the black-suited figure of Father O'Donnelly who, upon seeing the anxious face of a young man and the emaciated figure in his arms, felt no need of questions, for here in God's house he had witnessed stranger and sadder scenes. Opening the door wide, he stepped aside for Rick to pass, saying, 'Take her to my house. I'll call an ambulance at once! She looks in a bad way.'

'Thank you, Father, but no. I have a car outside so it will be quicker if *I* take her to the infirmary,' Rick replied.

Of a sudden, the bundle in his arms quickened and, pausing to look down, Rick was enthused and surprised by the strength in Queenie's eyes as she met his gaze. 'No, Rick,' she whispered, her heart filled with love and with immeasurable gratitude that here in this man's arms she felt safe and secure. In the midst of such feelings, other forgotten emotions had been awakened by the kisses he had rained on her. Now into her mind places and people all came flooding back to swamp her with relief, with thankfulness and with the wonderful sensation of belonging. In that same moment there had entered her heart a great quietness and somewhere deep in its core she felt a soaring and beautiful song telling her that yes, she *had* heard right. She and Rick were to be married! The how and when she knew not but somehow she truly believed that it must be so, for had her heart not always promised that it *would* be?

As she gazed up at Rick, and saw there in his eyes the glorious reflection of her own love Queenie felt its warmth, its tenderness and its ferocity. And when, enveloping them both, it reached out down the tortuous years, melting them away forever, she smiled on him and through her tears of joy she whispered, '*No* infirmary . . . Katy, take me to Katy, please.'

Rick gave no answer, for there was need of none. Instead he pressed her so close to him that through the thinness of his shirt Queenie could feel the beating of his heart. When he bent his head to blend his mouth with hers in the softest and most exquisite of kisses, in her mind Queenie gathered him into her arms, into her heart and into her very being. She was home. And home was paradise!

Chapter Eighteen

It was the most delightful April that anyone could remember. On this late Thursday afternoon, 22 April 1968, the preparation for the wedding festivities less than two days away had reached fever pitch, with Katy beginning to wonder whether she was on her head or her heels.

Rick had collected Queenie some twenty minutes back, so that the two of them could go to Rickham prison to see Sheila, briefly, and each other too, just as briefly till they met face to face in that church! Katy had reminded them both. Father Riley poked his head into the kitchen, his nose wrinkling at the delicious aroma of freshly-baked apple-pie. 'By! That smells a treat, Katy,' he said, at the same time beckoning to her. 'Look here, let's you and me take a breath of air, shall we? You've done nothing but run around in circles tying yourself in knots ever since Rick and Queenie fixed the date! Now, come on . . . outside with you!'

Grumbling beneath her breath, yet gladdened at the thought of a leisurely stroll around the grounds, Katy removed her apron and paddled after Father Riley.

Outside the sky was blindingly bright blue, dotted here and there with fluffy cream clouds scurrying along on the gentle breeze, and everywhere could be seen the promise of a glorious summer. In the extensive rolling grounds of the vicarage, all manner of life and colour was bursting forth, splitting, stretching and growing in an effort to throw off the restraints of a long and bitter winter. The small pink star-shaped flowers on the copper beech were only just being loosened by the wind, and blown about to cover the lawns like a living petalled carpet. The boughs of the cherry tree weighed heavy beneath the clusters of ripening buds just starting to open, and the sprawling rhododendron was a blaze of rich lemon blooms more vibrant in colour and size than even Katy could recall, she told Father Riley.

Blackbirds were busy winging their way down into the garden, their little feet stamping the ground to persuade out the unsuspecting worms which were promptly snapped up into those long vivid yellow beaks. When not hunting for food, the blackbirds were busy foraging for nesting material which they quickly bore up to the towering conifers by Katy's old cottage. Robins too, blue-tits and thrushes all hurried about the business of mating, nesting and feeding.

Amongst all this frenzied activity, there could be heard the building and refurbishment of yet another location for a loving pair about to set up home.

'Well, Katy. Do you think the two of them will be happy here?' Father Riley stood side by side with Katy, hands clasped together behind his back and every now and then emitting a small puff of grey smoke from the pipe clenched fast between his teeth.

Katy gave a broad smile and nodding her head towards the picturesque little cottage, she said grandly,

'Oh, aye! They will. I *know* they will. Me an' my man spent many a happy year in that there cottage . . . an' just think on what it'll look like when the work's finished, eh? An' what with the extra space bein' built on, well! It'll be like a little palace.'

'Certainly doesn't resemble a palace *now* though, does it?' Father Riley shook his head, taking stock of the workmen's tools piled high on the coal-bunker, the new doors and window leaning on the outside wall and the mountain of rubble heaped up across the old rose-garden. Then he shrugged his shoulders, took the pipe from his mouth and set off again in the direction of the vicarage. 'It's to be hoped it'll all be finished in time . . . less than two days to the wedding, and two weeks of a honeymoon. There! Not even three weeks and no time at all!' he said.

Bucking up her pace a step, Katy hurried after him. 'Oh, it'll finished, you'll see,' she promised, squaring her shoulders belligerently. 'Else I'll 'ave *somebody* dancin' to a tune, mek *no* mistake!' Laughing out loud, Father Riley stopped for Katy to catch up with him. 'Katy Forest!' he chided, 'will you never change? Do you mean to end your days always bullying?'

'No! Not at all! I don't mean to end me days, that's what. I shall go on forever!'

'And I believe you will . . . yes, I believe you will, you old rascal.'

Here, the two of them paused for a moment, with Katy observing, 'Strange, isn't it, how Queenie fled to the very church in which Hannah Jason lay sleeping her last sleep, yet neither Rick nor Queenie knew till Rita Marsden spoke of it?'

'Yes, it does seem strange, Katy. But then, God

works in mysterious ways, so they say. It seems that Hannah's husband was of that parish years ago and Rita couldn't bear for her sister to be in the prison for a minute longer than was necessary. You see, even the authorities have a warm and human heart when needs be.'

'Aye,' agreed Katy, not wanting to dwell on such sorry matters on a day like today, 'I'm glad Rick's close to Rita . . . she's been through the grind, what with her loyalties pulled in argumentative directions.'

'Close to Rita yes, but somehow I feel it'll be a long time before Rick and his *father* are on speaking terms and to be honest, I don't know *what* to say on the matter.'

'You don't? Well, *I* do! I say it's a sin and a shame what that man did! Him an' Snowdon both, an' the pair of 'em coming away scot-free if you ever did! Shameful it is! Downright shameful! An' I for one never want to clap eyes on the varmints, else I shan't be responsible for me actions!' Her head was shaking at such a pace and her face had grown so pink that Father Riley thought a change of subject in order.

'Still, it does seem that justice was done in the case of the woman Bedford and her tawdry colleagues?' he ventured.

'Oh, aye! It'll be many a day afore *they* set foot on free ground agin, eh? I'm glad the old Irish came to no harm though . . . tekken hersel' off home to Ireland they say. Well, best o' luck to the old 'un. If it wasn't for her, well, I dread to think *what* might a' become o' Queenie!'

Father Riley was walking on again, making sure to keep to a steady pace and in step with Katy. 'By all accounts Sheila's behaving herself, is she not?'

'She is! What with a new governor residing there an' Sheila's showin' the best side on 'er, I've a feelin' in me bones that it won't be too long afore the lass is set loose!'

'Let's hope you're right, Katy. I too can see it happening. According to Queenie, she certainly has made a great effort since they transferred her back to the open system.'

He pursed his lips and puckered his brows in contemplation before continuing, 'Surprised me though, when she decided to open the guest-house again, putting Maud and Nancy in full charge.'

'Best thing she coulda done!' declared Katy, 'that place will come to no harm wi' them two at the helm, eh?' Of a sudden, Katy jabbed a chubby finger into the fleshy upper arm of Father Riley as he swung it in keeping with his deliberately low step, 'Hey! Come on, let's be 'avin' you. I want a 'and wi' the veg'tables. Rick's coming back for dinner, last time 'e's to set eyes on Queenie afore the church a Saturday! An' I wants it to be a *special* meal 'atween the four on us.'

'Hmh! I don't remember being persuaded to help with the vegetables, Katy Forest! And anyway, come to think of it, I should have thought your powers of persuasion could have been put to better use in making Rick count the cost of staying in that hotel along Corporation Park these weeks. We've a spare room going begging, as I've told him time and time again!'

Katy was as much against that idea now as she had been all along, which she told Father Riley in no uncertain terms. 'An' it's too late now anyroad!' she reminded him. 'Which is just as well, for I never did think it a good idea to have a couple o' love-birds settling under the same roof afore exchanging the marriage vows! By! the very idea! And you a man o' the cloth.'

Katy's stubborn and blinkered ways never failed to amuse Father Riley. Sighing quietly, he thought he might get in the last word. 'Separate rooms, Katy me darling . . . separate rooms!'

'Stuff an' nonsense!' she retorted, turning at the kitchen door and cocking a haughty snoot at the naivety of a *priest*, no less. 'The way them two's 'ead over 'eels in love, brick walls wouldn't keep them apart. The sooner that lass is walking down the aisle, the easier I'll feel, an' no mistake!'

Having said her piece, Katy got back to her cooking, leaving Father Riley to throw his hands up in frustration, before following her into the kitchen where, under her eagle eye, he set to in scraping the potatoes.

Chapter Nineteen

'Queenie gel! How come you get lovelier while I get uglier?' Sheila demanded, her eyes moving about Queenie and taking in every detail, from the soft pink dolman-sleeved blouse atop a beige summery skirt, to the long slim legs and high-heeled white ankle-strap sandals. Bringing her gaze back to Queenie's face, she thought it remarkable that the splendid classic features showed no sign of the trauma suffered at the hands of creatures best forgotten. Only the hair still surprised her, for ever since Sheila and Queenie had been friends, some twenty years and more, Sheila could never picture Queenie without picturing those thick soft braids taken across the top of her head and back again. This here was a *new* Queenie, with short layered hair which fell attractively over her ears and about her lovely face in glorious deep waves. Sheila thought her friend as beautiful as ever, maybe more so. Sometimes, like now, it was as though all that beauty, all the gentle kindness inside her and all the warmth which made her the wonderful caring person she was, gathered in those eyes of hers, those dewy soft and striking grey eyes which once seen could never be forgotten.

Pulling her lips in as she resigned herself to the fact

that she never was a beauty and never would be, Sheila told herself that neither was she of the same calibre as this young woman sitting here now in the same loyal and concerned fashion she had done many, many times before. Reaching out to take the hand offered by Queenie, she smiled as Queenie replied, 'You *are* beautiful, Sheila . . . you in your own way, and happen me in mine! I don't know. But we both might do well to remember what Auntie Biddy used to say. "Beauty is only skin deep, lass. It's what's *inside* that truly counts." '

To this Sheila gave no reply, seeing the truth in it and regretting that she was beautiful neither on the inside *nor* the outside in spite of Queenie's reassurances to the contrary.

Taking away her hand from Queenie's loving grip Sheila extracted a cigarette from the packet on the table and lit up. She drew deep and hard on it, then after a fit of coughing and spluttering, she snatched it from her mouth and stamped it out in the ashtray. 'I *will* gi' the buggers up,' she promised, ''cause if I don't, the buggers'll gi' *me* up, eh?' Smiling awhile, she then asked, 'Rick outside, you say?' And at Queenie's nod, 'I appreciate 'is thoughtfulness, Queenie gel! You tell 'im that from me.' Of a sudden, there washed over Sheila's features a look Queenie couldn't recognize. It showed a softer and contrite Sheila, embarrassed almost and, when she spoke now, the voice too was quieter and her gaze dropped beneath Queenie's questioning look.

'You tell Rick as I'm *glad* he stayed outside. You see, I wouldn't want 'im to see me in 'ere like this.' She flicked a hand through her untidy dark hair and plucked uneasily at her grey cotton dress. 'I'm not proud o' mesel', Queenie gel . . . no, not proud o' mesel' at all.'

When Sheila's voice faltered and her bottom lip came up over her top in an effort to choke back the rising emotion, Queenie moved her chair over so that she could sit beside her friend.

'Hey! Come on now. Is this the girl who's allus telling me how to spit in the eye of fortune, eh? The same Sheila who in her own words "don't give a sod fer anybody!" ' she said, putting her arm around Sheila's shoulders.

At this Sheila giggled, then screwed her fists into her eye sockets, after which she wiped off the tears on her dress. 'Best get yersel' back to the other side o' that table, Queenie gel, afore the bloody screws catch sight on us havin' a cuddle! The buggers don't understand friendship the likes o' what *we* got. They'll think you're me fancy bit!' She threw back her head and cackled in the most raucous fashion, causing Queenie to see the funny side of it. Laughing, she thought the whole idea preposterous, but all the same, when out of the corner of her eye she saw one of the prison officers making her way to their table, Queenie was up out of her seat and round the other side in two seconds flat, after which she and Sheila collapsed in a fit of hysterics.

'Telled yer, didn't I? The buggers are *all* at it!' cried Sheila, the tears washing down her face, and her whole countenance putting Queenie in mind of Maisie Thorogood as was. 'Hey! Queenie gel, did I tell yer I've been to church a couple o' times? Only fer no other reason than to get some bloody peace o' mind!' she quickly asserted, 'but I've quite tekken to it . . . all that singing sort o' gets to be fun after a while. Tell me, gel, d'you think I'd mek a good nun?' Her face had fallen into a straight and quiet expression, and now, making her eyes big and innocent she stared at Queenie. 'What d'you think, Queenie, gel?' she asked in a serious voice. 'Would they tek me on fer a nun?'

Just for the briefest of moments, Queenie was taken aback. Then a well of laughter rose in her even though she was still not quite certain whether Sheila was serious. But no! Sheila Thorogood a nun? The image was too much, and of a sudden Queenie burst into laughter, with Sheila throwing herself across the table in a helpless fit. 'Nearly 'ad yer there, gel didn't I, eh?' she roared.

Queenie thought it good to see her old friend in fine spirits again, for she knew that in spite of the brave face Sheila put on, she really was desperately unhappy here. Reaching into her bag, Queenie withdrew a large white hanky which she handed to Sheila, who promptly wiped her eyes, blew her nose on it and returned it to Queenie. Queenie, wiping her own eyes on a dry corner, then squashed the hanky back into her bag. On looking up, she noticed with shock that Sheila's face had grown deathly white and she was looking in the direction of the door with big staring eyes. 'Lord love an' save us!' she murmured in a strange voice. 'It's the devil 'isself!'

Turning now, Queenie's gaze followed that of Sheila's. What she saw was a man talking to the duty officer and being pointed by him in the direction of Sheila's table. Quickly now, he came towards them, a tall dark-haired man in what looked to be the uniform of a seaman. He had a pleasant face and small, saddened eyes. Once at the table he snatched the cap from his head. Glancing at Queenie and giving a polite nod, he looked down to where Sheila's eyes had never left his face from the moment of first seeing him. In a small nervous voice he said, 'Hello, me beauty. I'm back to look after you, for it seems you can't look after yersel!'

Queenie had never seen the man before, but it crossed her mind that he might well be Sheila's estranged husband. When Sheila spoke, there was no doubt. 'Be all the bloody saints!' she said quietly. 'It's me ol' fella back from Australia!' At this point she got to her feet and threw herself into his arms, crying. 'Yer bugger!' she told him, laughing through her tears. 'Yer a sight for sore eyes, an' *that's* a fact! An' the kids? Ye've brought me kids?' When Bannion nodded Sheila laughed out loud and feverishly planted kisses on his cheek, his nose, his mouth. She would have gone on, but the duty officer had approached the table to instruct the pair of them to sit down.

Here Queenie quietly took her leave. She would have said goodbye, but neither Sheila nor her husband would have heard, wrapped up in each other as they were. So, gladdened by such a lovely sight, Queenie went outside to where Rick was patiently waiting.

An hour later Rick parked the car up at the end of Parkinson Street, there being no access into the devastated area. After they had stopped he leaned across to take Queenie's hand. 'Do you want to get out, my darling,' he asked, 'or would you rather take your last look from here?'

For a moment Queenie pondered on his words. 'My last look,' she repeated to herself, 'my last look at

Parkinson Street.' How strange and frightening a prospect, she thought. And yet it had been *she* who wanted to come here, she, who not twenty minutes since had stood in the churchyard where Auntie Biddy, the boy-child and his father . . . *her* father, were all at rest within an arm's length of each other; she, who had time and time again put off that visit, because she had not been able to find the strength within her to face it. Now, having faced what was not an ordeal after all, but a comforting and precious coming to terms, she was ready to say her goodbyes to her childhood home.

In answer to Rick's question as to whether she would take her last look from the car, Queenie shook her head, opened the door and stepped out. After a moment Rick too got out of the car, came to where Queenie stood, and together, hand in hand, the two of them walked to where the barricades stretched across the mouth of Parkinson Street. Here they stood, arms about each other, both silent, both lost in a train of thought which drew them even closer together.

As her trembling gaze roved up and down that long and ravaged street, Queenie's memories rolled back the carpet of time. In her mind's eye, twenty years and more sped away and she could see again old Maisie Thorogood and her colourful cart loaded down with bright dazzling yo-yos and painted balloons. She pictured the ancient, lonely Mr Craig sitting on his rickety stand-chair and dreaming of his sweetheart. Oh, and there was Mrs Aspen tiptoeing on her soap-box and peeping over the garden wall. Now Queenie imagined she could hear the old joanna playing a tune in the pub and the laughter of the riotous assembly there.

The longer Queenie stood and gazed down that familiar street, the more vivid became her memories and the more poignant grew her mood. Emerging proud amidst it all was the image of her darling Auntie Biddy, small of stature but immense of heart. Here she was stooping over the heated dolly-tub, the rising steam warming her cheeks cherry-red . . . there she was standing by the pot sink lovingly plaiting Queenie's hair and telling her those fascinating tales of goblins and little folk; now and then bending to plant a kiss on Queenie's cheek as the two of them laughed together. Of all the memories rushing fast into her heart, that one was the most exquisite to Queenie, the most vivid and the most painful.

Unable now to hold back the tears she let them break loose, running down her face and blinding her eyes till the whole of Parkinson Street became a blur. The mountainous piles of rubble, the splintered doors and gaping roofs, the towering cranes which till the morrow were silenced, all merged into one in Queenie's sight. She wondered whether the powers that be could ever really know what it was they were demolishing in the old quarter. Did they know that they were pulling down not just bricks and mortar, but a whole way of life passed on from generation to generation? Parkinson Street wasn't just a row of houses; it was a setting where flesh and blood people came into the world, worked, laughed, played . . . loved and died! You couldn't evaluate the dreams they dreamed, the pain they endured, or the ecstasy of the love they found. Just ordinary and wonderful people. All now gone and yet, Queenie thought, all still here, and always will be.

'All right are you?' Rick looked at Queenie, his great

love for her visible in his eyes. In that moment there was no more pain, only gratitude and a deep sense of peace.

'Yes, my darling, time now to let the past go and look to the future,' she said, smiling up at him.

At this he reached down to kiss her with the impatient fierceness of a man in love. When, after a while, they drew apart, he said, 'To think, my Queenie. The day after tomorrow we'll be man and wife. Won't that be wonderful?'

Snuggling contentedly into the crook of his arm as they walked back to the car, Queenie dwelt for a moment on how the wedding would not be the grand affair which Rita Marsden had wished and which they had not. It would be just a quiet service with Father Riley officiating, with Queenie wearing the long ivory dress worn by Katy at her own wedding and altered to fit Queenie's slim build. After a honeymoon in the Lake District their home would be the cottage. With Rick having bought into a new consortium of an import-export concern, the future looked bright; the only blot to Queenie's mind being the estrangement of Rick and his father. On the way to Parkinson Street, Queenie had dared to venture that Rick might one day make peace with his father. But Rick's face had taken on such animosity that it had shaken her. When he had said, 'I have no father!' she recoiled from ever broaching the subject again.

There was still a deep measure of fury in Rick's heart on that score, and Queenie could do nothing to change it. Yet, as she had already remarked to Rick concerning his bitterness at all these long and wasted years when they could have been together, the wasted years were a sin, yes. But not so much of a sin as was the waste in bitterness itself.

As for Queenie she held no grudges, for never before in the whole of her life had she been so gloriously happy. Now, in answer to Rick's question about how wonderful would be the day of their wedding, she paused in her step and looking up at him with adoring eyes, she said, 'And our lives will be wonderful my darling. All of our lives we'll be together. And oh . . . how I love you, and will always love you.'

Queenie's words were lost as, reaching down, Rick swept her up into his arms, and when again he took her to him, crushing her fiercely into himself and tasting her mouth in the most ardent of kisses, her heart soared and such feelings of ecstasy surged into it that she feared it might split asunder. Even now . . . even though she could feel his manliness against her . . . even though she knew that all of this was no dream and that at long last she and Rick were truly together, Queenie could hardly believe it.

But it *was* real. It was true. Soon they would be man and wife.

Now, as her lips were gently forced apart by Rick's probing tongue, the sensation it brought causing her whole being to weaken against him, Queenie conceded that Katy was right. The sooner marriage vows were exchanged, the better!

Of a sudden Rick lifted his head, gave out a whoop of joy, and swooping Queenie up into his arms, he swung her round to face Parkinson Street yelling at the top of his voice, 'She's mine at last! Do you hear? Queenie is *mine*!' After, gazing into Queenie's laughing eyes, he said in the softest murmur, 'Mine, forever and . . .' Here, Queenie placed a quieting finger on his lips. 'And ever!' she finished.

As the two of them walked away from Parkinson Street hand in hand and so very much in love, Queenie gave a last lingering look over her shoulder.

'Goodbye,' she whispered. 'Oh, Auntie Biddy! Do you see me? Do you see me and Rick? And do you know how happy we are, my darling?'

Queenie knew it wouldn't be too long before the sun set on Parkinson Street for the last time. But for her and Rick, the sun was only just beginning to shine. And Queenie prayed that it would go on shining till the end of their days.

A selection of bestsellers from Headline

THE CHANGING ROOM	Margaret Bard	£5.99 ☐
BACKSTREET CHILD	Harry Bowling	£5.99 ☐
A HIDDEN BEAUTY	Tessa Barclay	£5.99 ☐
A HANDFUL OF HAPPINESS	Evelyn Hood	£5.99 ☐
THE SCENT OF MAY	Sue Sully	£5.99 ☐
HEARTSEASE	T R Wilson	£5.99 ☐
NOBODY'S DARLING	Josephine Cox	£5.99 ☐
A CHILD OF SECRETS	Mary Mackie	£5.99 ☐
WHITECHAPEL GIRL	Gilda O'Neill	£5.99 ☐
BID TIME RETURN	Donna Baker	£5.99 ☐
THE LADIES OF BEVERLEY HILLS	Sharleen Cooper Cohen	£5.99 ☐
THE OLD GIRL NETWORK	Catherine Alliott	£4.99 ☐

All Headline books are available at your local bookshop or newsagent, or can be ordered direct from the publisher. Just tick the titles you want and fill in the form below. Prices and availability subject to change without notice.

Headline Book Publishing, Cash Sales Department, Bookpoint, 39 Milton Park, Abingdon, OXON, OX14 4TD, UK. If you have a credit card you may order by telephone – 0235 400400.

Please enclose a cheque or postal order made payable to Bookpoint Ltd to the value of the cover price and allow the following for postage and packing:
UK & BFPO: £1.00 for the first book, 50p for the second book and 30p for each additional book ordered up to a maximum charge of £3.00.
OVERSEAS & EIRE: £2.00 for the first book, £1.00 for the second book and 50p for each additional book.

Name ....

Address ....

....

....

If you would prefer to pay by credit card, please complete:
Please debit my Visa/Access/Diner's Card/American Express (delete as applicable) card no:

Signature .... Expiry Date ....